# Weave a Web of Witchcraft

Jean M. Roberts

ISBN: 978-0-692-05484-0

A huge thank you to my husband, who believed I could
write this book.

# Prologue

1690

Hugh stood at the summit of Trimont in Boston. His chest hurt as he struggled to catch his breath. God help him he felt old. The long winding climb up the hills had left him winded and his spindly legs ached. 'Twas worth the pain.

He turned his face into a brisk wind and stared out at the horizon. The deep blue of the Atlantic Ocean melded into the paler blue sky. A sudden gust of wind threatened to blow his hat from his head, he caught it in the nick of time. Large brilliant white cumulus clouds floated overhead, steered inland by the sea breeze.

Hugh squinted and stared out at the water, thankful that his sight had not dimmed with age. A small pop of white caught his eye; a sail, thought Hugh. He watched in silence as it grew larger and the brown-black hull of a ship came into view.

"Father." A voice called out. "Are you ready to start back down?"

Hugh, lost in thought, did not react until she called to him a second time.

"Father, we should start back soon. 'Tis a long walk down."

"A few moments more Ruth. I'll not make this climb again," he said as he dragged his eyes away from the sailing ship to smile at his daughter.

Ruth smiled in return, glad to see her father happy. Hugh pointed out the ship and together they watched it grow steadily larger. Sea birds wheeled and dived in the air above the ship. Mayhap, he mused, the ship had sailed from England. He imagined ocean weary passengers lining the deck, desperate for a glimpse of their new homeland.

Memories, mused Hugh, so many, many memories. Pent up memories, locked away for years flooded out. They washed over him like a high spring tide. Hugh wiped a tear from his face, overcome with emotion as if a dam had broken somewhere in his mind. Hugh thought back to his own journey; the smell of the ocean, salty and bracing, and the stink of the ship hold with its wretched passengers, the roll of the deck under his feet, and the deep black of a starlit night sky.

How young and brave I was to leave my home in England. Home, I haven't thought of home in many a year.

# Gosberton

Hugh lay on his back, a pile of scratchy hay under him. He studied a large spider as it spun its death trap, high in the ancient oak rafters of his father's barn. The translucent web was difficult to see in the shaded gloom close to the roof. The air inside was thick and warm; redolent of earth and animal. The drone of insects from the farmyard made him sleepy. Through the open barn door, he could see his stepmother's garden alive with bees as they gathered pollen from her flowers. A butterfly floated around the yard on a light breeze.

Perhaps the spider would catch a bee for its dinner. Hugh hoped it would not be a butterfly. No, it will be a fly, he mused, as he waved one away from his face with a lethargic hand. Poor stupid fly, I'm glad I'm not a fly, he thought.

Hugh yawned, eyelids drooping, as he watched the spider spin. His father's voice shattered his reverie. "Hugh, where are ye."

His eyes flew open. I've not got this stall cleaned out, he thought, Da will thrash my hide.

"I'm in the barn, Father." Hugh leapt to his feet and shook off any incriminating hay clinging to his hair and clothes. He snatched up the pitchfork and rushed to look as if he were hard at work, mucking out manure.

William Parsons entered the barn, leading his horse by its reins. He frowned as he scrutinized the state of the stall. Hugh struggled to concoct an excuse but drew a blank. "'Tis a fine day, is it not."

3

William rolled his eyes and sighed. He gave Hugh a wry smile. "Yes, 'tis a fine day." He reached out to pluck a piece of straw from a dark curl.

Hugh grinned at his father, there would be no punishment this time. Hugh leaned on his pitchfork and asked, "How did you get on in the village? Mam said you went to attend an errand."

"Aye," said his father, without further comment. He pointed at the stall. "Get this lot finished up. Brush down this beast and see he gets water; 'tis warm today."

"Yes, Da."

William crossed the barn floor, stopping at the door, he looked back at his son, his face unreadable. "Hugh, come and find me when you finish yer chores. We need to talk."

A ripple of apprehension flickered over him and formed a knot in his gut. Was he in trouble- again? Last week, Reverend Smith caught him as tried to kiss Goodman Whimple's daughter in the churchyard. Hugh grinned as he recalled Katherine's reaction. She slapped him, hard too, but 'twas worth it. 'Twill be worth getting in trouble for as well.

Hugh glanced up and saw a fly trapped in the web. It struggled in vain to free itself. My sympathies master fly, he thought. Finished with his chores, he put away his tools, and stepped out into the farmyard. He stood still a moment and raised his face to the sun, soaking up its warmth. Lazy chickens pecked at insects in the grass. Hugh took a deep breath and inhaled the indescribable fragrance of an English high summer afternoon. He sighed with pleasure.

But he could dawdle no longer, better see what Da wants, he thought. Hugh stopped just inside the door to let his eyes adjust to the gloom of the hall. He heard his stepmother, Alice, humming a tune as she stood over a table working a piece of dough. Next to her rolling pin sat a bowl of peeled apples coated with a light dusting of cinnamon and sugar. Hugh inhaled; the smell of spiced fruit made his mouth water. He grinned at her as he snatched an apple bit from the bowl and popped it into his mouth.

"I'm making apple pie," she said, lifting her head to smile at Hugh. She batted his hand away from her bowl.

"You only make pie for celebrations, what do we celebrate?" He asked but got no reply. What have I missed, he wondered?

"Get away with you, your Da is waiting on you," she said as she waved a flour coated hand towards the parlor.

"I'm done with my chores, Da," Hugh said as he entered the small room.

"Ah Hugh, good." William rose from his chair by the unlit fireplace. "Walk with me to the meadow, I want to check the hay."

They exited the house and followed the farm path which crossed through their fields of wheat. There had been ample rain, and the stalks were tall and healthy, anchored in the dark fenland soil of East Anglia. His oldest brother, Tom, expected a good crop this season. Hugh fell in behind his father as he strode ahead.

"Father, whatever it is, I give you my promise, I will not do it again."

"Whatever you've done, it can keep."

When they reached the top of the meadow, William stopped. He bent down and plucked a slender green stalk, chewing on it as he surveyed the land.

"The grass is looking fine, we'll have plenty of hay this season, if the weather holds."

Hugh studied his father's silent face. William was a man of few words, who kept his opinions to himself. He was strict, but not unkind. He could neither read nor write and was not a religious man. William attended church, the law mandated every soul attend service, and the churchwarden was quick to spot a delinquent sinner. But, if he did any praying, he did it in silence, for fine weather and a good harvest. Salvation came second to putting food on the table and paying rents and taxes.

"Hugh." His father spoke as they walked on through the grass. "You know this land will go to Tom when I pass."

Hugh nodded. He did not like the sound of this, was his father ill, he wondered? "I know Da, Tom reminds me every chance he gets."

"I have no land to give you, nor any money to leave you." William stopped and faced his son. "Your only hope to make a fair living is to learn an honest trade."

Hugh opened his mouth to protest, but his father silenced him. "Your brother Tom has found an apprenticeship for you. Johnny will help us pay for it." William paused and then said, "You're to be a brick maker."

Hugh stood stock still, not believing what he was hearing. He felt a rush of anger wash over him.

"A brick maker!" Hugh slashed out at the grass with a stick. "God's teeth, I don't want to be a brick maker. I don't want a trade. I want to farm."

"Mind your temper, boy. Don't you bark at me. We only want what's best for you, and this is the chance you need for some kind of future."

In that moment, Hugh understood what it meant to be powerless. He glared at his father. "Please Da, don't make me do this."

"My minds made up. I'll not change it."

Hugh kicked out at a clump of grass. "So, I have no choice?"

"No Hugh, you do not," William said. "You're fifteen years this summer and 'tis past time for you to grow up. Mam and I have indulged you long enough. I want you settled."

William stared out at the distant edge of the meadow. "Times are changing, Hugh. Goodman Thompson was at market in Boston a week since and came home with tales of riots in Leicester and other places. There are rumors about that Sir Charles Wyche plans to enclose Gosberton commons. He's already bought out some of the smaller tenants. The village is all abuzz with fearful talk."

"What's he about, Sir Charles?" His apprenticeship forgotten for the moment.

"He wants the land for himself." Bitterness crept into William's voice. "He can make more money farming himself then renting us the land. I fear for Tom. Sir Charles may decide not to renew the lease when I am gone."

"He can't do that," cried Hugh, "He can't toss Tom off the farm, Parsons' have always had this farm."

"He can Hugh, he can." William said. "'Tis why I want you settled down in a trade, no one can take that from you."

His father's stern face told Hugh that he would brook no argument. Feeling like the fly trapped in the spider's web, Hugh asked, "When do I go?"

"A week today, Son. Now, let's return to the house and give your Mam the happy news," said William. "Your brother Johnny will be here to congratulate you on your new situation and I expect you to thank him and Tom for their help."

If Hugh was honest with himself, he knew this day was coming. His father indulged him, the youngest son, for too long. Hugh had overheard his father and his two brothers argue about his future. Tom was the oldest son. Older than Hugh by eighteen years. He and his wife Agnes had taken up the new religious zeal spreading across England. Some called them Puritans. Agnes was always prattling on about God and covenants and saints. As his father's heir, Tom, with his wife and children, lived in the family home, making it all the more crowded. Maybe leaving home wasn't so bad after all, thought Hugh.

Hugh would miss his brother Johnny, though. He may have been second born, but Johnny had done well for himself. A smart ambitious man, he married well, above his station, some would say. He had caught the eye of Cecily, the only child and heir of a rich local yeoman. When her widowed father died, the year after her marriage to Johnny, she inherited his entire estate. It would be Cecily's money that would pay for his apprenticeship.

Hugh took his time as he walked back, his thoughts in turmoil. As he neared the farmhouse, he could hear the voices of his brothers, Tom and Johnny. Before opening the door, Hugh put on a smile for his family then stepped inside. Alice pulled him into a bosomy hug.

"Oh, my boy, what an opportunity, you are very lucky."

"'Tis God's will, not luck," said Agnes. "He has answered our prayers, and for that we are grateful."

"Well, I think Hugh's lucky that God willed it," said Cecily, winking at Hugh.

"Amen," said Hugh with a naughty grin. Agnes stomped off in a huff.

"You two are wicked," said Alice with a smile. "Hugh, go thank your brothers, and tell your father we will eat soon.

The family talked of Hugh's future over the supper table. Cecily declared Hugh must build her a new brick chimney as soon as he finished his apprenticeship. Why stop with a chimney laughed Johnny, Hugh will build us a new brick house.

Hugh savored every moment of his last week at the farm. He walked the fields and lay in the sweet meadow grass, trying to absorb the sights and smells and store them up in his mind, until he could return.

# Apprentice

Hugh rose with the dawn and packed his meager possessions in a rucksack. Today's the day, I begin my apprenticeship, he thought. He had a quiet breakfast with his family before he took one last ramble around the farmyard. William hitched the horse to his ancient farm cart and placed Hugh's bag in the back. Father and son rode in silence to Master Lawrence's imposing house. Hugh clambered down and surveyed his new home. A thin coating of red brown dust covered everything in sight, including the boxwood shrubs that surrounded the house and outbuildings. His father's knock dislodged a small red cloud of the stuff. Brick dust, Hugh decided.

A moment later, the door flew open and a diminutive female bustled out; she introduced herself as Mistress Lawrence.

"You must be Goodman Parsons, welcome, welcome." She spoke in a fluttery manner; her voice held a hint of sympathy. Hugh thought she must have witnessed many such partings between fathers and sons. She approached Hugh. "Well, my boy, this is an important day for you. Yes, very important."

"Yes, Mistress." Hugh observed that, unlike Alice's snowy white linen cap and apron, Mistress Lawrence's were a pale rust color.

"Well, get your things. Master Lawrence awaits. Come in, come in, if you please."

William lifted Hugh's rucksack from the stoop and they followed her inside. She darted across the wide hall waving her arms for them to follow. Stopping before a closed door, she rapped loudly, several times. Not waiting for a reply, she pushed it open and ushered them into the room. Without a word, she scurried back out the door, closing it as she left.

Hugh's new master sat behind a heavy oak table. Neat stacks of ledgers and loose papers, held in place with bits of broken brick, covered the top. Mr. Lawrence rose and greeted them as they entered. He nodded to William before he turned to Hugh, looking him in the eye. Hugh returned his gaze as they tried to take the measure of each other. Lawrence, a large man, had a plain inscrutable face. Unlike his wife, he exuded a no-nonsense, business-like demeanor. Hugh noted that Lawrence's hair was red. Jesus, did the dust stain his hair, Hugh wondered?

After a moment, Lawrence spoke. "You appear to be a stout fellow, my boy." His sonorous voice conveyed power and demanded respect. "I've one rule. Do as I say, when I say. Do that, and we'll make a fair brick man of you."

He turned to address William. "I expect you'll be wanting to sign the contract." Lawrence pulled a thick sheet paper from under a brick and placed it in front of Hugh's father. "Shall I read it aloud?"

William nodded his assent. Hugh, frozen in place, listened to the words that would change his life forever.

*I, William Parsons, do place my son Hugh Parsons in apprenticeship with Master George Lawrence for the period of seven years. I George Lawrence do take Hugh Parsons to be my apprentice and to train him in the trade of brick making and masonry.*

Hugh blinked back a tear. Lawrence handed his father a quill dipped in black ink.

"Where do I make me mark?"

"Just here." Lawrence, pointed to a spot below William's name. William took up the feather quill and scratched his mark on the page, careful not to drip any ink. He returned the quill then slipped his hand inside his coat pocket for a bag of coins.

"Here is the payment, 'tis all there if you wish to count it."

"No need." Lawrence flipped open his iron strong box and dropped the bag inside. Hugh jumped as the lid slammed shut with a loud thud. Lawrence reached out and shook William's hand, completing the contract.

"Take care of my boy," said William, his voice quavering. "He's a good lad, has a mouth on him sometimes, so you have my permission to beat him if he needs it."

He faced Hugh. "Do as you're told son, come and visit your Mam when you- when you can. And Hugh- make us proud of you."

He enveloped Hugh in his firm embrace then said farewell to Master Lawrence. Mistress Lawrence suddenly reappeared. She held Hugh's arm with gentle restraint in case he attempted to bolt after his father. Hugh shuddered as the door swung shut. His eyes burned with unshed tears. He swiped a hand roughly over his face, not wanting to cry in front of her.

"There now, 'twill be all right." His new Mistress gave him a kind smile. "Come with me, I'll show you to your chamber."

Hugh followed her to the rear of the large house and up a flight of stairs to the small room he would share with the senior apprentice, Robert. Later that night, after supper, Hugh stretched out on his bed, staring at the ceiling, unable to sleep. Seven years, he thought, I shall sleep in this room for seven years. It seemed an eternity.

The next morning Hugh rose early. And so, it begins, he thought. Master Lawrence was firm but fair. He had no sons so required the help of apprentices. Robert was in his fifth year and Master Lawrence needed Hugh to be ready to take over his share of the workload when Robert left. The work was hard but never grueling. The food was plentiful if plain. Hugh received a new set of clothes, including boots, each year at Christmastime. He also got a well-deserved clout upside the head when deemed necessary. He didn't love the work but over the years he made peace with it. Hugh could return to Gosberton, for a day's visit, one Sunday per month. Each visit brought painful changes. Hugh felt the rhythm of farm life slip away, replaced by a new routine of clay, fire, and bricks.

In the second year of his apprenticeship, his stepmother's health declined. A physician came from Boston to examine her and diagnosed her condition as dropsy. Her heart was failing and there was naught they could do. Tom's wife, Agnes, assumed the running of the household. Alice died in her sleep six months later. William Parsons remained stoic through his wife's illness, not wanting to burden her with his grief. But, her passing drained him, his vigor gone. He left the management of the farm to Tom and spent his days dozing by the fire. Hugh found his visits home unbearable, so much had changed. Agnes and Tom, ever pious, became more so. They spoke against the old papist ways of the church and embraced the new puritanical strain of their protestant religion that swept through East Anglia.

His father died the year Hugh turned eighteen. When Johnny arrived with the news, Hugh was sad but not surprised. Master Lawrence granted him two days off to attend the funeral. Afterward, he avoided the farm, the memories were too painful. He stopped going altogether after he quarreled with Tom over the sale of two cows. Johnny played peacemaker and kept in contact with both. He made frequent trips to Boston to conduct business, passing the brick pits on his way to and fro, and would drop by on his return journey.

June, of 1635, marked the start of Hugh's fifth year of apprenticeship. Near the end of the month, Johnny called in on him. He was investing in a fishing venture in the English colony of New Hampshire and was returning from a business meeting with his Boston agent.

"How are you Hugh." Johnny gave him a hug then eyeballed him. "You've grown! Tall as a man, and as strong, I wager!"

Hugh blushed at his brother's warm praise. "I'm past twenty years now Johnny, I expect I'm bout grown."

The brothers sat at Mistress Lawrence's scoured pine table. It was rare for her to let men into the heart of her domain but she enjoyed hearing Johnny's gossip from Boston. Hugh thought she was sweet on his brother, most women were. She poured them each a small ale and laid a platter of brown bread and cheese on the table. "Tell us the news of the world, Goodman Parsons."

She continued to bustle around the kitchen, checking on her dinner as it bubbled and simmered in various kettles suspended over the fire. She never strayed out of earshot, wanting to catch every detail. "Tell us about New Hampshire. What's it like? Is it full of wild beasts and savages?"

Johnny laughed and shared what little he knew. "I hear most folk live along the coast and fish. Further inland are

dense forests and bogs making the land unfit for farming."
He took a sip of ale before he continued.

"The bigger news is further south in the Bay Colony. I
hear folk have lined up to go there. There's so much land,
they give it away for free. I know several people who are
considering emigrating. Even our brother Tom talks of
leaving."

That surprised Hugh, he'd known no one who moved
anywhere, other than the bone-yard. "Tom would never
leave the farm."

Johnny shook his head. "He may have no choice. Sir
Charles has double his rents. Even worse, he has started
the enclosure of the commons. There was nowhere to
pasture the cattle, Tom had no choice but to sell."

"They'll survive, if anyone knows how to pinch a penny,
it's old Agnes." Hugh couldn't help but let bitterness creep
into his voice.

Mistress Lawrence joined them at the table and poured
herself a cup of cider. "'Tis a shame, what's happened to
your brother. The world is changing to be sure. My
husband saw a notice in Boston, just last week, advertising
for millwrights interested in going to America."

"I believe they're looking for men of all trades, not just
farmers and fisherman. They need carpenters, cobblers
and metal workers. I predict they'll need quite a few brick
makers. Mayhap you should go, make your fortune selling
bricks."

"Me!" Hugh rolled his eyes at his brother. "Emigrate to
America, are you daft, man? Mistress Lawrence, what have
ye put in Johnny's ale?"

"Why not?" Johnny looked and sounded serious. "You
can always come home if it's not to your liking." He
chewed on a piece of Mistress Lawrence's bread, waving

16

the crust at Hugh. "'Tis something to consider anyhow. How much longer is your time here?"

"He has two more years with us." Mistress Lawrence lifted the jug of ale and refilled Johnny's cup.

"Two years is plenty of time to ponder your decision." He took a sip and complimented her on her brewing, making her blush. The brothers spent the next half hour talking of Johnny's growing family and made plans for Hugh to visit.

It was late afternoon when Johnny rose to leave. He thanked Mrs. Lawrence for her hospitality. Hugh walked with his brother into the yard where his horse munched its way through a bag of oats. Johnny tightened the girth then swung himself up onto the saddle. Hugh handed him the reins and gave the horse a scratch on its nose.

"Take care Hugh," said Johnny, as he cantered out to the road. "Think on what I've said about Massachusetts."

In the summer of 1636, Hugh began his last year as an apprentice. On reflection, it had not been as difficult as he had feared. Master Lawrence taught him everything he knew about the business. Hugh had the knowledge required to manufacture bricks. Of equal import, he could build things with them. Hugh enjoyed the process of taking raw materials from the earth then adding heat to create a building block from which came chimneys, walls and houses. There was a simple beauty in it that resonated with him.

Hugh spent the final year learning how to run the business. 'Tis one thing to make bricks, but if you cannot sell them, you'll not earn a living.

"If you forget everything else that I've taught you, remember this," Master Lawrence lectured, "Never let the customer get the upper hand in a bargain."

Hugh spent years observing his master in action, a hard driving businessman; it was a rare day that a customer took advantage of Mr. Lawrence. When a customer arrived to strike a deal, Hugh watched from a corner of the room, making a mental note of the transaction. During his last months, Master Lawrence allowed him to negotiate the price for several orders. He did well.

"Now listen Hugh, you have a fiery temper, which you need to learn to control, else it will get you into trouble."

"I know, it's just that sometimes, I can't make it stop." He threw his hands up in frustration. "It grows out of control."

"You need to find a way, Hugh. Or twill drive off your customers."

As the days of his apprenticeship dwindled, Hugh began the search for employment. Master Lawrence helped him write and send inquires to several well-known London brick makers but received no response. Hugh felt discouraged, what had the last seven years achieved. Lawrence explained that times were tough. The economy was sluggish, even the cloth industry which always thrived, was under stress. Money was tight and there was less demand for bricks and building materials. Add to that the political upheaval in the county. When the King and Parliament sorted out their differences, things will improve.

"Don't despair," Master Lawrence clapped Hugh on the back, "Somewhere there will be a position for you."

# Decision

1641

Hugh's final day at the brickworks arrived with little fanfare. He spent it, as he always did, working alongside Master Lawrence. Later that afternoon, he packed his belongings in his old rucksack. He perched on the edge of the bed and gazed around his room. It surprised Hugh to feel ambivalent about leaving. It was not his choice to leave the farm; he had not wanted to come here. But the brickworks had, over the length of his apprentice, become home. He was fond of his mistress and had deep respect for Master Lawrence. Yet, if he wished to pursue his craft, he had to strike out on his own. It was time to go.

Mistress Lawrence surprised Hugh with a farewell dinner in his honor. She roasted a joint of beef and served it with all the trimmings. For dessert she made Hugh's favorite, a raisin pudding. Master Lawrence poured them each a glass of wine and made a toast to Hugh's future.

Early the following morning, Johnny arrived to collect him. Hugh slung his rucksack into the back of the pony cart. Mistress Lawrence took a break from her laundry to say farewell. She gave Hugh a hug and told Johnny she would miss his visits. Johnny thanked her for her care of Hugh. Master Lawrence was busy training the new apprentice and could not say goodbye. Hugh understood, it was as it should be. Hugh climbed onto the seat next to Johnny and with a flick of the whip, they were off.

The day was clear and warm; the hedgerows in bloom. The horse trotted along at a fair clip making for an enjoyable journey. Johnny was quiet, not his usual garrulous self.

"Are ye all right, Johnny, you've said nary a word?"

"Sorry Hugh, I didn't mean to ignore you, 'tis just a matter weighing heavy on my mind." Johnny gave him a weak smile. I'm meeting the County Sheriff this afternoon.

"Can I come with you?"

"Nay, you settle in. Cecily will be glad to see you." He pointed in the distance, "Look, we are home."

Johnny pulled the cart to a stop near the house. As Hugh scrambled down, the door flew open and Cecily bustled out, followed by her children. She greeted him with a warm hug, which he returned. "Welcome Hugh, we are glad to see you."

"Thank you, Cecily. I am happy to be here." He bent down to survey the four small children at her side. "Now then, who has a kiss for their Uncle Hugh?"

The greetings completed, Cecily untangled herself from her gaggle of children and ushered Hugh into the house. "You have to share a chamber with the boys, I hope you do not mind." He followed her as she climbed the stairs and showed him to an upper chamber.

Hugh laughed as he surveyed the room. "I am sure I will survive; I've slept in worse."

Hugh spent the rest of the morning fending off his young nephews, intent on prodding and poking him, when he least expected it. His nieces proved to be no better company; they ran shrieking to their mother whenever then laid eyes on him. Unused to the company of small children, Hugh found himself bemused and mystified by their behavior. After dinner he had an urge to stretch his legs. He crossed the road that fronted Johnny's house and plunged into the field that stretched away into the distance. He rambled for several miles, enjoying the solitude. It was early evening when he returned, Johnny too was back, and the family was waiting on him.

Johnny and Cecily were both quiet during supper. Johnny snapped at a servant who spilled gravy on a table linen. He's not himself, Hugh mused. Something is wrong. He was glad when the meal finished, the perfunctory conversation made him uncomfortable. Cecily rose to see to the children. Johnny took Hugh upstairs to his study room and shut the door behind them.

The brothers sat on ornate carved chairs, softened by cushions, that once belonged to Cecily's grandfather. The oriel window was open; a warm evening breeze rustled the papers on the desk. Johnny reached into a cabinet and pulled out a brown glass bottle. He grabbed two small pewter cups and poured a measure of dark fragrant liquid into each.

"'Tis a drink called Rum, comes from Barbados, an island in the Caribbean." He handed a cup to Hugh who took a large swig. His reaction was immediate. His eyes watered and his mouth was on fire. Christ's bones, he thought, as he choked and sputtered. Johnny reached over and slapped him on the back. When Hugh recovered, he pushed his cup back towards his brother. "'Tis a vile poison, I hope you did not pay overly much for it!"

Johnny laughed. "You must sip it Hugh, 'tis not for gulping."

Hugh took another tentative taste, his face screwed up with dislike. If Johnny can drink it, so can I, he decided, as the liquid burned its way down his throat. They sat in silence for a few minutes. Johnny picked up his cup and refilled it. He stared into his cup as he swirled the liquid around, as if looking for answers in the bottom of his drink.

At last Johnny spoke. "I've some news to tell you and it won't be to your liking."

"Aye, well let's hear it then."

Johnny blew out a deep breath. "Sir Charles Wyche, remember him?"

Hugh nodded.

"Well, Sir Charles, he is putting Tom off the farm and before you start yammering, I can do naught to prevent it. I spent the afternoon with the County Sheriff, and I've talked myself blue in the face, he cannot help us."

Hugh struggled to make sense of what he was hearing. Tom kicked off the farm. He felt his anger flare. That's our farm, the Parsons' farm, how could he. "What do you mean, he's putting Tom off the farm? Who the devil does that bastard think he is?"

"Watch your words now Hugh, the children may hear you. The law says 'tis his land, and when father died, he rented it to Tom on a year-to-year lease. This year, he says he'll not renew."

"What will Tom do? Johnny, are you going to just sit idle and watch it happen, watch Sir Wyche evict our brother from our family farm?"

Johnny's eyes narrowed, and he fixed Hugh with his steely gaze. "No, Hugh, what I will do is evict my tenants, who have farmed at Meadow Bottom for years, and give their farm to Tom."

He drained his cup and slammed it on the table. Hugh reached for the bottle of rum and poured them each another drink.

Over the next few weeks, Hugh helped Tom and Agnes move their belongings into the Meadow Bottom farmhouse. Tom, haggard and worn, looked as if he aged twenty years. Agnes too was subdued, exhaustion written on her face. The farm was smaller, less than fifteen acres, but at least it gave Tom a chance, other local farmers were

22

not so lucky. Gosberton was looking like a plague village, emptied of its population, not by illness, but by greed. Once the family settled in, Tom and Johnny's attention turned back to Hugh and his future.

After a family dinner, hosted by Johnny and Cecily, the three men adjourned to Johnny's study. Hugh dragged in a third chair and a new bottle of rum emerged from the cupboard. After several rounds, and some desultory talk between them about Meadow Bottom, Tom spoke.

When the reality of losing the farm sunk in, he searched for other land to rent, without success. He ran into an old friend who mentioned his nephew who immigrated to Massachusetts. Without speaking to Agnes, he went to Boston to meet the Vicar of St. Botolph's, a church known for its strong puritan leanings. The previous vicar was the fiery Reverend John Cotton, now a leader in the new colony. The current vicar helped families emigrate to Massachusetts.

"I could have made a fresh start in New England. In fact, the Reverend told me he received a letter from a parishioner who wrote to describe his one-hundred-acre farm." Tom shook his head in disbelief.

"A hundred acres! Imagine owning such a farm. Impossible to achieve such a thing in England today," said Johnny.

"The Colony is advertising for tradesmen. They need more than just farmers to make it successful."

Hugh was catching on to the purpose of this conversation. It appeared his brothers were trying to steer him into leaving England.

"Why didn't you go Tom?" Hugh asked, curious about his reasons.

"Agnes said she would not go. Didn't want to leave her mother. And I refused to take the old biddy with us."

Hugh and Johnny exchanged glances and burst into laughter. Tom grinned, a sheepish expression on his face.

"I believe you should give serious consideration to going Hugh. God knows there's naught for you here. And what with the trouble between the King and his parliament, who can say what may happen."

Hugh looked from brother to brother. "You really think I should do it?"

"Yes!" His brothers said in unison.

"Let's drink a toast then," said Hugh, "To America!"

# Arrival

1641

Seabirds, gulls and cormorants, circled and swooped overhead. Hugh stood at the ship's rail; head thrown back as he watched their antics. A warm breeze blew out of the west and carried with it the unmistakable scent of land. He closed his eyes, breathed deep and filled his lungs with the tangy mixture of sea and earth. Within the hour, the longed-for call of 'land ho' echoed through the ship. Hugh's spirits soared as the distant smudge became a distinct coastline. The captain, with his charts and instruments, determined their position to be about one hundred miles north of Boston. Hugh spent the next days watching the tree-lined shore slip past, anxious to see signs of life; a house, a wharf, a plowed field, anything. After several days, the captain predicted that they would arrive in Boston by the next morning.

The rattle of the anchor chain woke Hugh as it dropped into the deep harbor waters. We are here, he thought. His excitement made further sleep impossible. Eager for his first glimpse of the town, Hugh crept up the stairs to the deck, treading with care in the dark. Within minutes, other passengers joined him at the ship rail.

They watched the sunrise; its tentative rays illuminated the land before them. The first pink streaks of the new day fell on three small hills, but brightened to reveal a patchwork of buildings hidden in their shade.

"There." The man next to him yelled in excitement. "There be the town of Boston."

Hugh's face fell as he scanned the shoreline. A ramshackle row of wooden buildings ran the length of a narrow, crooked street. Town, he thought in disgust, 'tis naught but a cluster of hovels. The poorest farmer in Gosberton had a sturdier house than this lot. He had a sickening sense he'd just made the greatest mistake of his life.

The rail filled as passengers streamed up from below, excited to view their new home. Men and women, overcome with emotion, fell to their knees in prayer, thanking God for their safe deliverance. Hugh surveyed the faces of his fellow shipmates and noted a look of horror on many of the passengers. One hysterical woman swore to her husband she would not get off the ship, she would go back to England instead.

Could two places be more different, thought Hugh, his attention drawn back to the shoreline. The extensive London wharves overflowed with exotic goods and bristled with longshoremen and sailors. Ships stretched out along the Thames like a leafless forest. The *Dolphin*, the only ship docked in Boston harbor, sat off a solitary wharf. On a positive note, he reflected, there was not a single brick building in sight. At least I shall have work.

The crew, eager to get ashore, hustled the passengers aboard a fleet of row boats to ferry them to land, where a small crowd gathered on the wharf. As the new arrivals approached, the crowd, arms waving, shouted halloo's and greetings across the water. Many of the passengers had family and friends already established in the colony. Hugh stood aside and allowed families to go first, letting weary mothers get their excited children off the ship. When it was his turn, he climbed down the rope ladder that dangled over the side and squeezed onto a seat in the rowboat. Two muscular sailors rowed for shore. Hugh watched the pier draw closer and sensed, not for the first time, the enormity of what he was doing. As he stepped onto dry land, he swore he'd never set food aboard a ship again.

Prior to his departure from London, he received instructions from his new employer, Mr. William Pynchon of Springfield, Massachusetts. Hugh and Johnny met his agent in a small room, smelling of damp and mold, near the London docks. Hugh signed a three-year agreement to work for Pynchon as a brick maker for passage to New England. If he settled in Springfield after his indenture finished, Pynchon guaranteed him a division of land, enough for a house lot and raising crops. Johnny read over the contract.

"Are you sure 'tis what you want, I will happily pay your passage and you'll arrive a free man."

"Aye, I'm sure. You've done enough for me already, Johnny, and your hands are full with Tom and Agnes. This is what I want. I can use my skills as a brick maker and I get my farm, 'tis more than I could hope for here."

His face set in a look of determination, he asked, "where do I make my mark?"

And now, here he was, thousands of miles from Johnny and Tom, all alone. As Hugh picked his way through the throng, he bade farewell to his fellow passengers. A small elderly man on the edge of the crowd stopped him.

"Welcome to the Bay Colony, young man, what news do you bring of England?"

"I thank you for your greeting, Sir," said Hugh. "I must admit, I know little and understand less of the doings of kings and court or Parliament. But I'll strike a bargain with you, if you guide me to my destination, I'll tell you all I know."

The old fellow who introduced himself as Goodman Brown, agreed to lead Hugh to the Blue Anchor Inn, a short distance up the muddy street. Hugh's legs wobbled like jelly as he tried to walk. Goodman Brown stopped and gave Hugh his arm to steady himself.

"I seem to have forgotten how to walk!"

"Hold on to my arm, Hugh. I can still remember how strange it was to be on dry land again. Do not despair, it won't take long and you'll be running again."

They stood in front of a large wooden house; the largest Hugh could see. The door, right on the edge of the street, swung outward almost hitting them. A dark eyed, sharp-faced man, dressed in an elegant but severe suit of black clothes, emerged. He must be someone important, thought Hugh, he has an air of authority about him. The man acknowledged Hugh and Goodman Brown with a brief nod and threw a good day to them as he rushed by, headed for the wharf.

"Who was that?"

Goodman Brown laughed. "Well now Hugh, you're not in the colony an hour and already you have seen the great man himself. "Twas none other than the Governor, Mr. John Winthrop. He must have got word of the *Dolphin's* arrival."

Hugh gaped after him. He thought Winthrop looked more like a vicar than the leader of a colony, but then, he reflected, nothing looks like I imagined.

"Mayhap you'll hear him speak someday, he gives a wondrous sermon," said Goodman Brown.

When Hugh regained his balance, the two men resumed walking and within a few minutes found themselves at the door of the Blue Anchor. They settled at a rough wooden table, redolent of fresh cut pine, and sat side by side on a hard, backless bench. Despite the warmth of the day, a fire blazed in a large hearth filled with kettles and iron legged ovens. The aroma of cooking food made Hugh's mouth water and his stomach rumbled. Goodman Brown ordered ale from the innkeeper, Mr. Fairbanks, and a trencher of venison stew for Hugh. When the wooden flagon arrived, Goodman Brown and Hugh, taking turns, raised a toast to his safe arrival in the colony. Hugh took a sip and sighed with pleasure; at least they had good ale. He pulled a pewter spoon from his pocket and dug into the piping hot stew with gusto. God, it was good. The first bite made him moan with pleasure, a meal without salt beef or mealy biscuits, heaven. Goodman Brown smiled and waited as Hugh scarfed down his food.

"Now then Hugh Parsons, your belly's full and you've a good Boston ale before you." Brown adjusted his seat. "Tell me all the news from England."

Hugh wiped his face and hands on a rough linen napkin and took a last sip of ale. He admitted that before he boarded the *Dolphin*, he was ignorant of the religious and political machinations playing out in England. He got an earful aboard ship. When his fellow passengers weren't praying, they hashed out their grievances against the king and spoke of little save the wrongs done to them at home. Hugh recounted their tales of King Charles summoning parliament and a disastrous war with Scotland. As he spoke, other customers drifted over to listen. News from England, good or bad, was a rare treat. Hugh reported Parliament's petitions to the King, their concerns about his abuse of power and how Charles, dissolved the parliament in anger at their demands. His unsettling news set off murmuring amongst the men.

Turning the tables, he asked how the colony fared. Brown spoke of illness, death and the harsh conditions endured by the early colonists. Despite a sluggish economy, the quality of life was improving and many new plantations dotted the colony. New England needed a steady influx of families who would become consumers upon arrival.

"When did you arrive?" Hugh was curious about his new friend.

"Ah, I came with the governor in 1631." He scratched his head. "Ten years now; I've seen it from the start."

"Do you regret it? Leaving England, I mean."

Hugh watched as a wave of emotion swept over the old man's face. "I lost my first wife during the crossing. I lost my second and four of me children to fever. All that's left is my son and his family. But he's got a good life and four strapping sons." He shrugged his shoulders and gave Hugh a sad smile. "I have to believe it was for the best."

The noon bell rang. Goodman Brown rose to take his leave. "That's me dinner bell. Mayhap we will meet again."

"I look forward to it and when next we meet, I will repay your kindness."

Moments after the door swung shut behind Goodman Brown, a tall man ducked under the sill and entered the inn. As he scanned the room, his eye settled on Hugh. He pushed through the throng of sailors and made his way over to Hugh's table.

"Would you be Hugh Parsons, newly arrived from England?" Without waiting for an answer, he said, "I am Samuel Chapin, Mr. Pynchon's agent here in Boston. His office in London wrote, saying to expect you on the *Dolphin*."

"Aye, I am Hugh Parsons, glad to make your acquaintance."

Samuel sat and order a drink. "I see you have met Goodman Brown; Boston's one-man welcoming committee."

Hugh laughed at the description of the spry old fellow. "He picked my brains for the better part of an hour."

"So, tell me what is your impression of New England?" Samuel wiped ale from his lips as he set the flagon down on the table.

"I can't rightly say, I've not seen much. I have questions though."

"Ask away," said Chapin.

Hugh plied Chapin with queries about Mr. Pynchon, and his new home. Samuel described the workings of the colony for Hugh and told him what he knew about William Pynchon and his founding of the town.

"Yer ship, the *Dolphin*, carried thousands of pounds of goods for Mr. Pynchon. We will transport it to his warehouse in Springfield."

"How far is it to Springfield?"

"Overland, 'tis near a hundred miles due west. The road is naught but a rough Indian track and would take us weeks to make the journey. I have a faster route in mind."

Puzzled, Hugh asked, "How then shall we get there, Goodman Chapin?"

"By boat, of course," he replied, laughing at the grimace on Hugh's face.

# Preparation

Despite his fierce objections, Hugh found himself in a boat, on the water. Captain Holloway demonstrated how to man the oars of the dingy. For the next few days, Hugh helped him, along with Samuel and his crew, transfer supplies and goods to the *Abigail*, Holloway's boat that would take them to Springfield. His back and arms ached from rowing load after load out to the scallop. It was late afternoon when they transferred the last of the heavy cargo. Hugh surveyed the piles of crates and barrels and wondered how the sailors would fit onto the crowded deck.

Hugh groaned as stretched his aching back. "What's in these crates, anyway?"

Samuel seated on a barrel, pulled a cloth from his pocket and mopped the sweat from his forehead. He patted the side of the barrel. "This lot is goods for trading with the Indians."

"Indians. There are Indians in Springfield?" Hugh, so taken aback by the notion of living amongst savages, almost fell overboard.

Samuel laughed. "There are Indians everywhere lad. Mr. Pynchon makes his living trading with the savages. He hath even learned to speak their devilish tongue. He gives them scissors and knives and such novelty stuffs and in return they give him beaver pelts. Pynchon has set himself up as the biggest Indian trader in the colony. Truth be told, a man can make his fortune with the right skills."

Hugh shook his head. "Tradings not for me. I'll take a good farm any day."

"I thought you was a brick maker, come to earn your coin building chimneys and such."

"Aye, I make bricks, and I'm proud to say it. But I'm farm bred and raised, 'tis in my blood. And between the two, I will make my fortune." Hugh surprised himself with the passion behind his words.

"You're in luck, Farmer Parsons, I hear tell the Connecticut Valley is a veritable Garden of Eden." Samuel stood, replaced his hat and climbed into the dingy, "Now then, let us get ourselves back to the Blue Anchor. I believe we could do with a flagon of ale and a dish of Mistress Fairbanks' stew."

Hugh and Samuel rowed to shore and joined Captain Holloway at the inn. Over a shared trencher of steaming venison stew, thickened with sliced onions and root vegetables, Hugh questioned the captain about the next leg of his journey. Holloway, a seasoned mariner with tanned leathery skin and sailor's squint, had plied these waters for years. His permanent home was in Salem, a day's sail up the coast from Boston, but he spent more time at sea than on dry land. He'd made the journey to Springfield countless times and accrued a wealth of knowledge of the Bay Colony.

Holloway, pushed aside empty trenchers, sending spoons clattering across the table top as he unrolled a rough map of the coastline. Pointing out various landmarks, he drew a finger along their course. They'd sail out of Boston Harbor and head east towards the tip of Cape Cod. When clear of the Cape, they would sail west aiming for the mouth of the Connecticut River. The river was navigable for almost seventy miles; a series of waterfalls south of Springfield prevented them from sailing the entire route. Wagons would meet them at that point and carry the cargo the remainder of the way to the town.

His stomach full of stew and ale, exhausted from his exertions, Hugh rose and bid everyone good night. He tumbled into bed and pulled his rough woolen blanket up to his chin. His muscles relaxed as he mulled over all that Samuel and Captain Holloway had told him. What a strange place I've come to, he thought.

The following day was the Sabbath. Sunday was a day of rest, set aside for worship and communion, manual labor forbidden until Monday morning. The inn remained quiet and for a change Hugh slept past dawn. A thump on the head jarred him awake. Hugh cracked open an eye and glanced around. Sunlight glinted off the oil paper that covered the window and the imposing figure of Samuel Chapin towered over him.

"What the devil are ye about?" Hugh rubbed his head.

"Time to rise," Samuel said. "And watch yer tongue. I'd leave the devil out of my conversations lest ye wish to find yerself before the General Court. It's not long fore they bang the drum for meeting. Get yerself up and get dressed."

Hugh yawned and rolled over. "I'm not one for going to the meetings." He covered his head with his blanket. "Go without me."

"Then you will have to change." Samuel reached down and yanked back the bed cover. "Everyone goes to meeting here, everyone. A word of warning, the quickest way to ruin is to oppose or anger a clergyman. They hold the reins of power in this colony. My advice to you: honor the Sabbath, go to meetings regular like, and keep your bloody opinions on religion to yerself."

Chastised, Hugh rose and rushed to dress. Together the men hurried the short distance to the town's only meetinghouse. As they approached, Hugh studied the rough wooden structure and compared it to the beautiful ancient stone church in Gosberton. Squat and square with a steep pitched roof, Hugh found it ugly. Samuel explained that it was not a religious building but rather the civic center of Boston. The interior of the building was as unappealing as the exterior. No memorials, no baptismal font, no stained-glass windows, nothing that would distract the eye of a bored worshiper.

The furnishings consisted of rows of rough, backless benches divided by a central aisle. Men sat on one side, women on the other, in a precise pecking order laid out by the deacons. Galleries ran down either side and there was a raised gallery above. Just as Samuel said, it appeared all Boston tried to squeeze into the small building. The pair lucked out and found a seat in the upper men's gallery. Latecomers had to stand outside the open door for the entire service.

As Hugh watched, the ministers filed in below him, like a flock of lace collared black crows. He spotted the governor, John Winthrop among them. Samuel bent and whispered in his ear, "You're in luck, the Reverend Cotton will preach the day's sermon. That's him there." He pointed to a man of middle stature with a fleshy face and curly gray hair.

After two hours of haranguing sermon, dry psalms and still more lecture, Hugh felt anything but lucky. After a final lengthy prayer, the minister released his congregation. "Jesus, I thought he'd never stop talking." Hugh rubbed his stiffened back and buttocks. "I'm desperate to piss and my stomach growls with hunger."

"We best get a move on then, there's only an hour break before we reconvene for the afternoon lecture." Samuel grinned at the expression of horror on Hugh's face.

When they neared the inn, Hugh raced past Samuel, headed for the outhouse. He yelled at Samuel to order food and drink in the meantime.

Hugh slid onto the bench and took a long sip of ale. "Must we return, who will notice our absence in that crowd?"

Samuel punched him in the arm. "Shut up Hugh and eat, you sound like a whiny papist."

The afternoon lecture was shorter but held no more delight than the morning version. Hugh decided Reverend Cotton enjoyed the sound of his voice. As he glanced around the gallery, he noted some men appeared sound asleep, anchored in place by their neighbors, they did not fall over. At last the sermon ended; they were free to go. Back at the Blue Anchor, over another fine supper prepared by Mrs. Fairbanks, Samuel told Hugh to pack his belongings. Captain Holloway was ready to sail with the morning tide.

# Springfield

My God, Hugh marveled, as they made their way along the coast of Massachusetts, this is nothing but a vast wilderness. Their ship hugged the coastline, never venturing out of sight of land. Hugh's panoramic view of his adopted country was one of blue green waves crashing onto rocky beaches, intermixed with wide stretches of empty marshland. Empty of humans that is. Hugh lost count of the varieties of waterfowl that rose from waving grass and reeds, circling in flocks overhead or diving back to the water for a fish. Towering emerald forests made a brilliant green backdrop to both beach and swamp. Trees, trees, nothing but trees as far as the eye could see, marveled Hugh. Not a village, not a farm, not a house, nor a puff of smoke in sight. Hugh found he was both excited and frightened by the prospect of hacking out a farm from this untamed land.

As the scallop neared the tip of Long Island, part of the Dutch Colony of New Amsterdam, Captain Holloway gave orders to set the vessel on a northwesterly heading. He was aiming for the small settlement of Ft. Saybrook which guarded the mouth of the Connecticut River. It surprised Hugh to find he enjoyed this journey. Unlike the Atlantic voyage, with its endless days of empty blue ocean, there was plenty to see and much to learn about this land. Captain Holloway and Goodman Chapin pointed out topical features, birds and animals unfamiliar to Hugh.

On a serious note, Holloway shared tales of the Pequot Indian War of 1636. The Natives had attacked Ft. Saybrook, killing many settlers. They burnt warehouses, destroyed farms and blockaded the river, preventing river traffic to and from Springfield. Peace was restored the next year. Relations had improved with the local tribes, but the memory of the conflict lingered in the minds of the colonists who rebuilt their homes with trepidation.

They reached the fort in late afternoon, tying up at the dock. The ship stopped to deliver letters and goods awaited by the residents. Starved for word of loved ones left behind in England, a letter was worth its weight in gold. And, for the isolated settlement, news and reports from Boston and the rest of the colony were equally welcome. Hugh and the crew aboard the scallop were happy to spend the night on shore and eat a hot homemade meal before they began the last stretch of the journey upriver to Springfield.

After a hearty supper prepared by grateful Saybrook women, Captain Holloway built a bonfire near the wharf. He and his crew wanted to sleep on dry land, but needed to keep watch on the boat and its valuable cargo. The fort commander, soldiers and a handful of farmers joined them. Captain Holloway pulled out a bottle of rum and passed it to the Commander. "What do you hear from the local natives?"

"The Indians have been quiet of late; the men are most likely hunting or trapping beaver while their women prepare for the harvest and winter season."

"They'll come trading as soon as the weather cools," said a soldier, as he took the bottle for a sip.

Holloway pointed at his boat. "That's what we carry, trade goods for Mr. Pynchon."

Finally, Captain Holloway yawned and said, "We've an early start in the morning."

The next day the crew, a little worse for the rum, continued their journey, sailing due north. It was late

August and the days, although growing shorter, remained warm. The *Abigail* made stops at the small muddy settlements of Windsor and Hartford to deliver letters and goods that had traveled with Hugh on the *Dolphin* from England. The crew inquired about the native tribes. All was quiet, the locals reported. "Praise God," said the Captain, "If the Indians organized and launched a concerted attack, they could wipe us off the face of this continent and push us back into the sea."

The river narrowed as the scallop sailed further inland. Hugh scoured the shoreline for signs of life, he was eager to spot an Indian, having not yet set eyes on the original inhabitants of the land. The abundance of wildlife amazed him. Slender brown deer, drinking at the river's edge, bounded into the wood at the ship's approach. Samuel pointed out a beaver to Hugh who laughed at its unusual tail. Once he thought he saw bear but he couldn't be sure.

Early one morning, as he emptied his bladder into the water below, a canoe appeared out of the river mist. Startled, Hugh shivered as a frisson of fear rippled down his spine. He gawked as the two strange silent figures paddled past the scallop. Their hair was black as coal and worn in a braid down their back. One had a single eagle feather stuck at a jaunty angle in his hair. They wore no shirts despite the morning chill; their legs clad in leather garments. Indians, Hugh realized, those are Indians. The men in the craft, ignoring Hugh and the ship, disappeared back into the mist, headed downstream. He wished he could tell his nephews...

By late morning, the mist burned off and Hugh spied rough water, dead ahead. A series of low waterfalls blocked their passage. This was the end of his trip by boat, the remainder of the journey would be by foot or wagon.

Hugh knew this meant that he was almost at his destination. Eager to reach his new home, he helped the crew unload the vessel while Samuel Chapin set out on foot for Springfield. Chapin said he would return by nightfall with men and wagons to transport Mr. Pynchon's goods the rest of the way.

By early afternoon, all the crates and barrels sat stacked on the shore ready for the transport wagons. Hugh dipped his kerchief into the river and sponged his face and neck as he listened to the lazy buzz of cicadas. He stretched out on sweet meadow grass while Captain Holloway set to work with string and hooks to catch some trout. A sailor gathered fallen wood from the edge of the trees and built a small fire. When the coals were red hot, they grilled the fish, skewered on sticks. Holloway turned them as they sizzled. The smell made Hugh's mouth water. The men sat in a circle around the cooling embers and devoured the grilled fish.

Hugh groaned with pleasure as he ate a final bite. He licked the last drop of savory autumn fat from his fingers. "Captain Holloway, I do believe that was the best supper I have ever ate."

"Aye, 'twas mighty fine-," said the Captain. He cocked his head and looked toward the falls. "Ah, I believe Goodman Chapin returns with his wagons. Yes, there he is."

"Hallo. Hallo, there Captain, I have returned," cried Goodman Chapin. "Here is my help come to take our goods back to Springfield." Samuel introduced Hugh to his companions. "Hugh this here is Rice Bedortha, John Lumbard and Jonathan Taylor."

Hugh nodded his head in greeting at his new neighbors. "'Tis good to meet you, I am Hugh Parsons." The men shook hands.

Hugh noted that Samuel's wagons were not empty. "What is this lot then?" He pointed at the barrels.

"Oh, 'tis furs from Mr. Pynchon's warehouse. He wants them transported to Boston. They'll go out on the next ship bound for London."

The sound of evening bird song serenaded them as the late summer sun slid towards the horizon. Samuel reached into the first wagon and pulled out a familiar brown bottle that Hugh recognized on sight. "Men, I say we bunk down here tonight and get this lot loaded in the morning. I've a bit of rum we can share to help pass the evening; you can tell Hugh all you know about life in Springfield."

The next morning, Hugh rose and bade Captain Holloway farewell. Hugh shook his hand and thanked him for his kindness. "Good luck young man, I expect good reports about you, when I return." Holloway stepped aboard and with a last wave cast off his line; the boat came about and headed south. Hugh watched until it was out of sight.

They spent the next few hours reloading the cargo. The men worked, eager to get their delivery back home. With the wagons loaded they rumbled up the dusty track that paralleled the water. After a few miles, the tree-line fell away from the river giving Hugh his first view of Springfield. From his vantage point he saw a single row of a dozen or more drab wooden thatch-roofed houses and outbuildings strung out along the line of the river. In front of the buildings was a thin ribbon of brown, a road that ran the length of the entire settlement. Between the river and the houses were plots of golden crops, ripening in the summer sun. Gray wood-smoke curled from mud-clad chimneys. Somewhere a dog barked.

"Welcome to Springfield," said Samuel.

# Proposal
1645

Hugh once thought the weather in England unpredictable, but the volatile temperature changes in this new world never ceased to amaze him. It might be cold when it ought to be warm and warm when it ought to be freezing. On an early spring day, a light breeze blew from the south; the sky an unblemished periwinkle blue. The day started out cool, by noon the temperature had risen making for a pleasant afternoon. Just a fortnight ago, he had cursed the elements as he worked to kiln dry an overdue order of bricks. The cold damp dreary days made his life miserable and his brick soggy. A sudden change in the wind direction brought mild and dry conditions perfect for his bricks.

That morning, Hugh loaded his cart with his finished bricks and coaxed his mare up the street towards the Clark's house. Goodman Clark had hired him to build a new central chimney and hearth. It would replace the current wooden, mud plastered one that was not only a fire hazard but much too small to accommodate the Clarks and their growing family. He had made countless brick for Mr. Pynchon, but they went to repay his passage and indenture. This was his first independent order. Goodman Lawrence would have been proud of him; he had driven a hard bargain.

When Hugh arrived at the house, Goodman Clark directed him to the back, where he wanted the bricks stacked. As he pulled around to the side of the building, Goody Clark bustled out to inspect his work, checking the color and size of the bricks. After much hemming and hawing, she pronounced them satisfactory. With a sigh of relief, Hugh unloaded his delivery. As he stacked the last dusty red brick, he stood and stretched to ease the burn in the muscles of his back and arms. A trickle of sweat ran down his temple. He bent over and retrieved a kerchief from his coat pocket and mopped his face and brow.

A flash of red caught his eye; a woman slipped out the kitchen door. He watched, unnoticed, as she spread laundered linens over bushes to dry. As she leaned over, her dress rode up and he could see the edge of her red petticoats. It made him smile. Her linen cap was askew and a few curls escaped its confines. Her hair glinted like gold in the bright sun, teasing his imagination. She had been working hard, her exertions raised the color in her face, and gave her complexion a rosy glow. In that unexpected moment, she was as captivating a vision as he had ever seen. Mesmerized, Hugh stood and stared. She bent to lift a damp linen bed sheet from her basket and spread it to dry on a bayberry bush. As she stretched to throw the sheet, her dress strained across her back and shoulder, molding itself against her supple body. The sight of her sent a flare of desire coursing through his body.

Hugh knew who she was. He knew everyone in Springfield. Mary Lewis was her name; the Clark's serving woman. He had seen her about the settlement and at the meetinghouse on Sundays, but they had never spoken, only exchanged the polite greetings of strangers. Hugh had found her plain looking and when told she had a husband, lost interest in her.

It's funny how perceptions can change in a moment, he marveled. Hugh was desperate to speak to her but struggled to find the right words. He had always found himself uneasy in the company of women, having little opportunity to socialize with them since leaving England. He tried to imagine some gentle conversation, something, anything to say to her. An unintended sigh of frustration and despair escaped him. Startled by the sound, Mary whipped around and caught Hugh's staring eye.

"Humph, Goodman Parsons, is it not? Is aught amiss that you stare at me with such boldness?"

Hugh, his cheeks aflame, felt like a fool in front of her. "Nay, Mistress, my apologies, I did not mean to offer any offense."

"Well then, you can come and help me hang these last sheets, and then you may consider yourself forgiven."

Hugh broke into a grin at her saucy tone and hurried to assist her. If he could not conjure the words, it seemed she could.

Over the next few weeks, Hugh looked for and found excuses to call on Goodman Clark, hoping to see and speak with Mary. Mystified by their sudden popularity with Hugh, the Clarks were too polite to question it. On one occasion, he arrived to find Clark and his wife away from home. Mary invited him into the kitchen and gave him a cup of small beer to quench his thirst and a slice of baked cornbread, still warm from the new oven. He had just swallowed the last bite when she sent him on his way.

Hugh worked up the courage to ask Goodman Clark for permission call on Mary, as he had run out of excuses to visit. Relieved that Hugh Parsons was not interested in their own daughter, for whom they had high hopes, the Clarks assented to one visit a week after Sunday service and only if Mary had completed her chores to Goody Clark's satisfaction.

Courting under the watchful gaze of the Clark's made Mary uneasy. Goody Clark had a keen eye and a reproving tongue. Mary said she could spot a discretion from a mile away with one eye closed. At least it was summer and they could meet outdoors. Summer courtships were always happier for the couple. Nothing stifled a budding romance quicker than shivering around a smoking fire, in the dead of winter, surrounded by the entire household.

Once in a while, Hugh and Mary stole away and walked along the river's edge. Mary let Hugh hold her hand, but pulled away if a neighbor came into view. Several times they waded through the waist high grass of the long meadow and slipped out of view into the deep shade of the woods.

One evening, they strolled along the river path. The chirp of crickets provided background music for the eerie night call of the whip-poor-will. It was almost the summer solstice, daylight stretched deep into the evening hours. Mary asked Hugh about his childhood and why he had come to New England. He told her about Gosberton and his early life. "Enough about me, tell me about your village in England, what was it like?"

Mary rolled her eyes at him. "Not everyone comes from England. I am Welsh." She sighed, a wistful look stole over her face. "Llanvaches, near the Severn River. Have you heard of the Severn?"

Hugh shook his head. He knew nothing of Wales. Mary waved her hand at the river. "A mighty river, the Severn, not like this," she said, with a dismissive tone. "It is the border between Wales and England. 'Twas beautiful there. Llanvaches is no bigger than Springfield. It seems a lifetime since I left." She stared down at the water, lost in her reverie.

Hugh wanted to ask about her marriage, but feared what she might say. They stood side by side staring out at the water. "Tell me about your husband." He held his breath.

"I wondered when you would ask." She turned to him. "I married in my sixteenth year. He was the brother of my friend, Blanche. She's Blanche Bedortha now, married to Reice. Anyway, his name was Robert Lewis."

"What happened, why did he leave you?"

"He was a papist, kept to the old ways. Blanche and I, we attended the services of Reverend William Wroth after he came to Llanvaches. He established a new church, but Robert would hear nothing of it. We fought about it almost every day. In the end, he left; left without a word." She shrugged her shoulders, her face inscrutable.

Hugh studied her, trying to read her expression. "Did you try to find him?"

"Of course, but he up and disappeared, no one has seen him since. Alexander Edwards, who also hails from Llanvaches, has written home for me, trying to locate him, to no avail."

Hugh took a deep breath. "Do you want to find him?" His heart pounded as he waited for her reply.

"No." She smiled up at him.

Relief washed over him, he feared she yearned for him. "'Tis a long journey from Wales to Springfield. How did ye come to be here?"

"'Twas the Reverend, the Reverend Wroth that is. He organized transport for any in his congregation willing to leave. Blanche and I signed up as servants, and here I am."

A few weeks later, Goody Clark allowed Mary a Sunday off. After lecture, she and Hugh ambled towards the northern end of town. Leaving the road, Hugh led her down an ancient Indian track. Mary hesitated but Hugh grabbed her hand and pulled her along, he had a surprise

49

to show her. As they moved deeper into the wood, it became dark and close. Trees towered over their heads, the tops swaying in an unfelt wind, whispering and moaning in their own secret language. Brambles and bracken snagged at her dress. The still air was full of sounds and movement. An owl screeched nearby and they could hear the bark of foxes. Leaves rustled by unseen creatures left Mary jumpy and on edge. The thought of Indians and wild animals frightened her. More than anything she sensed a malevolent presence in these dense woods.

The ancient forests surrounding Springfield fascinated, not repelled Hugh. He had never seen stands of virgin wood; trees centuries old untouched by man. The forest landscape, so different from the flat watery fens of East Anglia, was a source of wonder. He loved to explore and would follow the trails made by men and animals for miles. He had no experience at trapping but hoped to discover a beaver den and earn a month's wages with its pelt.

They arrived at one of his favorite places, one he wished to share with Mary. Hugh held her hand as she stepped into a small round clearing. Shafts of sunlight gave it the illusion of a well-lit room. A deep layer of fragrant pine needles carpeted the forest floor. Mary's mouth fell open in surprise. Hands on her head, she twirled around, gazing up at the sky. "'Tis a fairy house."

Hugh laughed, grabbed her hand and swung her around. "Nay, Mary, there be no fairies here, we left them behind in old England."

Her smile dropped, with a serious expression she said, "'Tis, no laughing matter, there's fairies and worse here."

Hugh frowned. "What's worse than fairies?"

"Witches," she said with a shiver. "There are witches here, to be sure."

Hugh put his arms around her, trying to ward off her uneasiness and recapture their earlier lighthearted mood. "Don't be afraid," he murmured.

Unable to resist, he bent to kiss her. Mary surprised him by responding. Entwined, they sank to the pine floor of the clearing, locked in their embrace. Hugh moved his hands along her curves, tentative at first, her lack of resistance emboldened him. When Hugh tried to pull her skirts up, her ardor fled. With a tremendous shove, Mary pushed him off of her. Hugh suddenly found himself staring up at treetops and sky. He held a hand up to block the sun from his eyes. He sighed as Mary, eyes blazing, jumped to her feet.

"I'm sorry Mary, say you forgive me," he said, a forlorn look on his face. "I did not mean to distress you."

"Humph! I may be a poor servant, but I'm no doxy, ready to take a tumble with any man who will have me. I've not much to my name, but my reputation is unblemished." Anger shone from her eyes and she tucked her curls back into place and straightened her skirts.

Hugh got up and adjusted his breeches and pulled a pine needle from his hair. "Ye will have to seek a divorce from that bastard Lewis."

"Oh, why is that then?"

Hugh stood face to face with her. He tipped her chin up, so they looked into each other's eyes. "Because I am going to marry you."

# Divorce

Hugh lay, hands under his head, waiting for dawn. He had been awake for hours. At last, he heard the Lumbard's cock crow. He tried to eat breakfast, but his nerves were making him nauseous. He rushed through his morning chores, mouthing the words he would speak to Mr. Pynchon. His chickens appeared unimpressed with his speech as they pecked at their corn. Hugh milked his goat, acquired from a neighbor. He rattled off his speech in rhythm to his hands as they pulled on her soft teats.

The goat turned her head and gave him a long unblinking stare. "What do you think?" he asked. Chewing her cud without comment, she blinked then turned away.

Chores done, Hugh scrubbed himself as best he could and dressed in his Sunday coat. Mary joined him on the high road as he neared the Clark's place. She fussed over his clothes, ensuring he looked respectable.

"You'll do," she said, sending him on his way with a gentle smile.

Hugh practiced his speech as he strode along the road. He struggled to remain calm, but his nerves were getting the better of him; he felt his heart pound in his chest. After several deep breaths, he rapped on Pynchon's door. A young serving girl ushered him into a wood paneled hall and instructed him to wait while she inquired on his behalf. Hugh doffed his hat and ran through his speech once again, as he awaited her return.

"You're in luck, Mr. Pynchon departs for Hartford this afternoon, but he will see you." She pointed the way. "First room at the top."

Hugh bounded up the stairs and knocked on the closed door at the top the landing. A deep voice bid him enter. The room was small and warm. Someone had opened a garret window on the chance that a stray breeze might slip through and stir the stale air. Iron bound chests and bundles of fur choked the room; a pile of beaver pelts added to the pungent aroma. Pynchon sat behind a cluttered writing desk; his white head bent over an open book. He appeared to be scribbling figures in his ledger with fat ink stained fingers.

"Mr. Pynchon, sir, might I have a word?"

Pynchon set down his quill and glanced up from his writing. He leaned back in his chair. "Ah, Goodman Parsons, good day to you. As I recall, you received your house and planting lots at last quarter's meeting. Is farming to your liking?"

Excellent, thought Hugh, as he cleared his throat, a spot of conversation before I make my request. "Aye, Sir, 'tis good to have land under the plow again. But I own 'tis hard work, much harder than my father's farm in Lincolnshire."

"Aye, that it is Hugh, that it is." Pynchon nodded in agreement. "'Tis mighty work to plow virgin land. Still, at least you can make bricks for a living, when farming gets too hard. Now, how may I be of service to you?"

Hugh took a deep breath and tried to rein in his nerves. "Well, Mr. Pynchon, sir, it appears I have found me a wife, and I would like to contract a marriage."

Pynchon pursed his lips and nodded as Hugh spoke, giving him his full attention. "A man needs a wife, a helpmate, but I sense there is a problem. Who is the woman?"

"Mary Lewis, sir."

"Mary Lewis." Pynchon sat back, folding his arms across his chest, and studied Hugh. "You speak of Goodman Clark's servant, Mary Lewis?"

"Yes, sir."

"Humph. Is she not married already? And to a papist at that!" He waved his hands with a dismissive flourish as if to indicate his disapproval.

Hugh felt his jaw tighten, but remained calm. I cannot get angry he schooled himself. "Yes, Mr. Pynchon, sir, 'tis Mary Lewis I wish to wed. She is a good Christian, a virtuous hardworking woman. I can vouch that she is no papist, unlike the rogue who abandoned her years ago. Mary desires to secure a divorce from him so we can marry."

Pynchon pursed his lips and gave Hugh a critical look. "Well, I'll grant you there are few marriageable women in Springfield. Would it not be best to wait for someone more suitable, or perhaps look to Boston for a wife?"

"I am sure sir, Mary Lewis is a God-fearing woman, she is no papist. I believe she will make me a good wife."

Pynchon realized that Hugh remained standing and offered him a chair. Relieved, he sat on the rough wood, grateful to have a seat under him. The stink of the beaver belts made him nauseous. He dabbed his forehead with his kerchief before returning it to his pocket.

"She must petition the court in Boston for a divorce. You cannot wed until her first union is set aside."

"Aye, sir." Hugh nodded in agreement. "We hope you will assist us with her case. She is well known by numerous people here in Springfield. They grew up together in Wales and can testify to her faith."

Pynchon gave Hugh a piercing stare as if trying to read his mind. "If ye are determined, Hugh Parsons, I will see what I can do. I shall write to Mr. Winthrop in Boston to seek his advice." He pulled out a sheet of paper and took up his quill, waving towards the door.

The interview over, Hugh sighed with relief. "Thank you, Mr. Pynchon, sir."

Hugh suspected Mr. Pynchon would question his choice in Mary. He had not been sure himself if he would ask her for her hand until the words tumbled from his mouth. But if not Mary, who? Marriageable women did not grow on trees in Springfield. She had a prettyish face, and she worked hard for Mr. Clark, but then again, she had no choice, he thought, being a servant.

Hugh hurried to the Clark's house to share the news with Mary. He did not tell her of Pynchon's hesitation regarding the suitability of the marriage.

"What do we do now?" she asked.

"We wait for Pynchon to receive instructions from Mr. Winthrop." Hugh offered her an encouraging smile.

Mary's face fell as Hugh gave her the news. "How long will that take?"

"I cannot say. But the weather is fine and the roads are passable. I hope it will not take the post longer than a week or two to deliver a letter to Boston."

In early June, Hugh received a summons from Mr. Pynchon, delivered by a servant, to meet with him the following morning. Hugh hoped the news would be good. The same serving girl let him inside and once again directed him upstairs to Pynchon's study. This time, the piles of beaver pelts were gone along with their musky odor. Manuscript papers and several bibles lay in thick piles on the desktop. Pynchon set down his quill, sprinkled sand to dry his ink, then attempted to tidy the mess.

"I am writing a book," he explained without inviting comment. Digging under one stack he pulled out a folded letter. "I've had a reply from John Winthrop concerning Mary Lewis and whether she can seek a divorce from her husband." He held the letter out for Hugh to see though he could not read the contents.

Hugh held his breath, but sighed with disappointment as Pynchon read. "Mr. Winthrop instructs me to- 'gather testimony from those who know her to ascertain her good character and evidence to prove she is not a papist,' -and I am to forward this to him in Boston."

Hugh groaned. It could take weeks if not months, he thought. "Is there anything we can do to assist you, Mr. Pynchon?"

"Aye, I will need a list of those who know her and will speak on her behalf. I understand that Alexander Edwards hails from her village in Wales. Mayhap there are others as well. When I have the names, I will interview them. Patience, Goodman Parsons, use this time wisely, get to know the woman who would be your wife." He paused a moment. "I was down at Long Meadow yesterday. I see that you have made many improvements to your house lot. You have a fine-looking barn and kiln house. How is the house coming along?"

"Very well, sir. 'Tis small but it has a fine brick chimney."

Pynchon laughed. "Ah, I am sure it does. Well then Hugh, get me the names and I shall begin straight away."

The next morning, Hugh and Mary huddled in the Clark's kitchen to compile a list of names for Mr. Pynchon. Since neither of them could write, they asked Henry Burt for his help. He promised to give the list to Mr. Pynchon right away. There was naught to do but wait.

The summer dragged by, a slow progression of days. Hugh spent his spare time working on his house, sometimes until late in the evening. He hoped to have it finished by late August, all he needed was a wife. On a hot Sunday afternoon, Hugh and Mary exited the meetinghouse at the close of the noon lecture. Mr. Pynchon called to them, requesting they follow him to his house. He had word from Boston. They stood in the hall as he went upstairs to fetch his latest letter from Mr. Winthrop. Mary shook with excitement or nerves; Hugh was not sure which.

"What if he said no?" whispered Mary.

Hugh took her hand for a moment and gave it a reassuring squeeze. "Do not fret, he will not say no. If he does, I will ride to Boston and throttle him with my bare hands!"

"Hugh, hush, Mr. Pynchon will hear."

Pynchon returned, clattering down the stairs, the letter in hand. With painstaking effort, he unfolded it, smoothing out the creases in the paper. He appeared to read over it; his lips moving without speaking, as Hugh and Mary watched. Hugh held his breath, waiting for Pynchon to speak. At last, he lifted his eyes from the paper and fixated on Mary's face.

"Goody Lewis, the Court of Assistants has granted me permission to annul your marriage. You are free to marry," He pointed at Hugh, "this man."

# Marriage

October was harvest time in Massachusetts. The local corn crop looked to be a good one, for which the Springfield farmers were thankful. Autumn was not the ideal season to be married. December was a popular time, but Hugh was impatient; he wanted to marry as soon as possible, even if it meant forgoing a wedding dinner. But a harvest wedding did not prevent a pre-wedding eve celebration.

Hugh gathered with his neighbors for a celebratory drink. The small town had no true tavern or inn as yet, but Pynchon allowed Francis Pepper and his wife to operate an ordinary out of their home. Hugh built them a great chimney with a baking oven. Goody Pepper made bread and brewed ale which Goodman Pepper served in his large hall to the thirsty folk of Springfield. Francis stocked more potent liquor, rum and fortified wines, bought from Mr. Pynchon. Hugh, in a rare generous mood, paid for a round of fine Madeira wine.

Married men offered Hugh ribald advice for a successful wedding night. Samuel Chapin suggested that his wedding night was the last happy night of his life and encouraged him to make the most of it. The room burst into laughter; men nodding their heads in agreement, their wives making pursed lipped faces at each other. After a second round of drinks, contagious yawns broke out across the room. Gradually, people drifted home, tired from the day's labor. Tomorrow brought more of the same.

Hugh rose before dawn and completed his daily chores; a grin plastered on his face. Following a quick breakfast, he washed his face and hands and did his best to clean the dirt from his nails. Last night, he had laid out his clothes; a clean linen shirt and a red flannel waistcoat, Mary's wedding present to him. Outside, he bent to pluck a roadside flower and threaded it through the buttonhole of his jacket. There was a bounce in his step as he walked the short distance to the Bedortha's house. His bride spent her final night as an unmarried woman with her friend Blanche, who offered to help her dress for the ceremony.

Reice flung open the door to Hugh's staccato knock. He stepped outside and clapped Hugh on the back. "The women will be but a moment." He waggled his eyebrows at Hugh. "'Tis not too late to make a run for it." Reice laughed at his own jest.

"What is so comical that ye laugh so?" Blanche narrowed her eyes and frowned at her husband.

Hugh gulped as Mary floated out. Her eyes were bright and her cheeks had a rosy glow. She had on her Sunday dress; her red petticoats flirted from beneath her skirts. Blanche had sewed her a new linen cap, edged with a length of delicate lace. Blond ringlets framed her face.

Hugh gave her an approving smile. She smiled back. "Are ye ready?"

He nodded at her. "Aye, we don't want to keep Mr. Pynchon waiting."

The couples strolled up the street to the Pynchon home. They waited in the hall where Blanche and Mary admired the fine wood paneling. Someone had placed a vase of wild flowers on a table, scenting the room with their smell. Mr. Pynchon entered, dressed in his finery. He noted the two witnesses and asked if they were ready. Hugh and Mary nodded their assent.

Pynchon, who stood in front of them, turned to Hugh. "Hugh Parsons wilt thou take this woman in the covenant of marriage?"

"Aye, I will." Hugh nodded.

Turning to Mary, Pynchon addressed her. "Mary Lewis, wilt thou take this man in the covenant of marriage?"

"I will."

"As a magistrate, in the Colony of Massachusetts, and with all the authority therein, I declare that you are man and wife."

"That's it?" Hugh looked from Mary to Mr. Pynchon.

Pynchon lifted an eyebrow. "Married is married, Goodman Parsons. You have both declared your contract. Do you wish for a lengthy sermon?"

Hugh blushed and shook his head.

"Very well. Do not forget to see Mr. Burt and ask him to record your marriage in the town book. Do you know today's date?"

"No sir, I do not."

Pynchon picked up a small notebook and flipped through the pages. "Today is October the 27th in the year of our Lord 1645."

Hugh repeated the date and promised to see Henry Burt straight away. Pynchon turned to Mary and gave her a smile.

"Congratulations to you, Goody Parsons. I wish you a long prosperous life together."

"Thank you, sir."

'Tis done, thought Hugh, I am a married man. He turned and gave Mary a nervous smile, which she returned. The foursome returned to the Bedortha home where Blanche gave Mary a hug and waved as Hugh took Mary's hand and led her to his home; now their home. Hugh lifted the latch and pushed open the door. With a flourish, he ushered Mary across the threshold. The house comprised two rooms; hall and parlor, with a lean-to kitchen. Rough oak timbers, hewn from trees cut by Hugh himself, formed the framework of the house. Instead of expensive wood paneling, it had wattle and daub filled walls. Fragrant pine planks lay over a rock lined cellar. The most prominent feature, a large brick chimney, divided the house into two. Hugh grinned with pride as he showed Mary a small baking oven, built into the chimney.

Mary poked around the hall. "'Tis very small. The Clark's house is much grander."

"'Tisn't finished. I plan to build a second story." Hugh smiled and wagged his eyebrows. "When we have children."

Mary rolled her eyes at him. She stuck her head into the lean-to and poked through the contents of the barrels. "There's hardly any food stuffs, what are we to eat?"

A muscle tightened in Hugh's jaw. "Tomorrow, you can go see Mr. Pynchon's man at the warehouse and buy what staples you need. I have an account with him."

He stepped through the doorway into the parlor. "Come and see, in here. I had Mr. Clark's man move your belongings while we were at Mr. Pynchon's."

Mary crossed the hall and stuck her head into the parlor. Hugh stood next to the bed, his wedding surprise for his new wife. She sniffed as she entered, her gaze flicked around the room, ignoring the bed. Hugh pointed out her chest, tucked into a corner. Mary shivered and wrapped her shawl tight around her shoulders. "'Tis freezing in here."

The smile faded from Hugh's face as he watched her reaction to his house.

She looked around once more. "I should have stayed with the Clarks, I was better off as a servant," she said, with the toss of her head, "at least they kept me warm and well fed."

Hugh, bit his tongue, trying not to lose his temper. She's just nervous is all, he thought. He reached to embrace her and said, "I will keep you warm Mary."

Mary danced away from his arms. "Humph, I should have waited for you to finish the house afore we married. Blanche will laugh when she sees the inside of this place."

Her words stung. He had worked damn hard to get this place habitable for her. "Mary, you are acting unreasonable. Blanche's home is not better than this, and she hath no brick chimney. Twill be a fine house one day."

"Well, twill never be as fine a house as the Clark's."

"Jesus woman, are ye not married five minutes and already turned into a complaining shrew." Hugh knew he was losing control, but he didn't care. He grabbed his hat off the peg where it hung and stomped to the door. It was not right that his wife should speak to him in such a manner and tone, he told himself. Flinging open the wooden door, he turned and gave her a hard stare. He lifted his hand and shook a finger at her.

"Mayhap, you should have bided with the Clarks, and you may find yourself back there with them afore long." He choked out a bitter laugh. "Aye, I begin to see why your first husband left you." He stomped out the door slamming it behind him.

Mary raced after him. "Where are you going Hugh?"

"To the planting field," he shouted, as he strode out of sight.

The fall weather was cooperating. The days, cool and rain-free, made for ideal conditions for clearing land.

Hugh had started preparations for planting his fields, determined to sow his first crop come spring. His house lot, a long and narrow strip stretching from the river to the edge of the wet meadow, was eight acres. His grant also included acreage in the Long Meadow, where he grew hay for his animals. Beyond the meadow were tree lots where each man could cut his own timber. Across the river lay the planting lots, more land for growing crops. Hugh had moved his kiln to his house lot, but this took up only small part of the land, the rest he could clear for farming and for Mary's house garden.

Clearing virgin land was arduous and back breaking. The removal of trees and brush was the first step. Hugh used his horse to help pull the stump and roots from the ground. The long tentacles that anchored ancient oaks, beech and maples, reached deep into the earth. They resisted Hugh's efforts but gradually lost their grip and slipped free.

After an afternoon of intense labor, Hugh trudged home in a misty rain, his temper cooled; dissipated by his exertions. He led his horse to the barn, giving it feed and water. While he brushed the horse, he thought of what to say to his new wife. "Samuel was wrong, yesterday was the last happy night of my life," he said, out loud. With the animals settled for the night, Hugh crossed the yard. He watched the pale glow of the autumn sun slide behind the dark smudge of the tree line. As the darkness of evening thickened, the sudden screech of a great owl startled him, sending a shiver up his spine. He stood awkward before his own door. What the hell am I doing, he wondered, and reached for the latch. The door swung open.

"What on earth are you doing lurking out in the rain?" Mary waved him into the house. "Get inside and warm yourself, you look half froze to death."

Hugh entered. He gave Mary a wary look before removing his hat. He moved to stand by the hearth, reaching numb hands towards the glowing warmth.

"I've made you supper." Mary gave him a wan smile, waved her hands to show him the table. "A peace offering."

Spread before him on the table was a block of cheese and brown bread, smeared with a thick layer of butter. A stew bubbled over the fire and a jug of what Hugh hoped was beer sat on the sideboard.

"You found everything all right, I see?"

"Aye, I did, now come, come and sit Hugh." She pulled out a chair for him. "Let's eat our first meal as husband and wife in peace, please let us be friends, again."

Hugh's stomach grumbled as if in response, startling them both into laughter. "I guess that's your answer."

Mary laughed in relief and grabbed a trencher to fill with pottage. She placed the savory dish of pease, onions and a mixture of fresh and dried herbs in front of Hugh. A curl of steam rose from the food and teased him with its aroma. He realized he had not eaten since yesterday, having been to nervous that morning. Anger had fueled his belly. He sat and dug into the food. Mary joined him at the table. Hugh, pleased that she had set aside her earlier complaints, pretended it had not happened. Maybe 'twas her nerves, he thought.

After their meal, she cleared the supper dishes, and Hugh banked down the fire for the night, Mary led Hugh to their bed to quench a different hunger.

# Man and Wife

December 1645

For the next few weeks, Hugh and Mary struggled to adapt to life as man and wife and form a cohesive unit. But they rubbed each other like grit on an iron pot. A stray comment, like flint on steel, might spark an argument in a flash. Hugh used words as a hammer to pound out his meaning. Mary's voice was sharp and stabbing. She probed with her words, searching for weakness. Hugh found the remedy for marital discord in manual labor. He spent long hours working his land, making progress, despite the encroaching winter. He was in a race against the hard frosts of December and January snows that made ground work impossible. His dream of becoming a farmer inched closer, one tree stump at a time.

On a mid-December afternoon, Hugh and his neighbor stood in his planting field across the river. The slate gray sky threatened and the damp air smelled of snow. A biting wind was rising. Jonathan Burt shoved his raw hands into the deep pockets of his cloak and surveyed Hugh's progress. "You've made good work of the plow Hugh; I warrant you'll be able to plant near on five acres of Indian corn, come Spring."

Hugh grunted in response. Lifting his head, he watched the thickening clouds. "Storms a brewing," he said.

"Aye." Jonathan stamped his feet to keep them warm. "It looks to be snowing soon. There'll be no more plowing till March. Let's get across the river before the snow flies and me toes freeze."

Hugh headed for the river's edge and their boat. "Jesus, 'tis cold as a witch's tit out here!"

"What do you know of witches?" Jonathan snickered as he clambered into the craft alongside Hugh. "Besides you have your wife now to keep you warm."

"Humph. As you say, I have a wife. But 'twill be the size of my woodpile that will keep me warm this winter." The men, backs straining, pulled hard on the oars. A stiff wind whipped up tiny caps that danced on the icy water. They maneuvered the boat to a small dock and dragged it out of the river, trying not to wet their boots. After covering the craft with a tarp, Hugh and Jonathan trudged up the path from the river. Hugh shivered and yanked his cap over his ears as the first snowflakes fell.

Hugh said farewell to Jonathan and headed home. Although satisfied with his progress, he dreaded the thought of spending the impending winter months trapped in the small house with Mary. Brushing the snow from his cloak, he stamped the thick river mud from his boots and ducked under the door jamb. The house was silent save for the sound of weeping. "Mary, what's wrong?"

Hugh discovered his wife in a heap on the bed, crying. Something terrible must have occurred, he thought, as he knelt beside her. Hugh, with a gentle touch, lifted the hair away from her face.

"Mary, what ails you, what is wrong that you carry on so, are you hurt?"

Mary raised a tear streaked face and glared at Hugh. "My monthly courses have not come," she said, spitting out the words, one at a time. "I fear I am with child; two months married and I am already carrying a babe."

Her reaction to the pregnancy stunned and puzzled him. Hugh rocked back on his heels. "But 'tis good news. Isn't this what you desire Mary, a family. Why are you so distressed?"

"I'm afraid." A tear slipped from the corner of her eye.

Hugh reached into his pocket and handed her his handkerchief. "Afraid of what?"

"Afraid to die, Hugh. I am afraid to die. My own mam died in childbirth as did my gran. Did your mam not die birthing you?" Her voice quivered with emotion.

"Come now Mary," he said, "'tis in God's hands, there is naught ye can do." Hugh, unable to conjure any sympathy, attempted to brush off her concerns. "All will be well."

Mary did not reply but wiped her eyes with the bed sheet. Hugh stood and gave her an encouraging smile as she sat.

Unfamiliar with female emotions, Hugh believed the situation resolved. "What you need is honest hard work to take your mind off your worries."

Mary's head jerked around to look at him. Her expression sending signals that went unheeded.

"Come now, enough lolly-gagging, I've worked long and hard today. I'm hungry for my supper." Hugh took a step towards the hall.

"You want your supper, do you? Here is something you can chew on."

Hugh ducked as a shoe flew past his retreating head. Sighing, he searched the lean-to kitchen for sustenance. He cut himself a slice of day-old cornbread and poured now sour beer into a mug for his supper. After his meager meal, he banked down the fire, leaving just a glow of embers to light the hall. He could hear the wind keening outside, the shutters rattled in response. A few snowflakes blew under the door; it would be a cold night.

Hugh undressed in the dark room and hung his clothes on a peg. He crept into the parlor and slipped under the coverlet, trying not to awaken Mary. Tired as he was, sleep evaded him, his mind in turmoil. What have I done, he wondered; how will we survive this? The howl of a nearby wolf sent shivers up his spine. 'Tis an omen, he decided, before sliding into uneasy slumber.

The wind dropped during the night. The storm, a small one, pushed on, leaving a clear blue sky. Hugh rose early and tried not to disturb Mary. The house was cold as he set about rekindling the fire, feeding the hungry flames with fatwood until he could add sufficient larger logs to get a blaze going. The fire slowly shared its warmth with the room. He ate the last of the stale cornbread, washed down with plain water, before stealing out the door. He shut it quickly to avoid letting out the little heat that had accumulated.

Hugh checked on the animals in the barn, giving the goat a forkful of fodder. Reassured that all was well, he headed towards the Taylor's house. The snow was already melting, leaving small puddles in the rutted track. He and Jonathan were joining a work party to cut timber. With winter's approach, this was their last chance to fell trees this year. They worked collectively and divided the wood amongst them. It was theirs to use or sell, as they pleased.

Once away from the house Hugh's mood lightened, even the dark wood could not dampen his spirits for long. The stale smoky air of the house behind him, Hugh closed his eyes and inhaled the fresh cool air. How peaceful it was out here. Hugh greeted the men gathered in Taylor's barn; they were discussing a sickly horse. Nathaniel Bliss argued that the mare needed a mustard poultice, but John Matthews disagreed insisting that only comfrey root would do. Hugh, leaning against a hay cart, let out a loud yawn.

"What's this Hugh, your new wife keeping you awake at night?" Jonathan Taylor made a crude gesture causing the other men to laugh.

Hugh, embarrassed, turned to leave the barn.

"Aye, he's a lucky man, our Hugh," said Nathaniel, joining in the banter.

"She's a fine lusty looking woman, Hugh," said Taylor with a sly look on his face. "What man wants a filly when he can have a mare that's already broken in."

The men burst into rowdy laughter. The crude language turned Hugh's amusement to sudden anger. Hugh whipped around and grabbed Taylor by his cloak and shook him with a violence that shocked them all. "Do not speak of my wife with such an uncivil tongue, you rogue."

"Easy man, easy, he meant no harm," said Goodman Roberts, to Hugh. "Loose your hold on him, it was but a jest."

Hugh threw Taylor to the ground in disgust. "If you speak such words against my wife again, you will regret it, by God."

Taylor scrambled away from Hugh. John Matthews assisted him to his feet. "Twill be you who will have cause to regret if you lay your hands on me again." Taylor straightened his disheveled clothes, brushing at the mud on his cloak.

"Come away man," said Matthews, as he handed him his cap. "Do not provoke him further."

"Come now all of you. Goodman Parsons, Goodman Taylor enough of this foolish talk, save your energy for the ax, we have trees to fell." John Matthews led the way out of the barn.

Their jovial mood dissipated by the fight and the threats; the men trudged in silence following a trail that took them from town to the tree lots. The best conifers grew deep in the wood where lack of sunlight forced them to grow tall and straight in pursuit of the sun's rays. Hugh shivered as he fought his way through the abundant undergrowth. The quiet of the forest was unnerving. Hugh heard naught but the wind as it sighed and moaned through the trees. Goodman Bliss said the Natives were able to pass through the woods unheard and unseen. A silent band of warriors could surround them; none would be the wiser. Hugh put thoughts of Jonathan Taylor and Indians out of his mind and admired the massive oaks. He wished his father could have seen them. He was positive no one in England had laid eyes on such specimens in hundreds of years.

Late autumn to early winter was the best time to fell trees. The days were cooler, and even more importantly the sap had stopped rising and when cut the wood dried faster. Goodman Roberts was an expert axe man and Hugh admired the way he swung the ax with both his right and left arms. He, himself was just a novice, and he knew his arms would ache on the morrow. But it was worth the pain if it meant he could earn much needed money and have timber to improve his house and barn.

Hugh worked off his anger as his ax bit into the tree with a steady thunk. It was cold enough to see his breath but under his cloak he was sweating. When the men took a break, he made his way over to Jonathan Taylor who stiffened at his approach. "Jonathan, I am sorry, I know you spoke in jest." He stuck out his hand in a peace offering.

"Apology accepted." The two shook hands. Neither wished to pursue the incident further.

After a long day of felling trees, Hugh, tired and sore, approached his home with trepidation. He sank his ax into a log by the woodpile. As he checked on his animals, he thought to himself, God please let Mary be a in better mood. He threw the chickens a handful of grain and inspected the gate of the hen house, making sure to shut it tight. The closeness of the wolf concerned him; afraid it might return overnight. He did not want to lose any of his birds to the hungry predator. The temperature was dropping and Hugh shivered, despite his thick wool clothes. This is foolishness, he argued with himself, what manner of man am I, frightened of my own wife?

The house was quiet as Hugh stepped inside, sighing with relief he removed his cloak and hat, hanging them on a peg by the door. His nose tingled with the aroma from something savory bubbling away over the fire. His stomach growled with hunger as his mouth salivated with anticipation. He bent over the pot to sneak a bite just as Mary swept into the room. She carried a pan of golden corn bread, glistening with melted butter and honey. The smell made him groan with pleasure. Mary smiled at Hugh as she crossed over to his side and gave him a quick peck on the cheek. She sniffed and wrinkled her nose. "You stink Hugh Parsons," she said, as she laid the food on the table. "Go wash. I've a special supper waiting fer you. 'Tisn't every day a man finds he'll be a father. We must choose names, boy and girl, but I warrant it will be a fine son."

She shooed him towards an ewer of water and a linen cloth, placed near the fire. Hugh did his best to scrub away the day's grime and sweat. Bemused, he shook his head. Lord help me understand this temperamental woman, he pleaded, she blows hot and cold. They spent the rest of the evening in easy companionship. As he fell, exhausted, into bed, Hugh clung to a glimmer of hope that they could make this marriage work.

# Whispers

1646

A heavy snow fell in the early hours of December 25th, trapping Hugh and Mary in their house. The puritans of Massachusetts did not celebrate the birthday of their Lord. Christmas feasts, Yule logs and other ancient traditions, consigned to the past, were lingering remnants of their pagan ancestors. Only the papists, followers of Rome, clung to the old ways. Hugh and Mary, neither very good puritans, exchanged tales of Christmas celebrations from their youth. The old folk, reluctant to part with the customs of their forebears, continued to observe the holy days, albeit hidden from the condemning eyes of their puritan neighbors.

Hugh enjoyed himself as he shared stories from his childhood. "My grandfather loved to sing the carols at Christmas." He cleared his throat and broke into song, his voice a pleasant baritone.

*The goodman of this place in fere,*
*You to be merry he prayeth you here,*
*And with good heart he doth to you say,*
*What Cheer, Good Cheer, Good Cheer, Good Cheer.*
*Be merry and glad this good new year!*

Mary smiled from behind her hands, her toes tapping in rhythm to the song. "Hush Hugh, you should not sing such songs, someone will hear of it and report you to the magistrate."

"'Tis naught but idle conversation to pass the time, what harm can come from it." Hugh dismissed her concern with a wave of his hand. "And who could hear us on such a foul day as this?"

"The Devil and Reverend Moxon are always listening. Such talk is an invitation for either to make mischief for those foolish enough to tempt them."

Hugh, amused by Mary's fears, placed a finger to his lips and tiptoed to the door. He turned his head and put his ear to the wood. "Ssh," he said, making a twisted face at her. "They lurk just outside our door and wait on us to speak the word-," he paused, "Christmas!" Hugh shouted causing Mary to jump in her seat.

"Enough, man! Do not make light of such things." She patted his chair. "Come. Sit by me, the babe stirs."

Hugh crossed to room and lay his hand on her rounded belly. "I cannot feel anything," he said, his voice hushed.

"Be still," she said, as the baby fluttered in her womb. "There! Did you feel that?"

Hugh nodded; his eyes widened in awe as he felt the subtle movement under his hands. "'Tis really there, my little son."

"Humph, well think of him the next time your mouth runs away with wicked talk."

Hugh rolled his eyes at Mary and put more wood on the fire. "'Twill be a cold night and it smells of snow. The Devil and Mr. Moxon will huddle by their fires tonight and we are safe. Now, let us to bed, I'm tired."

Winter passed; a slow progression of frosty days and frigid nights. The ground wore a thick mantle of snow for weeks on end. The mountain of firewood, stacked outside the door, dwindled at an alarming rate. Hugh spent every spare autumn minute chopping wood, he hoped to have a sufficient supply to last through the coldest months. But the chimney was a hungry beast. It devoured their offerings in exchange for teasing flames that offered little light and disappointing heat. Despite the small size of the house, the edges of the hall were cold and gloomy.

The Agawam River, the town's link to the outside world, froze over for most of the winter. Boats carrying letters and information from Boston could not reach them; isolating from the rest of the colony. Icy roads and drifts of snow made even local travel treacherous.

Many days, the conditions outside prevented them from venturing no further afield than the barn, to see to the welfare of the animals. The Parsons spent their time huddled by the fire. Hugh built wooden molds for his bricks, listening to Mary's chatter as she sewed garments for their unborn child. On the darkest day of winter, they dreamt of the spring thaw. Hugh looked forward to planting his corn while Mary planned a kitchen garden to add fresh vegetables and herbs to their diet. If they had a surplus, they could use it barter or trade for other goods. Mary wanted piglets to raise, one to eat, and one to keep.

Weather permitting, they escaped the confines of their home to visit neighbors, sometimes together, but more often they went their separate ways. Such was the relief to speak to someone other than one's spouse, the fact you did not particularly like them or they you, mattered little.

With only the occasional communication from Hartford getting through, there was naught to talk about, save each other. No action or comment escaped the scrutiny of the Goodmen and Goodwives of Springfield. Any misdeed was chewed on, each detail savored. A word or a look could consume hours of conversation. Behavior, ignored or even unnoticed in the busy warmth of summer, merited dissection and censure. The bone chilling cold, the stale rationed diet, constant threat of illness and death brought the immortal soul closer to the surface. It was visible beneath the taut skin of winter.

On a clear, snow-free January day, Mary pulled on her sturdy leather boots and made her way to the Bedortha's. She walked with great caution along the frozen rutted road. It would be easy to twist an ankle, or worse. She was pleased to find Blanche at home, and the mistress of the house was equally glad to see her visitor.

The Bedortha home was practically identical to her own. Two rooms with a central chimney. The most striking difference was that the Parsons' fireplace was built of brick. Mary and Blanche settled by the fire for a long chat. They were soon joined by Elizabeth, Jonathan Burt's wife, and her children. "Sorry," she said, with an apologetic smile, "they all have coughs and sniffles, but I had to get out." She hung up their cloaks and shooed the children into the parlor. "Children, go and play while I talk with Goody Bedortha."

The three women discussed the progress of Mary's pregnancy, dissecting every ache and pain. Elizabeth, mother of four, offered her advice. When the subject was thoroughly covered, the conversation turned to the latest town gossip.

"Reice tells me that a new family has arrived in town. A widow and her three grown children. They moved into the empty house at the top of the street."

Elizabeth nodded as she wiped the nose of her eldest child. "Jonathan met her youngest boy, Samuel he's called. Says he's a large strapping lad. There's also another son and a daughter, both married. I hope to meet the widow at Sunday lecture."

Blanche opened her mouth to speak when Mary, squirming with pleasure, hushed her. She knew something the others did not. "Well, Goody Ashley told me..." She leaned forward and whispered like a conspirator. "The widow was run out of Hartford, down in Connecticut."

Elizabeth gasped. "What for?"

Mary's eyes gleamed as she spun out the tale. "Mrs. Moxon said the widow fled with naught but the clothes on her back. Her sons returned to fetch their belongings and set her up in the Moody's old house." Mary took a sip of her cider while Blanche and Elizabeth waited for her to continue.

"They say she fled under a cloud of suspicion. I do wonder what mischief she got up to." Mary cocked an eyebrow and smirked. "Maybe the widow was making merry with the wrong person."

Blanche sat back frowning. "Humph. Well, she cannot be too much trouble if Mr. Pynchon allowed her to settle here in Springfield. He's not one to stand for any nonsense, especially from a woman, widow or not."

Mary's face fell, disappointed at their response. A loud cry interrupted their gossip. Elizabeth lifted an unhappy child to her lap and wiped her runny nose with her apron. "Poor wee thing," she said, as she cradled the sick girl against her shoulder.

A determined knock startled the women. "Mary, see to that for me," asked Blanche, as she rummaged in a basket for a clean linen.

Mary rose from her seat by the fire and crossed the room. She unlatched the door and cracked it open. Eyes widened in shock; Mary gasped loudly as her heart leapt in her chest.

"Are ye going to stand there gaping or will ye ask me in?" The Widow Mercy Marshfield, the object of their gossip, stood on the threshold. Mary guessed her age to be slightly more than forty. A steeple hat, worn atop her linen coif, added to her considerable height. With her proud face, Mercy cut an imposing figure.

"Mary, your letting out what little heat we have!" Blanche, unnerved by her new guest's sudden appearance, waved her in. "Welcome, Widow Marshfield, please do come in."

The Widow stepped inside the now crowded room. "I am looking for Goody Burt, her husband said she was here."

Elizabeth, stood, surrounded by her four children. "Yes, I am here."

Ignoring the others, Mercy Marshfield stepped up to her. "I am told your little ones are doing poorly. I've brought a bit of horehound lozenge to ease their cough." She glanced around the room. "I'll not stay, I only stopped to leave these with you." She handed Blanche a muslin bag that contained the drops. Pivoting, she pinned her sharp gaze on Mary. Her lips formed a brittle smile.

"Good day to you, Goody Parsons." With that, she swept out the door, leaving the women with mouths agape.

When Mary returned home, she recounted to Hugh how the Widow Marshfield had materialized out of thin air, just as they spoke her name.

"What did Goody Burt do with the horehound candies?"

"I told her to throw them in the fire, but she licked one and said 'twas not but a lozenge and gave a piece to little Joseph."

Hugh laughed at Mary. "'Twas naught but being caught in your own gossip is all."

His attitude angered Mary. "The Widow Marshfield is not all she seems."

"The Widow Marshfield is but a decent woman, Mary, you make much of nothing, 'tis naught but idle woman talk."

"Ye may dismiss me Hugh Parsons, but I warn ye, the Widow Marshfield is not what see seems, she will do us harm, when all is said and done."

# Calves

By late March, the worst of winter was behind them. The days grew warmer and the time of the last frost approached. If the weather cooperated, Hugh could plant in mid-April, but first he needed to purchase seed corn. William Pynchon, with his extensive holdings and large warehouse, was the only man in town with a surplus. There was little coinage in New England; Hugh himself had a scant few pennies. A system of barter and trade underpinned the economy. Hugh had his bricks, lumber and physical labor to offer for the seed corn.

Hugh saddled his horse and led it from the barn. Mary was busy planting cold-hardy cabbage seedlings in her new garden. Once done, she would spread a thick layer of composted manure around the plants for fertilizer and to keep them warm.

"I'm off now to Pynchon's to get the seed." Hugh stopped by the side of the house to open the garden gate. His horse, in high spirits, whinnied as she pulled on the reins. Hugh smiled at the beast. "Feeling frisky are you, we are all glad to see the back of winter."

Mary twisted her head, her view of Hugh blocked by the corner of the house. "What did ye say?" she shouted at him.

"Shut the gate behind me." As he spoke the horse broke into a canter and carried them up the street. He hoped she'd heard him. Quite a few folk were moving their cattle down to the Long Meadow, where they would spend the spring and summer grazing on the sweet grass. They would pass his house lot on their way out of town and he didn't want a stray to get into his dooryard and the garden beyond.

At the warehouse, Hugh asked to speak with Simon Beamon, one of Pynchon's employees and a notorious drinker. He preferred to deal with him rather than Pynchon himself, a keen negotiator. After dinner was the best time to bargain with him. If he had one-to-many cups of cider with his dinner, Hugh could strike a deal in his favor. Beamon appeared from a backroom. He was a small, thin man with a large red nose that spread across his face. Crumbs covered his waistcoat.

"Goodman Parsons, what do you want?" Simon let out a loud, cider-scented belch.

Good, thought Hugh, he has eaten, and by the smell of him, he's had plenty of drink. "Ah, Goodman Beamon, I'm here to purchase a bushel of seed corn."

Hugh and Simon wrangled over the price of the corn, eventually agreeing on a trade. Hugh would cut timber for Mr. Pynchon in exchange for the corn. The deal was in Hugh's favor; Pynchon could have gotten twice the amount of work out of him. He smiled to himself as he mounted his horse. Mr. Pynchon will be angry with poor Simon if he gets wind, but a deal is a deal.

He rode home in a good mood, whistling a jaunty tune. As he neared his house, he heard voices coming from his dooryard. Female voices raised in anger. With a sigh, he dismounted and walked his horse towards the garden gate. He frowned to see it wide open. When he made his way around the house, the explanation for the argument became apparent. Standing in the middle of her garden was his wife, surrounded by trampled cabbage plants. A second woman was attempting to herd two rambunctious calves from the side of the kiln house. At the sound of his approach, both women turned and glared at him. He recognized Widow Marshfield at once. These must be her cattle, he thought.

"Look, look at the state of my garden. 'Tis destroyed, 'tis ruined." Mary's cap was askew and her face, splotched from the heat of her anger, framed a mouth which sprayed an angry staccato of words. She pointed an accusing finger at the widow. "Damn her, 'tis her cattle that hath destroyed my garden."

"Your gate was open, 'tis your own fault. If you took care to keep it closed my calves would have walked right past." The widow moved to catch her animals.

Mary looked to Hugh. He dropped the reins of his horse and moved to her side. He rubbed a hand over his face, his lips compressed into a firm line. The widow had a point, dammit. The gate was open. "I told you to close the gate behind me. There is naught we can do. Now stop your hollering and get inside."

Hugh watched his wife's hands curl into clenched fists. Her eyes widened in shock then narrowed to two thin slits. He groaned, here it comes, he thought, as a finger jabbed into his chest.

"Do not quiet me, Hugh Parsons. If you are not man enough to defend me, I will do so myself." She whirled around and directed her fury at the offending woman. "Be warned Widow Marshfield, if I spy one of your animals in my garden again, I shall.... I shall have it for my supper."

Widow Marshfield stopped in her tracks. Her face a ball of fury. "Goody Parsons, if you dare make a scratch on one of my cows, I will have you before the magistrate."

Hugh was losing patience. Was there anything worse than squabbling women? He needed to get control of the situation. First his wife.

"Mary, think of the baby, get inside." Turning to the other woman, he spoke. "Widow Marshfield, gather your animals before they do more damage. I will close the gate behind ye."

Mary, face scowling, stomped off. She slammed the door closed behind her. Hugh helped the widow get her animals out of the dooryard and latched the gate closed behind them. He returned to his horse, leading it to the barn. His pleasant mood shattered by the drama. He spent the next hour trying to salvage as many of the cabbage plants as he could, setting them back into the furrowed rows destroyed by the calves.

Mary's mood was frosty, she ignored his efforts to engage her in conversation. Hugh sighed; things had been going well between them. We never get ahead. She served him a chilly supper of beans and salt pork then they retired to bed. Gradually he fell off to sleep, the physical exertions of his day overcoming the turmoil in his head. Hugh felt he had only slept a minute when a cry jolted him awake. His wife was writhing in pain.

"What ails ye Mary, is it the babe, is there something wrong with the child?" Concern for his wife deepened the lines etched onto Hugh's face.

"I don't think so, 'tis my stomach, ah, it is cramping so!" Mary clutched at her belly. "Oh God, Hugh. 'Tis the Widow Marshfield, she's cursed me."

"Pshaw, do not accuse the poor woman, Mercy Marshfield is no witch." Hugh rolled out of bed. He grabbed the candle, taking it to the hall to light it. He returned a moment later. Mary was sitting up in bed, her face white and pinched with pain. Her distress did not prevent her from venting her anger at the widow.

"'Tis true, Hugh. Goody Clark told me that was why she fled Connecticut. They ran her out. Oh yes, the Widow Marshfield is a witch all right. She hath turned her evil eye on me."

Hugh rolled his eyes at his wife. "For God's sake woman, 'tis naught but a bit of excess wind in your bowels. There's no call to accuse the woman of spells and witchcraft. I'll make you a comfrey brew to settle yer stomach." He returned to the hall where he heated water and steeped the comfrey leaves to make a soothing tea. Mary sat up and sipped it gingerly.

She finished the tea and handed the cup back to Hugh. He set it on the table and returned to bed pulling the coverlet over them both. "Now then, no more talk of witches. I plowed a new section across the river yesterday and I need you to come and pick up rocks for me. Honest hard work will turn your thoughts to more important matters."

Hugh regretted the words the moment they flew from him mouth. Mary's face screwed up into a ball of fury. "You would have me risk my babe to pick up rocks. What manner of man are you, Hugh Parsons, that you would ask this of your wife?"

A man who wished to have food to eat next winter.

# Family

Spring passed into summer in a blur of work for the Parsons. Hugh sowed his corn in late April and watched with satisfaction as the crops sprang from the earth. Once planting was finished, he divided his days between making bricks and building chimneys for his neighbors and sawing timber for himself. His goal for the summer was to raise the roof and add a second story to the house before the babe arrived. Hugh worked from sunup to sundown in an all-out effort to get the job done.

The approaching birth put added pressure on Mary to complete her chores. On an early June morning she joined a group of women from the lower end of town at the Cooley's house. Rather than purchase expensive imported soap from Mr. Pynchon, they decided to try their hand at soap-making. The women, Mary included, gathered around a large kettle hung from a trivet in the center of the Cooley's dooryard. Sarah Cooley filled the kettle halfway with rain water. "Did you bring your ashes?" she asked, questioning each woman as they arrived. "Remember, no pine ashes, they'll spoil the soap with their tar."

Mary nodded and handed her pail to Sarah who added the ash to the water, one spoonful at time. As the murky gray liquid came to a rolling boil, Sarah Jones stirred it with a large paddle. "How do you know when it's ready?" she asked, her eyes burning from the noxious fumes.

"I remember my mam said when an egg floats in the water, the lye is ready to use." Sarah Cooley had an egg ready in her apron pocket which she dropped into the pot. After a few minutes the egg floated to the surface. Sarah Jones and Blanche, muscles straining, carefully lifted the kettle off the fire and let the ash water cool. Blanche hung a second kettle, filled with rendered lard, over the fire. Once the fat melted, Sarah Cooley slowly added the cooled lye water. The women, taking turns, stirred until their arms ached and the mixture gradually thickened and turned a pale-yellow color. Sarah Cooley judged it done when the spoon stood straight up in the porridge looking mixture. Together the women grappled with the hot kettle and poured the concoction into a rough wooden box. Goodman Cooley carried the box of soap into the larder where Sarah covered it with a muslin cloth.

"Now what?" asked Mary, as Blanche handed her a jar of salve to rub on her raw lye-burned hands.

"Now we wait. The soap must cure for several weeks before we can cut and use it. We must be patient."

The women treated themselves to a well-deserved cup of ale before heading home to prepare dinner and start the next chore.

A week later, Hugh arrived home after a long day of cutting timber. He pulled his kerchief out of his pocket and handed it to Mary with a smile.

"What is it?" Her eyes widened in delight as she unwrapped a large piece of honeycomb.

"Honey. Oh Hugh, is there more?" She broke a piece and greedily sucked the warm liquid from the comb.

"There is. I found it in a fallen log, the hive is huge. Reice said he knows how to smoke out the bees to collect the comb. We plan to try tomorrow."

The next afternoon, Mary joined Blanche at her house while they waited for their husbands to return. The women kept their hands busy carding wool which they would later spin into yarn. Mary lifted her head and turned toward the door. She heard the telltale creak of the garden gate. "They're back," she said, as she dropped the carders and rushed outside.

The sight of Hugh halted her in her tracks. Angry red splotches covered his face and neck and swelling reduced his left eye to a narrow slit. Blood dripped from a bruised hand. Streaks of dirt covered his breeches and a large tear in his shirt completed the picture. Oh God, thought Mary, biting her lip, he must be in pain, but Lord help me what a sight. She covered her mouth with a hand to hide her smile and choked down a giggle.

Blanche, racing out the door behind her, let out a loud gasp as she caught sight of Hugh. With his good eye, he shot them a look meant to be threatening, but the comical state of his face and closed eye only made Mary laugh all the more. Reice arrived, chest heaving and out of breath. He did not look much better than Hugh, his swollen face covered with stings. "Jesus, Hugh. I didn't know a man could run so fast." Reice bent over, chest heaving, trying to recover his breath.

Hugh turned and fixed him with a one-eyed stare. A laugh, rising from his belly burst out of him. Reice responded with a belly laugh of his own, both men pointing at each other. Mary rolled her eyes at Blanche who shrugged her shoulders in return.

Blanche took the honey from the men. "Willow bark tea is what you both need. 'Twill help ease the pain and bring down the swelling." Mary led the still laughing men down to the river's edge. She scooped up mud from the shallows and daubed it onto the stings on Hugh's face. She rinsed the blood from his hand and cleaned the abrasion. "What happened?" She turned his hand from front to back, assessing the degree of injury. A rare tender moment passed between them.

Hugh grunted and did not reply. Reice snickered; Mary looked at him, eyebrows raised.

"When the first bee stung him, he started to holler and leap about like a mad man. Lord help me, I could not but laugh at the sight of him. It made him so angry he slammed his fist into a tree."

"That sounds like my Hugh."

The willow tea, with a drop of honey, did its work and decreased the pain. Blanche decided the mud needed to stay on overnight. Mary didn't want the dried dirt falling into her bed and ordered Hugh to sleep in the barn. The next morning, after rinsing off the mud, his face looked almost normal. The swelling around his eye decreased to the point where he could open it. Blanche brought over a jug of honey and their share of the honeycomb, enough to make a few beeswax candles. Hugh judged a jug of golden honey worth a day or two of pain.

In mid-July, Hugh started construction of the second story edition to his house. Mary, hot and uncomfortable, choose to stay with Blanche at her house. It took a week and a frenzy of activity to remove the roof and frame out the two upper chambers. His neighbors helped him build a staircase that wrapped around the chimney, giving access the new floor. The upstairs rooms would be used for storage. When the addition was complete, Hugh moved all their chests and bags of grain up the stairs. The first floor, now uncluttered, left ample room for a cradle, and later a toddling child. Hugh, exhausted but elated, hammered home the final nail, just in the nick of time.

On a hot August morning, a sharp contraction woke Mary from a restless sleep. Fear gripped her belly as she mouthed her prayers in silence. Oh God, please let this child be born safe, she prayed. She rolled over on her side and nudged her snoring husband from a deep sleep.

"Hugh! Wake up Hugh, go and fetch Goody Lumbard, the babe is coming."

Hugh's eyes flew open, instantly awake. He grabbed his clothes off the peg and yanked on his shirt and breeches, then jammed his feet into his shoes. He flew out the door and raced to John Lumbard's house where he pounded on the door. A voice called out to stop knocking and wait a bit. After what seemed an eternity, Joan opened the door.

"Well, Hugh Parsons, today we will see you a father for the first time, 'tis a special day for you. God willing all will be alright."

"All will be well, Goody Lumbard," he said, "shall I go to the Bedortha's to fetch Blanche and send her to you?"

"Yes, get Blanche and then Goody Cooley."

Glad of the excuse to leave, Hugh hustled to the Bedortha's. Blanche, dressed and ready, opened the door to his knock. Reice sat at the table, a bowl of cornmeal in milk in front of him.

"Is it Mary? I had a sense that it would be today." Blanche picked up a basket of linens from the sideboard and prepared to leave.

Hugh nodded. "Goody Lumbard is with her now."

As she stood in the door way, she pointed a finger at her husband. "Stay out of the wine, Reice Bedortha. No celebrating before the child is born." She glared at Hugh for good measure and stomped out the door.

Hugh visited with Reice for a while and then headed to the Cooley's to see if Sarah would attend the birth. Benjamin shut the door behind his wife and slapped Hugh on the back. "What will ye do to pass the time Hugh? It's her first and it could be a long day's wait for the babe."

"I think I'll row over to the planting field to check me corn."

On his way to the river, he passed the open door of his house. A sudden howl, like a wounded animal, startled him. He cringed to think of Mary in such pain. But such was the way of life, he thought, ordained by God. Hugh spent the day weeding his cornfield. He rowed back across the river in the late afternoon and ate his supper with Reice. Blanche slipped out of the birthing room to check on her husband.

"How is Mary?" Hugh was worried. Mary had been in labor for over twelve hours.

Blanche patted him on the shoulder. "She is doing well and making good progress, but Goody Lumbard says it will be some time yet. It is her first after all, and all first babes like to take their own sweet time."

Hugh returned to his house, but rather than go inside where his presence was unwelcome, he bedded down in the barn. The sound of women's voices woke him. He stumbled out into the dooryard and tried to get his bearings. The chatter of birds let him know the hour was just shy of dawn. He stepped into the path of Blanche and Goody Cooley.

"Ah Hugh, I was just coming to find you." Blanche yawned. "You have a wee bonny lass."

Joan Lumbard, catching up with the others stopped to tell Hugh she would be back in the morning to check on Mary and the child. The women, tired, but ebullient at the successful birth, walked home, leaving Hugh in the yard. A crow announced the new day.

Not a son, he thought, not a son. Hugh stepped inside. By the firelight he saw Mary, wan and tired, on the bed. She gave him a weak smile.

"Well, Hugh, you have a daughter." She held out a bundle to him. "I hope she is not a disappointment to you." Hugh gingerly accepted the blanket clad baby and looked into the face of his child. He stared at her in wonder. So tiny, so beautiful, his girl, his own wee daughter. He thought his heart would explode with love.

"Her name is Hannah," he said, and handed her back to Mary. "Next time, we'll have a son."

# Illness

The following year brought few changes to Mary's life. Hannah thrived, praise God. Hugh remained Hugh. Their married life was like the river, sometimes the rocks were submerged, sometimes they rose above the surface, but their turbulence was ever present.

In October, Mary realized she was pregnant. The news distressed her friend Blanche, married before Mary, she had yet to conceive and feared she was barren. Mary and her friends assured Blanche that it would happen soon, and then she would yearn for her childless days.

As the year rolled by, their days fell into a chore centered rhythm. Mary and Hugh worked from dawn to dusk; when she finished one chore, she began another. Their days held little variety. They ate the same food, drank the same drink, wore the same clothes. Only the misfortunes and misdeeds of their neighbors added spice to their bland days.

On a rain cooled late-April morning, several women gathered at the Cooley house where two of the children lay seriously ill. Mary, Blanche and Pentecost Matthews helped Sarah nurse her little boys. Sarah bathed the feverish children while Pentecost brewed willow bark tea. Mary made a mustard plaster for their chest. The children sipped their bitter tea and were put to bed covered with heavy blankets, to break their fever. With naught to do but wait, the women passed the time spinning yarn and trading tidbits of gossip.

"What did Benjamin tell you about the trial, yesterday?" Mary gave Sarah a look of expectation.

"Ah, he said 'twas most fractious. Goodman Edwards was frightfully angry at Goodman Merrick for beating his boy, Samuel. Benjamin expected they'd attack each other in front of the constable and magistrate."

"Well, what father would not be angry? The child is only five, big for his age, but still only a child," said Mary. The other women nodded in agreement.

"John witnessed the incident when it happened. He said 'twas merely boys being boys. Goodman Edward's son Samuel knocked Thomas' son, Tom, to the ground and then tried to throttle him." Pentecost held the women's attention. "Goodman Merrick saw them rolling about on the ground and pulled little Samuel off his son."

"Doesn't sound like much too me." Blanche yawned; she'd hoped for a more exciting tale. She stood and offered to get a cup of cider for anyone who was thirsty.

"Well 'twas not much until Goodman Merrick thrashed the poor child, hitting him across the back three times with his stick. When my husband pulled the boy away, Thomas shouted that young Samuel should hang for trying to kill his son."

The women gasped in horror. Imagine a grown man calling for the hanging of a five-year-old boy. Mary clutched her belly as if to protect her unborn child. I would kill the man who tried to harm my child, she thought. I'm glad Goodman Edwards took him to court, he deserved punishment for such outrageous behavior.

The children slept fitfully for several hours; they woke in late afternoon complaining of thirst. Sarah pulled back the covers to check their fever. Mary heard her cry out and rushed to their pallet by the fire. A bright red, splotchy rash covered both children from head to toe. Measles! Mary shuddered, glad that Hannah was not with her.

Sarah Cooley's children recovered slowly from their ailment. To Mary and Hugh's relief Hannah did not contract the disease. Other families were not so lucky as the illness jumped from house to house. At lecture, Reverend Moxon prayed at great length for the sick children of Springfield, asking God to preserve their little ones. After the service, he called out to Hugh and asked to speak with him. Hugh and Mary remained in the meetinghouse while everyone else exited.

"Goodman Parsons, I wonder if we can speak about my bricks?" said Moxon.

Hugh cleared his throat. "I cannot make bricks at present. My time is taken up with planting."

"We had a bargain, Goodman Parsons. You agreed to build me a chimney." Moxon puffed out his chest to intimidate Hugh. It didn't work. Hugh stood several inches taller than Moxon and had about forty pounds on him.

A vein throbbed in Hugh's temple. He moved closer to the Reverend forcing the man to take a step backwards, almost falling over a bench. "We had no bargain Reverend. I said I would make the brick if I could and I tell you now I can't."

Moxon gave a nervous cough and his left eye twitched. "As you said, we had no firm bargain, but you led me to believe you could fulfill the order."

"Well I can't." He bent over to pick up Hannah and motioned to Mary to leave. "Ask me again after harvest."

Despite Reverend Moxon's protracted prayers, God did not spare his household. His youngest daughter was so ill she fell into a fit. She was sick for several weeks and all the local women, including Mary, took turns helping her mother nurse the children. They made a complete recovery.

Their neighbor's antics continued to provide fodder for gossip. Francis Ball was the talk of the town when he found himself in court for beating the wife of the Indian called Coe. Goodman Ball did not deny the act, but said he hit her only twice. The stick was not so big, he offered in his defense. William Pynchon, ever protective of his Indian friends, ordered Ball to pay the woman two wampum. He refused, saying he'd suffer a whipping before he paid a fine to an Indian. Pynchon banged his gavel and had him whipped on the spot.

On a beautiful May morning, the Springfield militia mustered on the meetinghouse green to practice military maneuvers. Hugh brought, not only his musket, but the pike, a long thrusting spear, he kept in the barn. The women, thrilled with a break in their monotony, took advantage, treating it as a holiday. They arrived at the green with blankets and hampers of food. The men marched up and down the green, practicing their drills, to the great delight of their children, while the older boys played at soldiers and Indians. Mary noted that young Samuel Edwards and Tom Merrick played together as if their prior incident had never occurred, although their mothers kept a wary eye on them. How quick to forgive are children, Mary mused.

Their maneuvers complete, the parched men joined their families. Francis Pepper tapped barrels of beer and cider to quench their thirst, courtesy of Mr. Pynchon. 'Twas a rare work-free day of frolic and Mary enjoyed every minute. She and Hugh strolled home at dusk; Hannah asleep in her father's arms. Hugh sang a ditty under his breath. We will all sleep well tonight, thought Mary, and in the morning, we'll pick up where we left off yesterday.

The illness which afflicted the Cooley children spread through the settlement, moving from family to family. By early June the children of Mr. Henry Smith were sick. Hugh brought home the news after spending the day working with most of the town's men on the main road, filling holes and cutting brush along the sides.

"I asked Mr. Smith if I could come by to purchase a quart of peas, but he said he was to distressed by the condition of his children. His mind was not on business," Hugh said, a sour faced.

"I'm glad to hear he worries so for his family." Hugh's lack of sympathy irritated her, what if it were his children, she wondered?

"I need the peas. I want to plant an extra quarter acre before it's too late." Hugh chewed his supper, waving his spoon around. "I'm sorry for the state of the little ones, but I need those peas and 'tisn't fair he holds a monopoly on seed, and I can get it from no one else."

Mary sighed but didn't comment, he's working himself up into one of his black moods, she thought. She watched as his emotions played out across his face. Suddenly, he sat back, the edges of his mouth curled into a sly smile. Ah God, he's got that scheming gleam in his eye.

"I think you should present yourself at the Smith house in the morning." He sat nodding his head, working out the details of his scheme. "Yes, you ask if they need your help nursing the children."

Mary rubbed her swollen belly. "Are you mad Hugh? What possible good could I be in my condition?" She waved her hands over her abdomen.

"If you do some nursing, Mr. Smith can pay you in grain, and I can have my peas." He gave her a smug smile, sure that his plan would succeed.

"Jesus, Hugh, would you look at me. Our babe is due at any moment. I can hardly waddle to the meetinghouse. How in the Lord's name do ye expect me to walk to Mr. Smith's and present myself as a nurse?"

Hugh's face fell. "Well 'tisn't fair that the man stops me from my planting, is all." A scowl crept over his features. "If he does, I swear he will regret it." Hugh slammed his cup down and flung off his napkin.

Mary rolled her eyes as he stomped out the door. Angry at the world again, she thought as she cleared the table. She stopped to rub her back. Please let this baby come soon. She piled her dishes in a bucket and took them outside to scrub them clean with sand and river water.

The next morning, Mary rolled out of bed, wincing as her swollen feet hit the floor. No boots for me today; she decided. Hannah, flush faced, stirred in her crib. She had a red raw rash on her bottom, which made her miserable when she wet herself. No air stirred in the hot house. Mary fanned her face as a trickle of sweat slithered down her neck. She propped the door open hoping to catch a breeze. After a breakfast of cornbread soaked in warm milk and drizzled with honey, Hugh rushed to the barn to care for the animals. The magistrate ordered a second day of roadwork, Hugh had no choice but to take part. He stopped at the house to get his dinner pail which Mary had packed for him.

"Are you determined you will not go to the Smith's? I need that blasted man to sell me the peas." Hugh clasped his hands to his chest and put on his please, please, please face.

Mary closed her eyes and sighed. "Hugh... ooh." Her eyes flew open; she fixed her gaze on Hugh.

"What?"

Mary lifted the hem of her linen shift and looked at her feet. A pool of liquid formed on the floor. She raised her head, staring at Hugh. "I'm sure. Will you fetch Blanche for me, the babe comes today."

Blanche arrived in short order as did several other women. They walked Mary around the room, even going outside for a short while to catch a breath of fresh air. Mary found this second birth less frightening; she knew what to expect. Her labor, shorter but no less painful, came to bear late in the afternoon. Red-faced and dripping with sweat, Mary pushed her child into the world.

Hugh left for home when word reached the work party that Mary had given birth. The work left his skin and clothes caked with mud. Wading into the river, he washed the sweat and grime from his body, dumping a bucket of cool water over his head. When he was presentable, he made his way to the house. He found Mary propped up in bed, Hannah asleep beside her. Blanche handed him a tiny bundle, which he unwrapped. A smile spread over his face; he had a son.

"Samuel." Hugh spoke aloud. "His name is Samuel."

The next morning Blanche came to check on Mary and the children. Hugh headed out for a day's work when she arrived. In late afternoon, Sarah Cooley charged in, out of breath and looking as if she had run a great distance. She leaned on the table and took a deep breath.

"What's amiss, Sarah? You huff and puff like the Devil himself has chased you here." Blanche handed her a cup of ale.

Pentecost Matthews stepped out of the parlor. "What is wrong, Sarah?" A worried frown on her face.

"Oh, my dears, I have heard the most grievous news from Goody Merrick who heard it from Goody Moxon, that two of Mr. Henry Smith's girls have died."

# Insult

Winter held Springfield in its icy grip; the short dark days of enforced idleness crept by. Travel was perilous. The Connecticut River froze over in late January making it impossible to cross. Main street was either buried under snow or rutted with ice-crusted puddles, that made walking difficult if not downright treacherous. If the ice was too thick, you were likely to slip and fall, risking a broken wrist or ankle. Thin ice gave way underfoot and your boot filled with frigid toe-numbing water.

When the snow was deeper than the knee, Hugh and Mary strapped on snowshoes to get around. The weekly trek to the meetinghouse for Sunday service was an ordeal. Mary bundled up the children in blankets and furs and tucked them into the sled which Hugh pulled through the snow. With its windows battened, the meetinghouse was dark and gloomy. The building was unheated save for a small personal brazier near Mr. Pynchon's seat. It was almost impossible to hear Reverend Moxon's droning sermon over the constant chatter of teeth. The smell of dank wet wool cloaks and unwashed bodies and the sound of phlegm filled coughs made for, at least in Hugh's opinion, an unpleasant day. Most Saturdays he prayed for deep snow, so he could keep him family home from the Sunday service.

Hugh found it difficult when the weather trapped him indoors with Mary and the children. The walls of the house seemed to contract and shrink although he had doubled the size of their home in August. The upstairs chambers were frigid, impossible to heat, and good only for storage this time of year. Downstairs the stale odor of cooked food mingled with tobacco and Samuel's dirty clout. Hugh longed to be outside if for no other reason than to fill his lungs with fresh air.

Their winter diet was bland and stodgy. The ate pottage with salt beef, pottage with bacon and pottage without meat. Every meal consisted of pottage. Hugh missed the fresh fruits and vegetables of summer and fall and the memory of grilled fish, hot off the spit, made his mouth water. Every winter he suffered from painful attacks in his bowels that struck without warning and took his breath away. Sometimes the pain came at night, causing him to cry out in his sleep. He would wake with teeth clenched; drenched in sweat. His restlessness woke Mary who would clamber of bed to make him a warm, milky posset to drink, but it did little good. Hugh told Mary it felt as if a wild beast lived in his gut and fought to get out.

The imposed confinement made him irritable. He was sharp with Mary and his daughter who wanted continuous attention. Samuel, his boy, was not an easy baby, and as proud as he was to have a son, the near constant crying was driving him mad. It seemed as if at least one member of his family was ill on any given day. Hugh was grateful for any excuse to leave the house. Late one afternoon in early February, he put on his heavy cloak and hat and announced that he had business with Reice Bedortha. Mary, who was sick with a nasty cold, gave him a baleful look but made no comment.

Once outside, Hugh pulled his snowshoes from a peg on the wall. His spirits rose with each step he took away from the house. Thank God Mary did not make a fuss about his leaving. He had naught to be guilty about. Children were woman's work. It was not his place to watch or tend to them when they were ill. But that did not stop his wife from complaining. Some days, Hugh thought, her tongue wagged from daybreak to sunset.

He needed to speak with Reice, who had mentioned, he wanted Hugh to build him a chimney come springtime. Before he molded and fired hundreds of bricks for the prospective chimney, Hugh wanted confirmation of the deal. With the extra money the chimney would bring, he could buy additional seed corn to plant on the ground he had cleared in late November.

Hugh headed up the street. He passed the door of Jonathan Burt, his house shuttered, smoke curled from the roof. As he passed Benjamin Cooley's, Hugh noted a crack in his mud clad, wood chimney. I must stop and tell him, on the morrow, Hugh thought, 'tis a danger if not mended. The house could burn to the ground if the wood caught fire. Mayhap I can talk him into a brick chimney.

Despite the extra effort required to walk in the snowshoes, Hugh was cold and shivering when he arrived at his destination. He removed the shoes and propped them against the wall near the door, near a second pair. Someone else was visiting the Bedortha's. As Hugh knocked, his ears picked up the sound of male laughter coming from inside. Blanche cracked opened the door. She was pregnant with her first child, and her large belly protruded under her dress. Hugh judged by her expression she was none too pleased to see him.

"Tongues have been wagging, I see. I shall have a house full before long," she said, "I told Reice to keep silent, but no, he must tell all. Well come in, your letting in the cold air."

Hugh gave her a quizzical look as he entered the house. As his eyes adjusted to the dim light, he saw Reice and Samuel Marshfield sitting on stools before the fire.

"Good evening, Reice," said Hugh, nodding at his companion, "Samuel, what brings you out on this cold night?"

"Good evening to you, Hugh. I've delivered a cask of sweet wine that Goodman Bedortha ordered off Mr. Pynchon. We were just tasting a wee drop." Samuel raised a wooden cup to his lips and sighed as he took a small sip. "Um, 'tis a fine wine," he said, eyes closed as he savored the drink.

"Samuel Marshfield, what can you know of fine wine, and does your mother know what you are about?" said Blanche, a sour expression on her face.

"Come Hugh, you must have a cup," laughed Reice, "Blanche, fetch a cup for Hugh."

Blanche shot her husband a look that no sober man would ignore; Reice was no sober man.

"Well then, seems I've arrived at the perfect time." Hugh moved in front of the fire and rubbed his hands to warm them. "I'll no say no to a tot of wine. Reice, you surprise me, I had no idea you were a wine man." Hugh laughed as he reached for the cup that Blanche offered him.

"Aye, well, my father died back home in Wales, God rest his soul. It seems he bequeathed me a few pounds. Mr. Pynchon took the bill of exchange and purchased a keg of wine for me instead. I figured, I'd toast the old man with wine, rather than pocket his money. So, raise a cup with me and drink to the old codger."

The three men lifted their cups in a toast to Reice's father, to Wales, to England, to old times, to times to come, and the babe soon to arrive. Hugh, warm from the fire and the alcohol, rose and took off his jacket, hanging it on a peg by the door. Reice hooted when he saw Hugh wearing his red waistcoat.

"See here, Blanche. Hugh wears his red flannel waistcoat!" His eyes danced.

"You're jealous, Reice, wanting one for yourself, maybe?" Hugh laughed at his friend.

"Nay, nay, but Blanche has made herself one, you will be like two bright berries on a bush, there'll be no mistaking the two of you when you're out and about," laughed Reice.

Hugh smiled and finished his wine. "Now then, Reice, what say we speak of your chimney?"

Hugh, who had less to drink, knew he had the advantage of Reice, who was rather the worse for it. He suggested a price well above the normal and seemed to have Reice convinced that it was a great bargain. Reice nodded his head in apparent agreement.

"Well, man, let us shake on this deal, and young Samuel here can be our witness," said Hugh, winking at Samuel as he reached to shake Reice's hand. "You'll have a new chimney by summer."

"You will do no such thing." Blanche lumbered to her feet and left her warm seat by the fire. She waddled over to her husband and put a restraining hand on his arm.

"You've had a skinful of wine husband," she said, eyes flashing as she glared at Hugh. "Do not be so quick to agree to anything tonight that you will regret come morn."

Hugh frowned at her interference and put his hand up. "Hold on, woman, this is between me and your husband, mind your business."

"Reice, listen me, I fear Hugh's bargain is no such a thing."

Hugh, stung by her inference he was trying to cheat her husband, said, "Gammer, you need not have said anything, I spoke not to you, but I shall remember you, when you little think on it!"

Blanche, eyes widened in shock, recoiled from Hugh as if he had slapped her with his hands, not his words. Her own hands curled into fists, how she wanted to lash back at him. Instead, she turned on her drunken husband and berated him for allowing Hugh to speak to her in such a manner. Reice squinted, one eye closed, and tried to focused on Hugh.

"Easy man, 'tis no good speech, my wife is right, I am deep in my cups and 'tis no time to seal a bargain. We should speak of this in the morn when clearer heads prevail." Reice turned to Samuel. "Now, I thank you, Samuel for delivering my wine and Hugh, we will speak on the morrow, but for now I am for me bed."

With that, Reice stumbled across the room, yanked back the curtain hiding his bed, and fell right across it, much to the chagrin of Hugh.

Blanche marched over to the door and flung it open. "Now then, Hugh and Samuel, you've overstayed your welcome the both of you, get yourselves home."

The men stumbled out into the night. The door slammed shut behind them, and the latch slammed into place. Hugh leaned on Samuel and laughed. "God man, what a cranky woman, Lord help Reice, I know not how he bides with her."

Samuel snickered as he headed off home.

# Blanche

March 1649

Blanche Bedortha rubbed her protruding belly, as she hobbled in a small circle around the work-table. My God, my ankles have disappeared, she thought, as she peered down at her feet. My legs look like tree trunks. Her swollen feet were painful, and it hurt to wiggle her fat toes. She paused a moment to massage her aching back, everything hurt. Winter is the worst season for childbirth, she decided, cooped up in the small house, how she longed to walk outside. God help me, she prayed, please let the babe come soon.

Her groans woke her husband. The reed Indian mat that partitioned off the bed did little to block any noise.

"Come to bed, Blanche, your pacing is keeping me awake."

"'Tis no use, I cannot sleep." She knew she sounded pitiful, but she couldn't help herself.

Reice yawned, threw back the covers, and slid out of the warm bed. He yelped when his feet hit the ice-cold floor and yanked on his stockings before slinging one of Blanche's shawls around his shoulders. As he pushed aside the mat, he noted a tear. The glow of the fire was visible through the rent. It needs mending, but thought it better to not mention it to Blanche.

Bleary-eyed, Reice padded across the room, stopping before his pregnant wife. He helped her to sit on a stool in front of the fire, then rubbed her back in a gentle motion. Blanche gave him a wan smile. I'm lucky to have him, she mused, Hugh Parsons would never do this for his wife, I wager.

"I know what you need," Reice said, leaping to his feet. "A tot of my father's wine, that will do the trick."

"Pour me some then, for I need my rest. Lord knows, I will get none after the babe arrives."

Reice filled the cup with sweet wine and handed it to his wife. Blanche took a sip and sighed with pleasure.

"Now then, back to bed with you," she said, waving him back to bed. "I'll be in before long, I promise."

The wine left a warm glow in her throat and belly, tension fled her body. One more cup, she decided, and then I'm to bed. Blanche enjoyed the pleasant flush that creep up her neck and spread across her cheeks. She yawned, stood and wobbled across the room. Ho now, she thought, as she swayed, my legs have turned to jelly. Taking careful steps, she made her way behind the mat to undress. As she removed her red waistcoat, one button came loose in her hand. Blanche lifted the garment to eye level, trying to get a better look. Instead of the button she saw a strange glowing light coming through the waistcoat. She squeezed her eyes tight then opened them again, first one then the other. A light like a candle flame bobbed before her. She shook her head and stared at it with narrowed eyes. Three times the flame moved over the fabric, tracing out a strange pattern. What's this, she thought, 'tis a queer sight. She lowered the waistcoat and stretched a hand out to the wall to steady herself. What trick is this? She raised the garment again, but the flame had disappeared.

Humph, 'tis but a trick of the wine, she decided, as she hung the coat up. She shivered as she removed her gown and slipped into the warm bed beside Reice, now snoring loudly. The room reeled around her; she put a foot out to make the spinning stop. At last, she fell into a deep sleep and dreamt of dancing candles and red waistcoats. A sharp pain in her belly and a wetness between her legs woke her. Her water had broken; the babe was coming.

Blanche tried to nudge Reice awake. He remained fast asleep. She rolled her belly over and hissed in his ear. "Wake up, Reice, wake up."

"Whaa, what is wrong?" Reice struggled to surface from his deep sleep.

Blanche shook him again. "'Tis the babe, it's coming."

"The baby!" His eyes flew open, instantly awake. Now oblivious to the cold, he leapt out of bed and rattled off his much-practiced instructions while he dressed. "I'm first to get Sarah and then fetch Widow Marshfield to tend to ye. Oh, and get Goody Burt." He stoked the fire to build up a good blaze before bounding out of the house.

Reice pounded on his neighbor's door, rousing Benjamin, who grumbled sleepy eyed, as he undid the latch to let him in. Sarah yelled from the parlor to assure him that she was up and almost ready. Leaving the Cooley's, Reice made his way as fast as possible to the Widow Marshfield's house, the full moon lit his way.

Mercy Marshfield had been expecting Reice for several days. A leather bag of herbs and jars of slippery elm sat by the door. She had Samuel move the birthing stool, made by a local carpenter for the laboring women of Springfield, to the Bedortha home in anticipation of the birth. By the time they arrived back at his house, Goody Burt had changed Blanche into her oldest shift and held her arm as they walked around the room. Goody Lumbard arrived not long afterward. Reice, trying to be helpful, stacked armfuls of firewood next to the hearth.

When there was no more for him to do, he made his way over to his wife and wrapped his arms around her in a gentle embrace. "I'm off now, Blanche."

"Pray for me, Reice. I hope to God to see you when this is done." She moaned as a contraction hit.

"Don't fear my love, I'll see ye and my new babe afore long." He placed a gentle kiss on her forehead and ducked out the door, striding up the road towards the Pepper's to while away the time.

During the next hours, women came and went, as Blanche labored to bring her child into the world. Mary Parsons let her hatred of Widow Marshfield prevent her from attending her childhood friend in her moment of need. She claimed she could not leave her children, but Blanche knew she resented Widow Marshfield. She had tried to dissuade Blanche from asking her, but Blanche insisted. Widow Marshfield, though not a midwife, was skilled at childbirth. Her calm but authoritative manner kept all the women busy and the expectant mother focused on the task at hand.

By late afternoon, Blanche felt the urge to push. The women positioned her on the birthing stool. Widow Marshfield knelt between her legs and felt for the emerging head. Before it crowned, she scooped up the slippery elm, easing it around the baby's scalp. With the next contraction, she ordered Blanche to push. The women gathered around and urged her on. With a grimace of determination on her face, she grasped the arms of the stool and bore done.

"'Tis almost here. Now then, Blanche, you shall have your child with the next pain."

Blanche, fatigued with her efforts, nodded her head. Goody Burt wiped the sweat from Blanche's face and murmured words of encouragement.

With the next wave of pain, she gritted her teeth, dug her nails into the wood and pushed. A searing pain, as her body tore, made her cry out. The head born, she panted, waiting for the next contraction to begin. With a final push, her son slid out of her body and into the waiting hands of Widow Marshfield. Blanche remained on the birthing stool while she awaited the after birth. Goody Burt cleaned the baby and wrapped him in a warm towel. Mercy helped the new mother, tired and sore, sponge herself off and then assisted her back to bed. Goody Burt presented her with a squalling bundle. Blanche, her pain forgotten, unwrapped him, a look of adoration on her face. She pressed a soft kiss on his forehead then offered him her breast; he latched with gusto.

The women cleared away the detritus of childbirth, while Blanche and the baby rested. Goody Burt returned home but sent her husband to find Reice, who was waiting for news of his wife. He had spent the afternoon hours at the home of Francis Pepper, passing the time in the company of his neighbors. He had enjoyed many a toast to his future child and was rather the worse for it.

Widow Marshfield was tending to Blanche when Reice burst through the door singing an old ditty. He plunked down on the edge of the bed and gave his wife a sloppy kiss. His breath smelt of beer.

"Praise God, for your safe travail." Reice choked on his emotions.

"Aye, praise God." Blanche patted his arm. She hadn't realized he had been so worried.

Blanche raised up on her pillow and proffered the babe to Reice. He held his son, gazing at the little face. He gave his wife a quivering smile, his eyes welled with tears as he looked down on his child.

"What will you name him?" asked Widow Marshfield, as she gathered her things and prepared to leave.

"Joshua."

Blanche spent the next day resting, trying to regain her strength. Neighbors stopped by with food and gossip. Widow Marshfield called in each morning to check on her. Three days after giving birth, Blanche got up and dressed. She did a bit of housework and made preparations for dinner. As a pottage bubbled on the fire, Blanche put Joshua down in his cot. Tired herself, she lay down on her bed, ready for a nap.

A pain woke her not long after she fell asleep. Moaning, she sat up, rubbing at her chest. Sharp and stabbing the pain returned, just below her left breast, strong enough to take her breath away. Mayhap I should get up and move around, she decided, and I shall feel better. I have no time for this. Her crying wet newborn needed her. Reice would be home soon, hungry and looking for his dinner. She fed the baby and then her husband, all the while rubbing at the pain.

The next morning, the pain worsened, spreading down her left arm. She massaged her jaw, it too ached. Concerned, Reice fetched Widow Marshfield to nurse her. Despite treatment, the pain continued unabated for several days. By the next week, the worst had past and Blanche was improving.

Mary Parsons spent several hours a day helping Blanche with the housework. Not wanting to cross paths with Widow Marshfield, Mary watched and waited for her nemesis to depart before she walked up the street to the Bedortha's house. Mary chatted about neighbors and what they were up to during Blanche's confinement, as she flitted around the room brushing away dust from the mud caked chimney.

"Hugh hath told me that Reice will not agree to a bargain for a chimney." Mary gave Blanche a sideway look hoping to get a rise out of her.

"Humph, 'tis surprising he would speak, even to you, of his treacherous dealings," countered Blanche. She had known this topic would be raised soon enough and had prepared her response. "My husband says he will go to his grave err he strikes a deal with such a dishonest man." Blanche watched as Mary flinched, her barb hit home.

Mary had no response, disappointed at losing the upper hand to Blanche, yet again. But Blanche was not done with her yet. "Indeed, I have heard many men speak ill of Hugh's dealings. Did he not argue with Mr. Moxon and John Matthews about bricks? Your husband is too greedy, and twill harm him in the end I fear."

Mary opened her mouth to respond, but her mind went blank. Blanche continued her attack.

"I am all amazed that he lets you come here to nurse me. Did he not encourage you to nurse Mr. Smith's children last year when they were dying? Did he not hope for payment?"

Baby Joshua let out a wail, a grateful distraction. Damn-it, Mary groused to herself, why does Blanche always seemed to outwit me. Mary lifted the baby out of his cradle and brought him to his mother to be fed. As she handed Blanche the baby, she said, "I wonder you continue to let that witch into yer house. She envies every woman's child; I would not have her near mine."

Exasperated, Blanche shot back. "Mary, you do her wrong. The widow is an upstanding Christian. She will only tolerate your slanderous speech for so long. My advice to you is to stop your tongue wagging about witches, 'twill not end well."

# Wool

April 1649

It had rained during the night; Hugh fell asleep to the rumble of distant thunder. He stepped outside at dawn to a pink sky morning. Water dripped from the eaves and a stiff breeze ruffled the early spring grass. Eager to plant his summer wheat and corn, Hugh hoped Springfield had seen its last frost. The sooner he sowed his crops, the sooner he could get on with his overdue brick orders. Mary had planted her kitchen garden with cold hardy onions and cabbages, set in neat even spaced furrows.

Hugh glanced at Mary as he reached across the table for a second piece of cornbread. "I need to speak to John Matthews today about his bricks." He took bite. "Do you want to come with me?"

Mary looked up, surprised at his offer. "Yes, I haven't seen Pentecost in a while."

"We'll leave after morning chores." He smiled at Hannah and tousled her blond curls.

For the first time since last autumn, they left their heavy cloaks behind. Hugh perched puddle-loving Hannah on his shoulders to keep her dress and shoes out of the mud. Mary carried Samuel, who at six months old, remained small for his age.  Hugh spied a mother rabbit and her kits, all but hidden in a clump of dead grass. Hannah clapped her hands and squealed with delight when the startled animals scurried to safety.

As they passed a patch of primrose, Mary bent to pick a blossom and handed it to Hannah. "My Gran said if you eat a primrose flower, you can see the fairies." She pretended to swallow the pale pink flower. "Oh, my." She made a funny face and pointed to the trees. "Look, there are fairies in the woods!" She danced in a circle, making Samuel smile and Hannah giggle in delight.

"I spoke to Jonathan Burt this morn about starting the corn tomorrow; if the rain holds off. The Indians over at Long Hill are getting ready to plant."

Mary glanced over at Hugh. "'Tis not too soon, then? Blanche says Reice will wait another senight til he throws his corn."

Hugh laughed. "Then his corn will be a week behind mine, just as it was last year." He stopped to adjust Hannah who was wiggling on his shoulders. "Jonathan and I will row over with John Lumbard to the planting fields just after first light. Maybe you can row over in the afternoon and help."

Mary made no reply. Hugh sighed and gave her a sideways glance to gage her reaction. The scowl on her face and the hard set of her jaw told him she did not want to cross the river. Did she think he enjoyed the planting, a muddy, back breaking business, he wondered?  Her help would speed the process.

"If you don't want to throw corn," he said," can you go see Benjamin Cooley and ask after some seed? I've a mind to plant a small plot of flax. Simon Beamon says Cooley will sell the seed and buy back what we reap in the fall for his weaving. I'd not mind the extra shillings in my pocket come fall."

A clanging in the Matthew's workshop gave them a clue as to John's whereabouts, a loud curse confirmed his location. Mary and the children headed towards the house. Hugh ducked into the shop; a pile of new barrels stacked outside.

Pentecost waved to Mary from her open door. Tall and spare, with clear gray eyes and an intelligent face, she was the rare woman who could both read and write. Her spotless reputation and aversion to gossip intimidated many women. In comparison, Mary's only claim to superiority was her fertility. Pentecost and her husband were childless. With a wide smile, she ushered Mary and the children into her hall. "I'm glad you have come Mary, I needed a distraction."

"Oh, aye, from what have I distracted you?" Mary made to sit on a stool, but Pentecost fussed at her.

"Nay. Nay, you must sit in the chair, twill be easier with the babe.

Pleased by the attention, Mary sat and settled Samuel on her lap. Pentecost perched on the stool next to her. "'Tis the strangest thing. I've searched all morn for a half-pound of wool. I planned to take it to Goodman Cooley on the morrow." She threw her hands up in exasperation. "Where I put it, I cannot say."

Mary's glance flitted around the tidy room, so different from her own messy home. "And you have looked everywhere?"

"Everywhere." Murmured Pentecost. "Even John has looked."

"Where could it be?" Mary gave her an impish smile. "I don't know, except, the witch has witched it away." She laughed gaily at her clever answer.

Pentecost tilted her head and looked askance at Mary. "I wonder you talk so much of a witch. Do you think there is a witch in town?"

Mary's eyes twinkled. "I do. And I know her name." She gave Pentecost a sly wink. "The witch came into your house and witched away the wool."

Pentecost squirmed on her seat and gave Mary an uncomfortable look. "Oh, and who is this witch you speak of?"

Mary leaned close to Pentecost as if someone might overhear her. "Widow Marshfield."

Pentecost's hand flew to cover her mouth, her eyes widened in surprise. "Nay! I do not believe you. 'Tisn't true."

"Oh aye, 'tis." Words spilled from Mary's mouth, unheeded. "Did not Anne Stebbings tell me, when we were both in Mr. Smith's chamber, that while she lived in Windsor, down in Connecticut, the Widow Marshfield fell under suspicion of witchcraft? 'Tis why she's here."

With pursed lips, Pentecost shook her head in disagreement. "'Tis naught but idle gossip. Goody Stebbings should watch her tongue, as should you, Mary. Mr. Moxon is a friend of the widow and he sees no ill in her."

Although disappointed in Pentecost's response, Mary ignored the warning in her neighbor's eye. "Have you not seen the lights in the marsh of late? The whole town talks of it."

"You are not the whole town Mary Parsons." Pentecost spoke with undetected sarcasm.

"No, no. 'Tis true, I swear 'tis true." Mary's head bobbed as she forged ahead with her tale. "The lights have only appeared in the marsh since she came to town. They are a sign of a witch. The devil lights her way to him." She finished with a flourish.

Pentecost frowned at Mary. She put down her spindle and yarn and rose to check on her stew. The conversation made her uncomfortable. As she stirred the pot, she looked over at Mary. "I would not spread such stories. No good will come of it."

"No good will come of what?" Both women jumped as John Matthews entered through the open door.

"Oh, John, you gave me a terrible fright. Did you need something?" A blush spread over Pentecost's cheeks. Her husband gave her puzzled frown.

"Good day to you, Goody Parsons." He nodded in Mary's direction. "I've just come for some tobacco." John walked to a corner cupboard and took out his clay pipe and a small canvas bag which contained his tobacco. "Hugh and I will share a pipe."

"Mind you stay well away from the street. You do not want Goody Taylor to spy you with your pipe. She will run to Merrick's and tattle on you both."

John grunted in agreement and headed back out the door. Pentecost handed Mary her wool carders and asked her to card the wool while she spun. "No more talk of witches."

The next day, planting day, dawned bright with a few thin clouds in the morning sky. There was little chance of rain. Hugh whistled while he prepared for the day, happy to start his spring planting at last. Not even his son's illness could dampen his mood.

Samuel woke with a stuffy nose that made it difficult to nurse. His skin was hot and Mary worried he had a fever. She decided it was too cold to take him across the river and expose him to the chill. They had only a small unheated hut for shelter. After Hugh left, she baked cornbread and added onions and cabbage to her kettle, along with a small bit of salted pork. With preparations for supper complete, she bundled up the children and set off to the Cooley's to inquire about flaxseed.

Goody Cooley invited Mary and the children inside then went upstairs to find her husband. Despite its large size, the Cooley's house appeared crowded with people and goods. Sarah Cooley had given birth to her third child, a son named Eliakim, in January. Storage chests, table and stools, cots and beds crowded the parlor. A large weaving loom filled the center of the hall. Along the walls were shelves stacked with wool and linen cloth woven by Benjamin. He also stocked cloth from England and had bolts of Kersey, red cotton and a rare bolt of black silk. Baskets of wool, spun by the women of Springfield, lined the floor.

Benjamin bustled into the parlor. "So, Goody Parsons, you wish to grow flax."

Mary nodded. "I've a small plot set out in my garden, not to big, I don't want to overdo it."

"Well you'll need to plant this seed fast, 'tis almost past time to sow. 'Tis a rare seed, it prefers cold weather."

"Aye, I shall plant it out on the morrow then." Mary pocketed the small bag of seeds.

"Oh, and mind now, the young plants do not thrive with competition, you must keep the weeds out. Tell Hugh to come see me if he has questions."

As she stepped out the door, Mary heard her name called. John Matthews, accompanied by his wife, stopped at the Cooley's door. "Look, Mary, at what I found after you left yesterday."

Pentecost held up a fuzzy ball.

"'Tis a ball of wool."

"'Tis *the* ball of wool," Pentecost said with emphasis. "I found it hidden under a basket in the parlor. Is Goodman Cooley at home?"

"Aye, I've just left him," said Mary. nodding back at the house. "He sold me some seed. I thought I would try me hand at flax." Mary turned to leave.

"Goody Parsons, may I have a word with you?" John asked, then said to his wife, "Pentecost, go sell your wool, while we speak."

They watched Pentecost step inside. John turned back to Mary a frown fixed to his face. "Now then, Goody Parsons, my wife tells me you spoke of a witch in Springfield."

"There is a witch. In fact, the witch taught me how to try a witch." Mary ignored the warning look on his face. "A widow who used to live in Windsor taught me. She now lives amongst us here in Springfield."

"Who is this widow, why do you not name her?"

"She hath three children, a married daughter and two sons, can you not guess."

Exasperated with her coyness, he pressed her for an answer. "I have no wish to play at guessing games, tell me of who you speak." John locked her in a gaze that dared her to speak the name aloud.

Mary, caught up in her tale, did not realize the danger of her accusation. "Why 'tis the Widow Marshfield. 'Tis common knowledge the Windsor magistrate accused her of witchcraft. The Devil hath followed her here to Springfield, and she has begun her mischief."

Goodman Matthews rocked back on his heels; his expression hardened. "I believe no such thing, and neither does my wife. The widow is naught but a good, upstanding woman. You smear her name, Goody Parsons."

Mary stomped her foot and waved a hand at him. "She deserves no good name. The widow is a witch." Grabbing his arm Mary, pulled John close. "She hath envied every woman's child till her own daughter gave birth. And now that child has died. So too, has her cow."

John stumbled back from Mary and pulled his arm free. "What are you saying, Goody Parsons? What hath the child's death to do with Widow Marshfield, her own grandmother?"

"She hath put a spell on her daughter's child and her cow, and both are dead."

"Goody Parsons, does your husband know you make such slanderous statements about the Widow Marshfield?"

Mary opened her mouth to reply but stopped short when the Cooley's door opened, and Pentecost and Sarah stepped out. Before the women reached them, John bent close to Mary's ear. "You will speak no more of this nonsense to my wife, do you understand? You will tell her no more tales of witches."

# Meadow

The day began badly. Samuel was sick, again. Mary rocked him until late in the night. The only one who had gotten any sleep was Hannah, the girl could sleep through the Second Coming, he thought. Dawn saw him and Mary bleary-eyed and cranky. When he left the house for the planting fields, Mary was rocking Samuel, trying to get him to sleep.

Hugh rowed across the river and spent the morning surveying the sodden fields. The wet spring had him worried about his crops. If the rain didn't stop soon, the corn would rot. Late in the morning, he saw John Matthews row over to check on his field. Hugh made his way across to John's field, boots squelching in the thick mud. John's field looked no better and some of his corn seed had rotted in the waterlogged field. Hugh was about to take his leave when John reached out an arm to stop him.

"I've wrestled with my conscience these two weeks, Hugh, and I must tell you I have gone to the Widow Marshfield."

Hugh, head tilted and brows drawn, said, "Oh aye, what about?"

"Er... about your wife."

What now, he thought. "Mary? What are you talking about, John?"

"Ah.... well, the thing is, Mary told both myself and Pentecost that Widow Marshfield is a witch. I tried to caution her but I fear I failed. She is telling others. Therefore, I felt it only right to tell the widow she is being slandered by your wife."

Astounded, Hugh's jaw dropped. What on God's earth was the woman thinking? He corrected himself, she wasn't thinking, that was the problem. The widow was a proud woman and a friend of both Reverend Moxon and Mrs. Pynchon. She will not tolerate Mary besmirching her good name and reputation. She will sue us in court, I know it.

So, here he was on the riverbank, burning with anger, whacking reeds and grass. What good was all his hard work if Mary's actions cost a large fine? When he had his anger under control, he rowed back across and headed home. Hugh burst through the door. Mary, holding Samuel in arms, stumbled backwards. The baby cried. Hannah whimpered, looking from her mother to her father's angry face. Hugh told her to get her corn doll and go outside to play.

"For Christ sakes, Hugh, you've scared me and the children near to death. You know Samuel is unwell. I just got him to sleep and now you have awakened him."

Just the sight of her made his anger flare. He could barely speak. "Never mind the children," he said, through gritted teeth, "I've just come from John Matthews, and what do you think he spoke about?"

A wary look flickered across Mary's face. She turned her back to Hugh to give herself a chance to concoct a response. She laid Samuel in his cot before the fire.

"I know not of what you speak. What tale is John Matthews spreading about me?"

"You know not!" he shouted, "you know exactly of what I speak. Accusing the Widow Marshfield of being a witch, that is what I am speaking of."

Hugh paced around the small room, unable to sit. He repeated back to her what John said she had told Pentecost and him about the widow being a witch.

"Have you lost your mind, woman. 'Tis slander to utter such things. If the widow complains to Mr. Pynchon you will answer to him in court."

Mary blanched as Hugh's words struck home. "It will not come to that," she muttered, under her breath.

"It will, and if you lose, your punishment may well be a whipping. Is that what you want? I've a mind to let it happen to teach you a lesson."

Mary jutted out her chin. "Well, 'twas only a jest."

Hugh flung himself onto a stool, running his fingers through his hair. His anger dissipating. "Let me think on it. I will hear no more talk of witches. Do you understand?"

Samuel's wail pierced the tension between them. His little face was tear-streaked and red from crying. Mary, shoulders slumped, sighed, but picked him up and carried him outdoors while she checked on Hannah.

A burning, nervous energy replaced Hugh's anger. He was restless and his legs twitched. His desire to flee the house overcame him. I will walk to the Long Meadow and check on my land, he decided. He packed food and drink in a wicker hamper and grabbed his cloak and hat. As he exited the house, he informed Mary, still trying to comfort her son, of his intentions. She opened her mouth to issue a retort but changed her mind and said nothing. But, her scowling, tight lipped expression made her feelings clear. She was angry, he was leaving. Hugh stared her down, he did not care.

Hugh tramped down the muddy track, hugging the river's edge to the meadow. The river, swollen from the rain, raced past him. He frowned to see branches and old logs sweeping past, they would make crossing the river dangerous. Debris on the path gave evidence that the river had breached its banks during the night. The morning's clouds had dissipated, mayhap they would get a break from the incessant rain. With each step, Hugh could feel the morning's tension leave his body. It was good to be outside, away from Springfield, his wife and his troubles.

It was not far to the meadow, only about four miles from his house, but Hugh took his time getting there. The sights and sounds of nature soothed his spirit and restored his mood. He stopped to admire a patch of wildflowers, blooming in the warm spring sun. Beggar's Tick and wild raspberries sprawled along the track. In the distance, he spotted a doe and her fawn grazing on new shoots of meadow grass. The sound of his footfall must have alerted them to his presence; the deer turned tail and with a few graceful leaps escaped into the safety of the wood. Intent on watching the animals, Hugh failed to notice the silent approach of a hunting party. The Indian's sudden presence startled him. They walked single file and carried two long poles between them from which hung a dozen beaver pelts. Hugh stepped off the path to let them pass. They are headed for Springfield, he guessed, to sell the furs to Pynchon, who will send them on to London and make a huge profit for himself. The natives nodded at Hugh as they passed.

It was late afternoon when he arrived. The road crested, and the meadow spread out before him. The green grass danced in a warm breeze, making a soft swishing sound. Wildflowers dotted the meadow. Hugh bent to pick some Merry Bells. Inhaling the sweet scent, the last of his tension blew away.

The town surveyor had divided the large meadow into plots, each householder received a share. Trees, rocks and bushes marked the boundaries of each man's parcel. By town decree, the owners had until summer to build a fence to enclosed their land. Hugh made his way to his section of the meadow. Several cows grazed nearby. A few families had established homes in the meadow. Alexander Edwards was the first to do so, wanting to be closer to his cattle, which he kept year-round on the meadow.

Hugh brought bread and cheese for his supper, which he ate at his leisure, undisturbed by crying children or a fussy wife. By God, he loved his son, but the child was always ill. He was certain that no child had ever cried so loud so often. Tonight, his only company was a family of ducks, making their way down to the river. Hugh threw them a few crumbs from his bread. After his light meal, he got out his pipe and tobacco. No need to worry about who was watching, he could in smoke peace, free from the prying eyes of his neighbors.

The night was fine and dry and Hugh, exhausted, slept well despite the rough conditions. A raucous chorus of birds woke him before dawn. He broke his fast with the rest of the bread and cheese, washing it down with the last of his ale. He rinsed out his jug with river water. Hugh went by the Edwards house on his way home to get fresh milk for Mary. It would be his peace offering. The Edward's owed Hugh money for some bricks, he would ask them for milk to offset some of the debt.

As Hugh approached the Edward's house, he saw a gentle curl of white smoke rising from the chimney. At least someone in the family was up and about, getting the fire stoked for the day's use. He heard someone in the barn talking to the cows. He called out a greeting as he entered. Sarah Edwards crouched under a large black and white cow, her strong hands manipulating the udders as a steady stream of creamy milk filled the wooden pail at her feet.

Sarah twisted her head around to see who had hailed her, while the cow, ignoring Hugh, chewed on her cud.

"Hugh Parsons, what brings you out to the meadow so early this morn?" Sarah's strong hands didn't miss a beat as she questioned him.

"Good day to you, Goody Edwards. 'Tis no concern of yours what I do here. I slept here last night and I'm headed home. I was hoping you could give me some milk to take with me."

"Has Springfield run out of milk?" Sarah's caustic manner of speech grated on Hugh, threatening to spoil his good mood.

"Goody Edwards, might I get a jar of milk from you without further ado, and I will count the milk against your debt."

Sarah Edwards would not let him off the hook. "I wonder what could bring you out here at night? 'Tis a strange thing, to my mind. You expect me to believe you've come all this way for naught but to sleep in the meadow." She turned her head to give him a sly look.

Hugh bit his lip. What is it with women? Why must they wheedle out every detail of a man's life, he wondered? "For the love of God, woman, quit your pratting and give me some milk." Hugh, red-faced and losing patience, tried to remain calm. Why was this woman being so difficult? He wished now he had not stopped but just gone on home.

Sarah's smile turned hard and brittle as she returned his stare. By God she is a bold woman to treat me so, he fumed.

"Well 'tis no call for rudeness, Goodman Parsons, I cannot give you any milk, 'tis already spoken for. I will give you some eggs instead."

"I do not want eggs, Goody Edwards. I'll have what you owe me in milk, if you please." The effort to remain civil set his vein throbbing once again.

"No."

He stared at her. She stood, pails of steaming milk in her hands.

"No, you cannot have any." And with that, she brushed past him, headed for the house, leaving Hugh slack jawed, standing alone with the cow in the barn.

# Trial

The knock came as expected. Thomas Merrick stood outside in the late afternoon sun, sweat stained his shirt. Like Hugh, he had spent his day working in his planting field. Hugh opened the door to him, watching the subtle transformation of Merrick's face from neighbor to town constable. His agreeable nature fought with the need to project a mien of officialdom; somehow failing at both. Thomas' accent gave away his Welsh origins, as did his short stature. Hugh towered over him. But Thomas had inherited the tough fighting spirit of his ancestors who had battled the English for centuries. Hugh did not intimidate him. The men exchanged greetings before Thomas got to the point of his visit.

"Well, Hugh, you know why I'm here."

"I'm sure I have a good idea, have your say."

Thomas cleared his throat and proceeded with his summons. "I summon you, Hugh Parsons, to appear before Magistrate Pynchon next Saturday, the 29th of May, to answer to the charge of taking tobacco in the street."

Hugh, who had been holding his breath, hooted with relief. He called Mary to come outside. Mary crossed the room and joined Hugh in the doorway.

"Here is the constable come to summon me to court on Saturday."

Mary looked from Hugh to Merrick, unsure what was happening.

"Someone has complained on me for smoking my pipe and I have to answer to Pynchon for my offense." He smiled at her, feeling a sense of relief.

"Hugh, you look as if you were expecting something worse."

"I don't know what you can mean Thomas. Now then, can I offer you some cider, you look like you have worked up a mighty thirst."

"Well, I'll not turn you down, but first, I've one more summons to read." Reaching into his bag he pulled out a second scrap of paper. He turned to Mary, giving her a hard look. "Mary Parsons, I summon you to appear before the magistrate on Saturday the 29th of May. I charge you with the slander of Widow Marshfield."

Thomas Merrick jumped back as the Parsons' door slammed shut.

Saturday morning saw Hugh up with the dawn as usual. He had a few hours of work to complete before he and Mary were due at the meetinghouse. Thoughts of Mary's case filled his head. His own trivial case did not concern him. The fine for smoking was small compared to what he would have to pay if they lost Mary's slander case. Yesterday evening, after the children were asleep, they talked about what to do and say in court. Hugh decided that it would be best for Mary to admit to everything and fall on the mercy of the magistrate. She would grovel for mercy and hope for the best. Mary was not happy with the plan but agreed to it.

As they rounded their house, they heard Constable Merrick bang his drum to summon the townsfolk to the meetinghouse. Court cases were tried on Thursday evenings, following the town meeting. But Mr. Pynchon called a special court session on Saturday to read the compiled printed laws of the colony and required every able-bodied adult to attend. Henceforth, none could claim

136

ignorance of the law as a defense when presented in court for a breach of the law.

All along the street, folk popped out of their houses, headed towards the town green. The population of Springfield was close to one hundred adults and three times as many children. By half nine in the morning, it appeared to Hugh, they were all accounted for, mingling on the steps of the meetinghouse.

The Widow Marshfield stood to one side of the building, surrounded by her children and friends. Hugh ignored them. He guided Mary to a spot near the door where they chatted with Jonathan Taylor and his wife. Hugh rolled his shoulders and cracked his knuckles, he wanted to get this over with. The sound of laughter coming from the Marshfield group grated on his nerves. He gritted his teeth, trying to fight off the anger. Where the hell was Pynchon, he wondered? At last, the door to the Pynchon residence opened, and the magistrate emerged, followed by his wife and family.

William Pynchon strode across the meeting green. Sunlight glinted off the shiny silver buttons of his black coat. On his head he wore a tight-fitting skull cap, reserved for court days. He stopped to greet Reverend Moxon before leading the way into the meetinghouse and made his way to his magisterial chair. The town people filed in after him. Just as on lecture days, the men and women sat on opposite sides of the building. The open shutters let in light and fresh air. But it would soon heat up, making the room stuffy and hot.

Pynchon banged his large wooden gavel; the room fell silent and everyone seemed to sit up straighter. Before the reading, Mr. Pynchon swore in Henry Burt as town clerk. Burt was one of a handful of Springfield men who could read and write with any proficiency. His election as clerk was as expected. Then, William Pynchon, in his most commanding voice, read the laws of the Colony of Massachusetts to the assembly. There were few surprises; most people appeared bored.

Pynchon rattled off the last of the laws then paused for breath and a sip of ale to wet his dry mouth. After a quick glance around the courtroom he called for questions. There was some murmuring before Goodman Sikes asked for clarification of the statutes concerning hogs and pigs. Discussion ensued before Pynchon declared the matter needed further review. He would present his findings at the next town meeting. With a bang of his gavel, he ordered the constable, Thomas Merrick, to call the first case, which was Hugh's.

Hugh rose from his seat, walked to the front of the room and stood before the magistrate.

"Who complains of Hugh Parsons?" questioned Pynchon.

"I do," said Thomas Merrick. "I have witnessed Hugh Parsons taking tobacco in the street nearby his house."

Hugh glared at Thomas, wanting to choke him. He had spotted the constable smoking his pipe down by the river just two days ago. The gall of the man.

"Constable, are there any other witnesses?

James Bridgeman, in a pompous voice, testified that he too had seen Hugh smoking. With that, the magistrate banged his gavel. "Hugh Parsons, I order you to pay a fine of 10 shillings. Constable call your next case."

Thomas Merrick complained of Richard Exile for the same offense, he received the same fine. Pynchon asked the courtroom if anyone else had witnessed someone smoking in public. Hugh stood and shot James Bridgeman a black look. "Aye, sir. I passed Goodman Bridgeman smoking in his yard this very morning."

Chagrined, Goodman Bridgeman paid a 10-shilling fine. As Henry Burt finished recording their fines, William Pynchon called for the next case. Hugh held his breath as he watched Thomas Merrick turn and search for Mary.

"The Widow Marshfield complains of Goody Parsons and accuses her of slander. Goody Parsons, approach the magistrate if you please."

Mary blinked and swallowed hard. She handed her son to Blanche, seated next to her. She patted Hannah on the head and told her to behave. Mary wound her way up the aisle and stood facing Mr. Pynchon. The constable called the Widow Marshfield to approach the bench. Supported by her son, the widow rose and stood opposite Mary, her face hidden behind the wide brim of her hat.

"Goody Marshfield, please inform the court in what manner hath Mary Parsons slandered you."

With a soft voice she spoke to the jury. "Goody Parsons hath impugned my good name and upstanding reputation with her idle tongue, your Honor, she hath called me a witch."

The courtroom gasped as one. Slander was one thing but to accuse your neighbor of witchcraft was a dangerous thing. Pynchon focused his stern gaze on Mary.

"How do you plead, Goody Parsons?" Mary mumbled an answer which Pynchon could not hear. "Speak up, woman, so all may hear your plea."

Hugh watched as Mary stiffened her spine and jut out jaw, he recognized that look. "Not guilty, your Honor."

The courtroom buzzed with excitement. Many, if not all the women present, had heard Mary speak of the widow and witchcraft. Her plea baffled them. Aghast, Hugh bit his lip to silence his howl of anger. Damn her, he thought. How could she do this to them? She didn't stand a chance of being acquitted. Half the town had heard her gossip about the widow. This would cost him.

"Widow Marshfield have you a witness?" inquired Mr. Pynchon, as the room settled.

"I do. I call Goodman Matthews and his wife Goody Matthews."

The Matthews stepped forward and swore an oath on the bible to speak the truth. The magistrate asked them in turn to describe what they heard Mary say concerning the Widow Marshfield. Both repeated the tales Mary had told of magical wool and the widow's jealousy of other women's children. John describe his conversation with Mary and how she said the widow had taught her to recognize a witch. Pentecost Matthews shook as she recounted Mary's story of marsh lights and her conversation with Ann Stebbings. When the Matthews finished their testimony, the magistrate once again looked at Mary.

"Goody Parsons, have you aught to say in your defense?"

Mary stood stiff and unyielding in front of the judge, eyes blazing she denied ever uttering such words. Her words dashed any hope Hugh had that she would confess and beg for mercy. Mr. Pynchon bent over and exchanged words with Henry Burt then spoke with the jury before once again banging his gavel.

"Goody Parsons, I find you guilty of the act of malicious slander of the good name of the Widow Marshfield. I sentence you to be well whipped on the morrow after lecture with twenty lashes by the constable."

The courtroom was abuzz. Twenty lashes was a fearsome punishment for a man. 'Twas a brutal sentence for a woman. Hugh watched Mary recoil as the magistrate's words hit her like a punch to the gut. The blood drained from her face and she made a low whimpering sound, as her knees buckled under her. Thomas Merrick grabbed her by the elbows and kept her upright. Hugh was thankful he did not let her fall, adding to the indignity of the moment. The magistrate gave Mary a steady stare, taking in her distressed state. He turned from her and sought Hugh in the crowd.

"Goodman Parsons, will you approach."

Hugh rose from his bench and moved forward as the magistrate leaned over talking with Henry Burt. He took his place next to Mary who grabbed his arm for support. Hugh gave her a grim look and shook his head at her. His frustration written all over his face.

"Goodman Parsons, the court will accept the payment of a fine of three pounds in place of corporal punishment, if you agree."

Hugh glanced at his frightened wife. She choked back her tears and gave him a pleading look. She looks scared, he thought, good, mayhap she will have learned her lesson. He took his time responding. He had half a mind to let the punishment stand. Who will care for the children while she recovers? Better to pay up. He would have to pay in Indian corn, he had no coin. This would cost him almost his entire crop for the year.

"Goodman Parsons, what is your decision? Will you pay your wife's fine, or shall I have her whipped as ordered?" Demanded William Pynchon.

"Aye, I will pay the widow."

Mary sagged with relief. Hugh took her arm and lead her down the aisle. He stopped to scoop up his children and headed home.

# Curse

June was one of Mary's favorite months. It was mellow, warm and dry. The spring rains had ended, and the heat of summer had yet to build. It was a time to be outside. Goodwives carried their butter churns and spinning wheels into the dooryard and sat outside to do their sewing. Women visiting their neighbors gathered under the shade of large trees while their children played around them. In the aftermath of the trial, Mary stayed close to home. She tended her garden and her flax plot; teaching Hannah which plants were weeds and needed pulling. Samuel remained fussy, another excuse to stay at home.

Blanche stopped by on a bright morning to visit. It was a beautiful day; the women sat beneath the canopy of a large chestnut tree on blankets spread on the ground. After a fitful morning Samuel was asleep. Mary carded wool while Blanche rocked her son Joshua to sleep. Hannah, humming to herself, played nearby, making mud cakes.

"I wager your ears have been afire this week. The gossip was about naught but you and the widow."

Mary sniffed and tossed her head. What do I care what others say about me, she thought?

"Mrs. Moxon said Hugh should have had you whipped, 'tis the only way to stop your wagging tongue, and Goody Chapin said she hoped that Hugh had boxed your ears to teach you a lesson."

"Oh, and what will still her wagging tongue, I wonder?" Mary pouted, disappointed to hear such harsh words spoken against her. She sat without speaking for a few minutes, staring into the distance. She sighed, shaking her head. Blanche watched her, saying nothing.

"You know, I only meant it as a jest." Mary blurted.

Blanche rolled her eyes in disbelief. "What mean you a jest? You buzzed about town telling any who would listen that she was a witch."

"'Tisn't true," said Mary, glaring at Blanche. "Pentecost and John gave false testimony against me. They twisted my words to make it seem so."

"Ha." Blanche scoffed. "You say that now that a jury hath judged you guilty. Every Goodwife in Springfield would give the same testimony."

Mary shot Blanche a petulant look. "Well, I swear I shall never speak that woman's name again, as long as I live. I hope she never needs my help; she will not have it."

"Good," said Blanche, "and whilst you're at it, mayhap you can swear never to speak of witches again… ah look you, here comes Joan."

Mary looked up from her carding to see Joan Lumbard, a baby on her hip and a basket over her arm. The hem of her dress was wet through; her apron covered with purple stains. She had been berry picking in the meadow all morning and had brought blackberries to share. Mary popped a fat, still warm berry into Hannah's mouth. The child squealed with delight as purple-black juice dribbled down her chin.

"How are you, Mary, dear?" she inquired. "And how does little Samuel fair today?"

"He seems better this morn, thank you for asking. 'Tis good to know I have true friends, not like that Pentecost Matthews and her husband."

Joan gave Mary a quizzical look as Blanche sputtered, "Lord help us, here she goes again."

Mary had been dreading Sunday, having to face the entire town again. Everyone would stare at her. She shuddered at the thought. Hugh was not sympathetic and said she only had herself to blame. He had told her to plead guilty and beg for mercy, but she could not bring herself to grovel. What harm had she done? No injury had come to the widow. It was all rather unfair.

Hugh advised her to hold her head up and act like nothing had happened. He could pull that off, she thought, but not her. The sound of Thomas Merrick banging his drum drifted in the open door. Hugh was eager to set off for lecture. He wanted to complete his deal with Mr. Henry Smith before the service began, but Mary dawdled over Samuel.

"For God's sake, Mary, let's go." Hugh shouted at her from outside.

Out of excuses to linger, she picked up Samuel and headed out the door, closing and latching it behind her. Hugh had hitched the cart to the horse and was loading Hannah into the back. Mary hurried to catch up, and together they made their way up the street to the meetinghouse green. Hugh was grumpy about being late. They were among the last family to arrive; most had already taken their seats. Heads turned and Mary received many reproving looks as she and the children squeezed their way to her spot on the bench. She settled the children, hoping Samuel would nap for an hour or two. Reverend Moxon and his family arrived and proceeded up the aisle. Mrs. Moxon and the children took their seats in the front bench while the Reverend made his way to the pulpit.

Moxon gazed down on his little congregation. His black hooded eyes swept across the women, settling on Mary. Her cheeks were burning and her stomach churned. She dreaded what was coming. Moxon commenced with a long-winded prayer. A scripture reading followed before

Moxon launched into his sermon. Mary rarely paid attention to her minister's words. His harsh Yorkshire accent grated on her nerves, and she had never developed a taste for the bombastic lecture style of the New England Puritan minister. It was so different from the services of her childhood which retained a whiff of incense and Catholicism. The memory of those long-ago days brought a rare smile to her lips.

The words slander, gossip and neighbor reverberated around the room, jolting Mary from her reverie. Cheeks aflame, she knew in an instant he spoke about her. There was a subtle shift of bodies as women moved to distance themselves from her. She itched to leap up and flee the room. Instead Mary drew on Hugh's words. She sat up straight, spine stiffened and forward looking, not quite meeting Reverend Moxon in the eye but still looking forward. How she hated him in that instant. Who was he to sit in judgment of her? His wife was no better than her. Mrs. Moxon enjoyed her share of gossip, she even laughed when Mary spoke of Widow Marshfield, saying she deserved a bit of heat for her attitude towards the rest of the women of Springfield. Mary thought Mrs. Moxon jealous of Mercy Marshfield. Lost in her thoughts once again, she did not realize the lecture was over, and the congregation was getting to their feet to sing the last Psalm of the service.

On their way home, Hugh announced that he would pay Widow Marshfield the next morning. "I want you to accompany me."

His request left her speechless. How can he ask this of me, she wondered, it would be humiliating? Tight-jawed she said, "I will do no such thing."

"This is a problem of your own making and you will see it through, else I will speak with Mr. Pynchon about a whipping."

Mary studied him from the corner of her eye. She saw the serious set to his face. My God, he means it. "Very well," she said, at last. "If you desire to see me humiliated, I will accompany you."

"What I want, wife, is to teach you the value of a civil tongue. If you will only be polite and offer the widow an apology, she may forgive us some of the fine."

Mary's jaw dropped. "Apologize, apologize for what? I have not to apologize for. 'Tis the Matthews who are in the wrong not me."

Hugh shook his head. "It matters not who is in the wrong, what matters is that if you act contrite it may cost me less corn."

"'Tis all you care about, Hugh, your money," Mary shot back in anger, "You care nothing for me." Mary stomped ahead reaching the house before Hugh who found the door slammed in his face when he arrived.

Mary woke the next morning in a foul mood. Hugh might drag her to Marshfield's house, but she would make him pay for it. After a breakfast of coarse oatmeal and stony silence, Hugh loaded the corn into his cart and hitched up the horse. Mary wanted to leave the children with Blanche but Hugh insisted they accompany them. Hannah and Samuel would make her appear more sympathetic.

The widow lived near the top of the road, just past the meetinghouse. All their neighbors were out and about. The men headed to their planting fields or the woods to cut trees. The women were doing chores and minding their children. Doors and windows all along the street were

147

flung open to catch the still cool morning air. Mary was certain that all eyes were on her as she made her way past.

When they reached the Marshfield's house, Hugh tied the horse to a bush in the dooryard. He yelled a hallo to the house. Samuel stuck his head out the open door.

"Good Morning, Goodman Parsons, Goody Parsons, you'll be wanting to see my mother, I expect, I'll fetch her."

Samuel disappeared behind the open half-door, they heard him calling his mother. Widow Marshfield took her time. Mary saw a vein throb in Hugh's temple and knew he was losing patience. At last, she appeared at the door. Mercy Marshfield gave Hugh a perfunctory greeting but ignored Mary, whose frozen smile slipped from her face. The widow's grown children joined her in the dooryard.

"I see you have brought my corn, Goodman Parsons, is it all there?" Her voice and manner imperious.

Hugh bit back a sharp retort. "'Tis all here and accounted for. But, before I hand it over, my wife wishes to say something to you."

The widow's expression hardened, she glanced with disdain at Mary, then turned back to Hugh. "Tell your wife there is nothing she can say to me."

Hugh let out an impatient sigh and rubbed his hand over his eyes. He took a deep breath and tried again. "My wife would like to apologize," he said, "She meant no harm."

"Well, let us hope she has learned a valuable lesson and thinks on the damage she does with her wagging tongue."

Mary's hand itched to slap her smug face.

"Ah, she has, she has." Hugh nodded his head at Mary. Clearing his throat, he went on. "Widow Marshfield, I hear tell that you might abate some of the fine, which is a great hardship on me and my family. Perhaps you will be so kind as to abate us 20 shillings." Hugh was doing his best to keep an even tone to him voice. It surprised Mary he was managing so well.

"I will not abate a thing," she replied, "Your wife has said the witnesses had taken a false oath."

Hugh's eyes closed, his fists curled and Mary watched his lips move as he cursed under his breath.

"'Tis true," said Samuel, as he moved towards his mother. "Your wife will not admit her guilt."

Hugh remained silent, but Mary could tell he was furious. He slung the bags of grain from the cart, throwing the last one down with a loud thump. A trickle of corn spilled out, landing at the widow's feet. As Samuel Marshfield bent to lift a bag, Hugh whirled around, pointing his finger at the widow. His face was dark with anger and his voice shook.

"If you will not abate, it will be as lent. It shall do you no good, it shall be but as wildfire in your house and as a moth in your clothes."

The widow's eyes widened in fear as she clutched at her chest. Her daughter gasped aloud, and her sons formed a barrier between their mother and Hugh. As if on cue, baby Samuel let out a piercing wail. Hannah grabbed her mother's dress and hid her face in the folds of fabric. Hugh barked at Mary to walk while he grabbed the horse's reins, ripping leaves from the bush, sending them flying. The widow remained silent as Mary scurried out of the yard not daring to glace over her shoulder. She could sense their eyes boring into her retreating back.

They walked home in silence. Hugh's anger visible on his face. Mary made no attempt at conversation. It would only lead to a fight, and she was tired of fighting. When they reached home, Mary hurried into the comfort of her house. Samuel was still whimpering as she laid him in his cradle. Hugh took his time putting away the cart and tending to the horse. She heard him as he stomped up to the door, but he did not enter the hall.

"I'm going to the meadow." And with that, he strode off.

# Dorchesters

The summer solstice approached; the days lengthened, and dawn came early. Hugh rose, trying not to wake his family. Pulling his clothes off their pegs, he dressed in the hall. Mary and the children remained fast asleep. Hugh gave thanks that Samuel slept through the night. Hugh stood over his cradle and watched him, thumb tucked into his pink mouth, his blond hair curled like a halo around his head. He looks like a little angel, he thought.

A cock crowed, announcing the dawn, as Hugh slipped out the door and picked his way down to the river's edge. He stopped to admire a large spider web, dotted with dewdrops that sparkled like gems in the early morning light. An eerie mist rose from the flat surface of the water. Safe from the prying eyes of neighbors, Hugh lit his pipe. He sat on a tree stump enjoying the sound of morning bird song. From across the river, he could just hear the lowing of cattle. A large splash caught his attention. A family of river otters frolicked among the cattails and reeds at the river's edge. What a carefree existence, he mused, beholden to no one. Hugh knocked the ashes from his pipe and with a sigh, rose to begin his workday.

Mr. Pynchon had ordered a community workday. He wanted a wooden walkway built over the wet meadows, connecting the main street of Springfield to the Bay Road, the road that led to Boston. Pynchon demanded all able-bodied men and boys take part; no excuses accepted. Hugh disliked these enforced workdays, false camaraderie grated on his nerves. Besides, he had work of his own that needed doing. To make up for lost income from Mary's fine, he agreed to make bricks for Henry Smith and

Reverend Moxon. Because he was in a financial bind, they took advantage, negotiating in their favor. Now, instead of working on their bricks, he would have to spend the day sawing logs with no profit in it for him.

The weather had turned warm of late, the air thick as day old pottage. The sun burned his neck, and biting flies buzzed around his head, landing on his face and hands. The workers laid cut logs on the marshy ground and topped them with thick planks of wood, forming a raised path. They worked for hours in the heat with only a brief stop to eat. Hugh, hot and sweaty, his boots and breeches caked with mud, trudged home exhausted from the work site.

His simple dinner had long burned off with the strenuous work of sawing, he needed to eat. But first, he wanted to wash. Bypassing his house, Hugh headed straight for the river. He threw a wooden bucket, tied to a rope, into the water and poured the cold contents over his head. God that feels good, he thought, as he doused himself and rinsed the mud and flecks of wood chips from his body. Time to eat; he strode to the house but stopped short at the barn. Tied to the door stood a horse he did not recognize; it appeared to be chewing on his hay. Voices drifted from the house on the thick humid air. Damnation, he groused, I'm tired and hungry, and it appears I've a house full of people. As he stepped through the open-door, conversation halted.

"Hugh," said Mary, leaping to her feet. "You're home at last. Come in and meet my cousin Sarah and her husband Anthony Dorchester, just arrived, this very day from Boston."

"Cousin Sarah," said Hugh, nodding at her husband. "Welcome to Springfield." Hugh sat at the table. "Mary, get me some ale. I see you have some already, Anthony."

"Aye, but I won't say no to a second." He held his cup out to Mary to refill, thanking her when she did.

"How was your journey?" asked Hugh. "Was the crossing rough?"

Hugh listened, sipping his ale, as Dorchester described the voyage from England to Boston and from there to Springfield. "It sounds much like my own," he said.

Anthony opened his mouth to reply when Hugh's stomach growled loud enough to startle the man into silence. Hannah laughed, clapping her hands, and exclaimed that father had a bear in his stomach. The adults chuckled as Mary put a trencher of food in front of her husband. He dug in, spooning up chunks of venison and vegetables. He waved his utensil at Anthony telling him continue his tale.

Mary and Sarah sat before the open door, hoping to catch an evening breeze. Hannah skipped in and out between them. Sarah had a harsh cough that racked her thin body. With her blond hair and fair skin, she resembled her cousin, but she lacked Mary's healthy glow.

"What's wrong with Sarah?" asked Hugh, in an offhand manner.

"She fell ill a week after we sailed; she lost a babe in Boston before we headed to Springfield. I pray that now we have arrived at our final destination, she can regain her health." Anthony spoke in a hushed tone, not wanting Sarah to overhear their conversation.

"Oh, so you plan to stay in Springfield. Where will you bide til you have a house?" Hugh watched as Anthony bit his lip, then glanced over at Mary. He caught a look pass between the pair before both turned and stared at him.

"What here?" Hugh sputtered as understanding dawned. "You want to stay here, with us? Mary, have you lost what little sense God gave you?"

"Hugh, please," pleaded Mary, "Sarah is my cousin, she is family, and she is ill. You would not turn them away."

Hugh pursed his lips, eyes narrowed. He gave his wife a hard stare, his fingers drummed on the table top. Hugh decided they discussed this before he arrived home. Mary must have given Anthony reason to believe he would approve.

Hugh leapt to his feet. "Mary, outside, now!" Mary scuttled out the door and Hugh made to follow.

"I can pay."

Hugh stopped in his tracks, turned back and looked at Anthony. "You can pay?"

"Yes, I've not a lot, but I can pay you some, in coin at that. I will also work for you. Help with the brick making, sawing, weeding, whatever you need." Hugh heard the desperation in his voice and gave him a grim smile.

"Mary!" Hugh pointed at Sarah. "Put that woman to bed, she looks dead on her feet."

The two families adjusted to communal living. The Dorchesters had their own kettle which hung over the fire next to Mary's. Hugh appreciated the extra help that Anthony provided but resented the presence of his sick wife in the house. The days grew hot and sticky. Mary kept the windows, open day and night, ever hopeful of a cooling breeze. She spent her days cooking, cleaning, tending her vegetable and flax garden, and tending to Sarah and her own son, who somehow never seemed to improve.

Samuel turned a year old in June but weighed no more than a child half his age. Mary worried and prayed over him. Springfield had no resident physician. The sick had to rely on their own herbal lore and that of their neighbors. Mary tried every suggestion offered. She made tisanes of herbs and spices which she spoon-fed to Samuel. She grew Lungwort and Elecampane in her yard garden, just outside the door. She dried the leaves and stems and then steeped them in boiling water, adding just a drop of honey to cut their bitter taste. Both were good for lung ailments. She traded eggs with Goody Pritchard for some of her coriander, which was good for all ailments. Mary made chest plasters of dried mustard and applied them Samuel's tiny chest. Anything that might lessen his fevers and near constant coughing.

Sarah Dorchester's condition was grave. Hugh and Mary had not realized quite how sick she was the night she and Anthony arrived in Springfield. The Atlantic crossing and the miscarriage had sapped her strength, but there was something more insidious at work. Despite a few weeks of Mary's ministrations, Sarah rise from her pallet by the fire only with great exertion. Mary struggled to care for both her cousin and her son, but neither improved.

At sundown, Hugh closed and latched the door to the house to keep out marauding pigs, escaped dogs and the odd, curious Indian. Two small windows let in minimal air, creating a miasma of stifling heat, the sweet decaying smell of sickness, and the pungent odor of the unwashed human body. The sunlit whimpers of an ill child grated on night-time senses and the quiet cough of day amplified in the dark of night. It became a nerve wracking, sleep destroying sound that only the unconscious could ignore.

The days shortened but summer retained its grip on their lives. August nights were hot and sticky, and the thick air enveloped them like a warm wet blanket. Hugh often found his house unbearable. He preferred to hike down to the meadow and sleep in the open air. His exhausted body and mind unaware of the nocturnal activity of the meadow's inhabitants, as they moved around his inert limbs with indifference.

Hugh lay in the meadow one night, stretched out on a bed of sweet-grass, his hands for a pillow. He stared at the night sky, marveling at the beauty of the stars. In vain, he tried to block out thoughts of home. He felt guilty about leaving Mary to care for both his son and Anthony's wife, but he found the atmosphere of his house intolerable. It was not just the physical conditions but the emotional state of his home that troubled him. He wanted to love his little son, but it was clear the boy was not thriving. It seemed to Hugh that the child clung to life. Mary spent endless hours rocking him, singing to him, fussing over him, praying over him, to little avail. Hugh imagined all the tasks Mary could accomplish if Samuel was healthy. Her flax plot was in dire need of weeding, and it was ages since they'd had clean clothes. Hugh could not remember when he'd had a decent meal, one that was not undercooked or burnt. And poor little Hannah spent more time at the Bedortha's house than at her own.

And it wasn't just Samuel. Sarah Dorchester was dying, all could see it, but none would admit it. The flesh was all but gone from her bones, her body wracked by a painful cough and her appetite gone. Everyone admired Anthony. He worked long hours for Hugh and for anyone else who would hire him. He told Sarah he wanted to salt away money to buy land and build a house, but Hugh knew the truth of it. Anthony hated the sickness as much as Hugh did and knew in his heart that his wife's death drew near. Hugh would never say the words aloud, but in his heart, he prayed that God would end the suffering of his child and Anthony's wife sooner rather than later.

# Knife

The first Sunday of September dawned cool and clear, no cloud dulled the brilliant, azure sky. A fierce storm, harbinger of autumn, blew through during the night and chased away the lingering heat and humidity of summer. The wind had picked up just before dusk, rustling the thick, green leaves of the oak trees and ruffled Hugh's hair as he went about his evening chores. Scanning the western sky, he saw a bank of ominous, slate colored clouds. Before they sat down for supper, Hugh and Anthony shuttered the windows and latched the barn door against the mischief making wind.

"We shall have quite the blow tonight." Hugh ladled steaming stew into his wooden trencher. "Umm, this smells good, have you ever tasted turtle stew, Anthony?"

"Nay, 'twill be my first." Anthony cast a dubious eye on his meal and poked at the chunks of meat with a cautious spoon. He speared a piece and chewed. "Humph, 'tis not bad, not bad at all."

"You must catch them whilst they be sleeping in the cool of the morn. Once the sun heats their blood, they be the devil to catch." Hugh laughed as he described his method of catching turtles.

As Mary joined the men at the table, a faint rumble of thunder echoed around the room. The storm was still some ways off. "We should light a candle," she said.

"Why? 'Tis plenty of light from the fire." Hugh rose from his seat, crossing the room to look out the window.

"Ah, 'tis the old ways of which she speaks. My Gran always lit a taper during a storm. The Devil is about his

159

business, she would say, but the light will keep him away." Anthony smiled at Mary as he reminisced.

Hugh scoffed. "'Tis a waste of a valuable candle, is all."

The storm rolled through a few hours later. Lightning ripped through the black, night sky, illuminating the house with its eerie light. Booming thunder rattled the walls and sent Hannah scuttling from her pallet, seeking refuge beneath the coverlet of her parents' bed. She burrowed into the space between Hugh and Mary, falling back to sleep. Hugh shifted to make room for her then swore under his breath. A trickle of cold water found its way through the thatch and dripped onto his head. Hugh sighed; he'd get no sleep until the storm passed. He prayed there'd be no damaging hail to wreak havoc on his crops, so close to harvest. The sound of thunder grew distant as the storm barreled eastward towards the coast. Hugh moved his sleeping daughter back to her own bed, tucking her beneath the covers. The house fell silent save for the drip of water coming off the roof. Hugh returned to his bed and slipped into a dreamless sleep.

The next morning, Anthony and Sarah, unused to such ferocity, marveled at the strength of the storm. Oak leaves and small twigs, stripped from trees by the wind, littered the dooryard and large puddles reflected the now cloudless sky. The families fell into their usual Sunday morning routine. Church doctrine forbade all work, including cooking, on the Sabbath but farm animals still need tending. Hugh took Hannah outside with him as he attended to his early morning chores. Mary shouted at her to not get her boots wet splashing in the puddles.

Mary's morning was no less busy. She had to feed Samuel, care for Sarah and prepare to attend Sunday lecture. She readied a light meal of bread, cheese and some dried fruit they could eat during the noon break. She packed the food along with a jug of cider into a hamper, covering it with a linen cloth. With the fine weather, they could picnic under a tree on the meetinghouse green. Hannah would enjoy running about outside and tire herself out before the afternoon service.

Before they left, Mary fed Sarah a bowl of porridge, thinned with broth, and lowered her to a pallet next to the hearth. Too ill to attend lecture, Sarah would spend the day resting by the fire. Hannah, who was still outside, throwing feed to the chickens, skipped to the door.

"Mam!" She shouted, "Mr. Merrick is playing his drum."

Thanking Hannah, Mary grabbed her cloak off the peg and slung it around her shoulders. She lifted Samuel from his crib, wrapped him warmly in a blanket, and carried him under the flap of her cloak for extra warmth. Hugh picked up his musket and powder horn, it was his turn to bring his weapon to lecture. Each week, the magistrate assigned six men the duty of protecting the congregation during services. A single building housing the entire population of the town was a tempting target for raiding Indians intent on inflicting death and destruction. Anthony, kissed his wife's cheek, and told her he'd be back at noon to check on her. He left his musket propped next to her chair, loaded, primed and ready to use, if need be.

Together they made their way up the street, greeting neighbors as they went. Mary hummed a little song for Hannah. Hugh welcomed the Sabbath as a day of rest, although there were still chores to do, they were minimal. But he resented the long hours spent at meeting, subjected to Moxon's droning lecture. On this bright September day, Hugh stared out the east facing window. Sunlight streamed through the open door and a cool breeze kept the building comfortable. Hugh studied the dust motes that floated before his eyes. Every once in a while, he glanced over at the hour glass which sat on the deacon's table. At the end of every hour, Henry Smith reached out and flipped it over. He was known to set it down with a loud thump at the end of the third hour, alerting Moxon, who frequently lost track of time.

Reverend George Moxon ended his final prayer of the morning, and seconds later, his congregation bolted out the door, eager to get to the outhouse. Hugh rejoined his family outside, glad to stretch his legs. He smiled at Hannah as she chased a friend, the children happy to be free for a few minutes. Anthony, concerned about his wife, left to check on her.

Hugh and Mary sat beneath the canopy of a chestnut tree. They spread their cloaks on the ground to make a comfortable place to sit and eat their noonday meal.

"I hear Mr. Henry Smith has a cow for sale," said Hugh, between sips of cider. "I think I'd like to buy some beef to salt up for the winter."

"How can we pay for a cow, Hugh?" asked Mary. "What, with my fine, you said we are behind in our savings."

"We won't buy the whole cow," Hugh explained, "I was thinking of splitting it four ways. I shall ask Anthony if he would care to go in on the purchase, then if we can find two others, I will only have to pay a quarter of the cost."

Mary, nursing Samuel, nodded in agreement. "'Tis a good idea, I tired of salt pork winter last. And, the beef broth would be good for our Samuel."

"I think I'll have a quick word with Griffith, he might like to go in on a quarter share."

Hugh stood and looked around for Goodman Jones. He spotted his wife and gaggle of children sitting nearby. She told Hugh her husband went home to eat his meal in peace. Griffith Jones, a small, wiry Welshman, lived between John Matthews and Reice Bedortha. Bluff and unruly, he was fond of his pipe and would never say no to a pint of cider. Unfortunately, the man was notoriously near-sighted. Returning home from Francis Pepper's one night, he mistook a tree for a marauding Indian. He shouted to alert the night watch, then raised his musket and fired. The loud noise roused his neighbors, who once they overcame their fear of attack, had a good laugh.

Griffith, Hugh thought, had more likely gone home to smoke a pipe than to eat. Reaching the dooryard, Hugh avoided a large pig that nosed about. He stuck his head inside the open door. "Hallo, where is the man of the house?" He hollered, not wanting his friend to mistake him for an Indian and shoot him. "'Tis Hugh Parsons."

"Ah, Good-day to you, Hugh." Griffith came to the doorway, pipe in hand.

Hugh smiled and stepped inside. There were several knives laid on the table, including an old rusty one.

Griffith shook his head and frowned at the row of knives. "This is strange. I couldn't find a single knife, but now I see they are all here."

Hugh laughed. "Yer wife said you came home to eat in peace, are you ready to return to the meeting?"

"Soon enough, Hugh, there's time yet. I'm about to have a smoke, will you join me?"

"I'll gladly join you." Hugh reached into his pocket to remove his ever-present clay pipe.

The men lit the tobacco and enjoyed the first few pulls in silence. "Now then. Are you here for a reason or just to smoke my tobacco?"

Hugh opened his mouth to reply when a large sow poked her head in the door. Griffith grabbed a stout stick and thwacked her on the haunches. "I don't know what's gotten into that pig, but she's determined to get into the larder." A second blow sent the animal squealing back outside.

"I'm of a mind to buy a quarter share of a cow. Dorchester's in, what say you?"

"Hum. T'would be nice to have a bit of beef. I can trade that beast of a pig for my share." He gave the invading creature a final whack then turned to Hugh. "Yep, I'm in."

The men knocked the ashes from their pipes and pocketed them. "We'd best hurry," said Hugh. "Don't want to be late."

Griffith rolled his eyes and latched his door. The empty green and the sound of warbling voices let them know they were late. Waiting until the psalm finished, the two slipped inside and slid onto the back bench rather than take their assigned seats. Hugh noted that Anthony had not returned, mayhap his wife had need of him.

The lecture over, Hugh and Griffith approached Benjamin Cooley on the green and asked if he wanted to be the fourth man in their purchase of the cow. He agreed, and the men made an appointment with Henry Smith for the next day, lest anyone purchase the cow from under them.

When Hugh, Mary and the children returned home, Anthony sat outside the door with his musket in hand.

"What ho," said Hugh, a concerned frown on his face. "Is something amiss?"

"Indians." said Anthony, "A crash, and some footsteps woke Sarah as she dozed. She thought we had returned from meeting. But when a bare leg walked by she realized t'was some intruder and cried out."

"Oh, Lord save us! Did they take anything?" Mary, in a panic, rushed into the house. After laying Samuel in his cot, she flew into the parlor to check her belongings. The lid of her chest lay open, the contents strewn about. It did not appear that any valuables were missing. She ducked into the lean-to kitchen.

"The devils," she cried, "they've taken my cornbread."

"They might have taken more if Sarah had not woken up, mayhap she scared them away with her cry," said Anthony.

Mary returned to the fireside to check on Sarah who shivered with fright or fever.

"Sarah, dearest, how terrified ye must have been." She laid a cool cloth on her cousin's hot forehead. "We should never have left the door unbolted."

"Oh Mary, I have never been so scared." Sarah trembled as she reached out to grasp Mary's hand. "How can you stand to live here knowing those savages are about?"

Mary gave her a hug and brought her a cup of warmed cider to ease her anxiety. Hugh went to report the break-in to Constable Merrick while Anthony remained on guard duty. They ate their cold supper, minus the cornbread, in subdued quiet. Hugh and Anthony patrolled the property at dusk, then latched the door on the night.

The next day dawned cool and clear. Hugh and Anthony together with Griffith and Benjamin went to bargain with Henry Smith for his cow. When the men agreed, the animal was led to Cooley's barn. It would take a few days to prepare everything they needed to slaughter and butcher the cow. None of the four men had the skills needed to do the job, so they hired their neighbor John Dibble, who had worked for a butcher in England, to assist them. They would give him the cowhide in payment. The women scoured out their meat barrels and went to Pynchon's warehouse to stock up on salt, brown sugar and saltpeter.

Benjamin set up a scaffold and trestle table in his dooryard for Dibble's use. He arrived with his ax and a set of sharpened knives. Goody Cooley fed the men breakfast before sending the children to the Parsons' house. She did not want the little ones getting underfoot during the butchering process. Once the animal was dispatched, the men muscled the heavy carcass onto the scaffold where it hung, blood draining into tubs. Dibble then set about butchering the beef. The joint owners drew lots for the various cuts and delicacies. Hugh rubbed his belly and made known his desire to have the tongue. There's nothing better, he told Anthony, then boiled tongue. He was disgruntled when Dorchester chose it, on the first round. Damn him, Hugh thought, he knew I wanted it. Still, I have the tail which will make a tasty soup. By the end of the day, the meat was all packed. That night the Parsons feasted on fresh beef for the first time in years.

# Tongue

Late August brought an end to summer rainstorms. The
humidity dropped; earth and sky dried out. Muted shades
of tan and brown replaced Summer's verdant palate of
green and gold. Although the warmth of the afternoon sun
lingered in the dying days of summer, the cool breeze of
morning whispered that change was coming.

September was a month of anticipation. Harvest time
drew near, all must be ready to leap into action when the
wheat and corn were ripe for harvesting. As the days
progressed, signs of the coming autumn were visible in the
fields and forests. The ears of corn and wheat ripened,
promising a bountiful harvest. Hugh, with Anthony's help,
spent his days cutting his wheat and stacking it into neat
sheaves. Indian corn, once oozing with milky goodness,
shriveled in its papery husk, waiting for the hand to severe
it from its withered stalk. The Parsons' larder filled with
the bounty of their hard work. The beef from the
slaughtered cow, packed into barrels of salt, would
provide meat for winter meals. Preparation was the
difference between a plentiful winter and just surviving.

Mary struggled to find enough hours in the day to finish
her chores. Between caring for Samuel and Sarah and her
household duties, she labored from dawn till late at night.
She found time to make a vegetable pickle with carrots,
swedes, onions and cauliflower mixed with vinegar and
spices. It would add flavor to their bland winter meals.
But, no matter her accomplishments, it was never enough,
and Hugh harped on her to do more. She dreaded his
return from the field or kiln house. He would question
what she had done that day. Thank God, she thought,

tomorrow is the Sabbath, and Hugh cannot expect me to labor in the fields.

Hugh arrived home alone, tired and quarrelsome. Anthony, had taken a job with Mr. Henry Smith, Mrs. Smith would feed him his supper. He poured himself some cider and sat at the table waiting for his own meal. Mary handed him a trencher of leftover food from their dinner. She had already eaten and returned to making a poultice for Sarah whose violent cough tore through her body. Hugh refilled his cup several times as he ate in silence. Oh Lord, thought Mary, he'll be in his cups soon enough and then he'll start.

Hugh lit his pipe and drew up a stool by the fire. "You spend too much time tending to that woman." He had a scowl on his face as he waved his cup in Sarah's direction. "'Tis not profit in it."

Mary glared at Hugh as she wrung out a cloth and placed it on Sarah's feverish forehead. "Why must everything be about profit? She is my cousin, what should I do, let her lie there in distress?"

Hugh groaned. "Can you not spare a few minutes to help thresh wheat? I cannot do this all myself, you can at least throw the corn from the door."

Mary felt her hands ball in rage. "How can you be so hard hearted? 'Tis all about money with you. If you need more help, why then do you not hire someone? Jonathan Taylor is always eager for extra work."

"Why pay for labor that my wife should do? 'Tis Dorchester who should hire someone to care for his wife." As if summoned, the door opened and Anthony stepped inside. He greeted Hugh and Mary; unaware he had been the topic of their conversation.

"How is Sarah this evening?" He perched on a stool by his wife's side. She gave him a weak smile as he patted her hand.

"She is feeling poorly, but I got her to eat a bowl of porridge."

"I could not do this without your help, Mary, and I cannot thank you enough."

Hugh snorted, saying, "Thanks do not help bring in the harvest."

Mary and Anthony remained silent. They were thankful when he stood and stretched, yawning. "Och, I'm for me bed."

Anthony Dorchester struggled to find pleasure in this time of bounty his resilient spirit deflated by the slow decline of his wife. The next morning, the Sabbath, she was too ill to rise from her pallet, let alone attend lecture. Anthony thought to cheer her by cooking the beef tongue he had salted. He asked Mary if she thought it might do his Sarah good, and she agreed, it would be a treat for her and raise her spirits. Antony took out the tongue and a second piece of beef from his barrel. He rinsed the meat in a bowl of cold water, removing the salt before slipping it into his kettle.

"We are leaving now Anthony," said Mary, as she and Hugh headed out the door with the children. "We shall see you at the meetinghouse."

"Yes, thank you, Mary. I will see Sarah settled in her bed before I leave."

Mary and Hugh walked in the cool morning air. Hugh was quiet, Mary decided he had a sore head from his cider. As they passed their neighbors, the Burt's house, Hugh reached out and took Samuel from her.

"Here, let me carry the child for you."

Mary gave him a quizzical look, but handed the child over.

"'Tis a beauty of a day."

"Aye, 'tis most wonderful." Mary was unsure why Hugh was being so pleasant, but she didn't question him. They walked on in peaceful silence. When they approached Thomas Merrick's place, Hugh handed the boy back to Mary. Without a word, he headed towards the house. Mary stood in the street for a moment and watched his receding back.

"Where is Hugh off to?"

Mary turned around, recognizing Reice Bedortha's voice. He and Blanche were coming up just behind her. "Good day Reice. Good day, Blanche. I cannot tell you, he said naught, just struck off towards Merrick's."

"Are you to wait for him, or will you walk on with us?" questioned Blanche, as they watched Hugh disappear around the corner of Merrick's barn.

"Who knows what that man is up too?" Mary asked, with a hint of anger in her voice. "He keeps his secrets close and tells me naught. I will walk on with ye."

Mary did not lay eyes on Hugh until the lecture drew to a close. Anthony Dorchester entered right before Mr. Moxon, but Hugh did not take his seat. Close to noon, Mary looked back over her shoulder and saw Hugh standing outside the meetinghouse door. At lectures end, Mary made her way outside. She glanced around the meetinghouse green and saw no sign of Hugh. Typical, she thought, shrugging her shoulders, leaving me here with the children. "Hannah, to me now, we're off home."

Anthony arrived ahead of her. "Mary, your home, come and see." Anthony stood by his kettle with a large spoon in his hand, a puzzled frown on his face. As she approached, he bent over his kettle and stirred the contents. He lifted the piece of beef he was cooking for their dinner. Mary stood and watched, unsure of the problem.

"What is the matter, is something wrong with your beef?" asked Mary, coming closer. She reached his side and glanced into the kettle as he stirred the spoon. She turned back to Anthony; one brow raised in a questioning tilt. "What am I looking at?"

"Where is the tongue? The tongue is not in the pot." His voice shook with frustration.

"Perhaps Sarah removed it, it being cooked." She offered with a shrug.

"Sarah has not risen from her bed." Anthony pointed at his incapacitated wife.

Mary walked over to the Dorchesters' salt tub and frowned down at the contents. "You put it in the kettle, did you not?"

"Damnation. You know I put it in the kettle Mary. You stood there and watched me." Anthony straightened and turned to her, his face red and angry. "Where is Hugh?"

Mary was wondering the same thing. Was this his errand? He was angry when he did not draw the straw for the tongue. Did he sneak back here and take it out of Anthony's kettle to spite him? Is that why he was late? Mary went over to Sarah, crouching down beside her, she touched her forehead, she was feverish again. Mayhap, the Indians came and snatched the meat from the pot. "Sarah, did you hear anyone enter the house since we left for lecture. You would have heard the door; it squeaks so when 'tis opened?"

As if on cue, the squeaky door opened, and Hugh stepped inside. Mary and Anthony turned in unison and stared slack jawed at him. Hugh gave each a puzzled look. "What?" he said, "why do you stare at me so?"

"The tongue is missing." Anthony gave him a searching look.

"Did you check your tub, mayhap you forget to put it in your pot." Sounding not the least bit disturbed that the tongue was missing, Hugh poured himself a cup of cider. He grunted at Mary and said he was hungry.

"I did not forget to put it in the kettle, your wife witnessed me do it." Hugh's answer frustrated Anthony.

Mary set a plate of food in front of her husband. He dug into the beans and took a bite of cornbread. Mary remained standing next to him. His indifference to Anthony was maddening, but also suspicious. Did he do it, she wondered? How can he sit there and eat his meal? "Are you not curious or concerned about the disappearance of the tongue."

Hugh stopped chewing his food, cocked his head to the side as if he were giving serious consideration to her question. After a moment, he picked up his spoon and with a slight smile on his face, he directed his reply at Anthony. "No, I'm not."

Mary feared Anthony would explode, he was so furious. But what recourse did he have? If he pushed Hugh too hard, Hugh would toss him and Sarah out. To stop Anthony from saying anything more, Mary said, "Anthony your broth tastes like it could use more herbs. Why do you not cut thyme and rosemary to add to the pot? Twill do Sarah good."

Anthony dragged his angry eyes away from Hugh as he took a deep breath. His response was terse. "Your right, Mary, some thyme will be a welcome addition to my empty kettle."

Hugh ignored him and continued eating. With Anthony out of earshot, Mary turned on her husband.

"Where have you been this morning? You were not at lecture."

Hugh returned her baleful stare. "I was, you just did not see me, 'tis all."

Before she could question him further, Hannah came through the open door. "Mam, I'm hungry."

"In a moment, love." Mary turned back to Hugh, but he stopped her cold.

"Feed the child, Mary, now."

Mary glared at him, but did as he said. She made a plate for her and Hannah and placed them on the table. Just as they sat down, Hugh scraped the last of his beans from his trencher. Mary did not offer to serve him more. Hugh rose, tossing down his linen napkin. "I'm off to the meadow, I need to stretch me legs." With that he grabbed his hat and sauntered out the door, leaving Mary flabbergasted.

Seeing Hugh depart, Anthony returned to the house. He added the herbs to his pot, stirring it well. He came and sat at the table with Mary, asking if Hugh had any more to say about the missing meat.

"Nay, he spoke no more on it. 'Tis passing strange though, that he is so incurious about it."

"Hugh thinks only of himself, not of others." Anthony said. "What do you believe happened?"

"I think I know," said Mary, almost to herself. She peered up at Anthony, her eyes large and troubled. "Mayhap a witch has magicked the tongue away."

"Magic," he said, rolling his eyes. "Who would have witched it away?"

"Hugh."

# Death

The temperature dropped steadily as September, cloaked in the vibrant colors of autumn, drew to a close. The days grew shorter, and nightfall came too soon for the harried farmer. So much to do, the dawn whispered urgently, hurry, hurry, time is running out. All of nature's bounty seemed to ripen at once; pumpkins, beans, corn. Fall was also the season to slaughter the summer fattened pig, the tantalizing scent of smoking hams filled the air. The first snow of winter could fly as early as mid-October in Springfield, bringing an abrupt halt to the harvest season, woeful was the farmer who had dallied, believing he had time to bring in his crops. The need to fill the cold cellar with root vegetables, the meat tub with freshly salted beef and pork, to fill the grain bag with corn, barley and wheat was the what drove the farmer and his wife out of bed in the dark and kept them out in their fields and work shed past twilight. Come winter, they could rest, their larders stocked, and dream of spring.

Hugh trudged home at noon for his dinner. He had been working since dawn, harvesting corn, hacking each cob from its stalk, one by one. He was tired and ravenously hungry. As he walked up from the river's edge, he noted with disgust that Mary had yet to cut her flax. Damn her, he thought, it needed to be done soon or it would be all for naught. More money wasted. When got to the house he stopped and removed his mud-caked boots before entering the house in his bare feet and swiped at the mud clinging to his clothes before entering the house. Sarah Dorchester was dosing by the fire, and Hugh could hear Mary singing to Samuel in the bedroom. He called out to her to let her know he was home.

"You'll be wanting your dinner I suppose, I'll be right there, let me put Samuel down, he's feeling poorly."

He's always poorly; thought Hugh, grumpily.

Mary entered the room and bustled about getting food on the table for her husband. "Where is Hannah?" asked Hugh, between mouthfuls of beans.

"I sent her home with Blanche to give her a break from this sickness."

"Humph." Hugh chewed on his cornbread, nodding in agreement.

Mary poured him a mug of beer and placed it down on the table near his trencher. She ran her fingers through the hair that had come loose from her plait, trying to fix it into place. Hugh glanced up at her, she looked tired, with dark circles under her eyes. Her white shift was dingy and her apron stained. Hugh could find no evidence of the pretty woman he wed but a few years ago. He shouldn't have permitted the Dorchesters to move in. Sarah was taking up more and more of Mary's time, she practically had to feed her. Hugh motioned for her to sit.

"Have you eaten? Why not sit a spell and rest?"

Mary grimaced and shook her head, "If I sit, I'll not get back up again, I am that tired." With hands on her hips, she arched her back, stretching her aching shoulders and tense neck muscles. "Ahhh," she sighed, "I should check on Sam."

She turned and walked towards the bedroom. Hugh didn't know where it came from, but he felt an overwhelming desire to touch her. He reached out and grabbed her arm. Without looking up, he turned over her hand, rubbing soft circles on the delicate skin on the inside of her wrist. Just as quickly, he released her, dropping her hand. Mary stood there a second more, neither speaking. With a soft sigh, she moved past him and into the bedroom. Hugh bent back over his plate.

Her scream shook him to his core. He leapt to his feet, covering the distance between them in seconds. Mary stood at the edge of their bed as if frozen, one hand covering her mouth, the other reaching out towards the bed. Panic filling her eyes, her whole body trembling.

"Jesus, Mary. What is wrong?"

A low, long wail came from her open mouth, growing louder with each second. Hugh pulled his eyes from his wife to look towards their bed. In the center of the blanket lay his son. God save us, he thought, the child was pasty white, his face coated with a sheen of sweat, and his blond curls matted to his head. His eyes rolled back, only the whites showed. As Hugh stared in horror, a bubble of foamy saliva emerged from his tiny, pink mouth. Samuel's arms and legs waved and thrashed about as if controlled by a mad puppeteer.

"Jesus, help us!" cried Hugh, horrified at the sight of his child, he looked at Mary, "do something for Christ's sake, do something." Suddenly, the baby's face turned blue and his entire body went limp.

"Go!" Screamed Mary, reaching out for her son, "go find Goody Cooley, make her come."

Hugh spun on his heels and ran. He burst, barefoot out the door, shoes, cloak and hat forgotten, such was the urgency. Legs pumping, he flew up the street, impervious to the rocks that bruised his feet. He reached the Cooley's house and flung open their door without knocking, scaring Goody Cooley and Goody Burt as they sat and spun wool by the fire.

"Goody Cooley, I need you most urgently, you must come." Hugh, chest heaving, stopped to catch his breath. "'Tis our Samuel, he is having the most dreadful fit, I fear for his life."

Without a word, Goody Cooley rose and set aside her wool. She, like most Springfield mothers, had lost babies of her own. She was well acquainted with the fear and anguish she saw on Hugh's face. She directed Goody Burt to go ahead to the Parsons' and see that a kettle was put on to boil. Then Goody Cooley grabbed a basket off a peg and filled it with items from her medicine cupboard, handing it to Hugh to carry. She flung her cloak round her shoulders; she was ready to go. Together, they hurried back to Mary and Samuel.

As they passed the Bedortha's door, Blanche stepped outside. "What is amiss, Hugh? Is it Cousin Sarah?" Concern was written on her face.

"No, 'tis Samuel, he had a most horrible fit." Hugh hurried past without stopping, he shouted over his shoulder at her. "Keep Hannah away from the house."

Back home, Hugh opened the door for Goody Cooley, bustling her inside. Mary was in the hall holding Samuel. "Does he live?" He asked.

Mary lifted her head, tears streaming down her face, she nodded. "He lives."

Goody Cooley took the child from her arms. Mary reluctantly let her. She ordered Hugh to clear the table; he swept the remains of his uneaten dinner onto a tray and carried it into the lean-to. She set him down on the table, unwrapping him as she did. Eyes closed, his little body was limp and still, save for the rise and fall of chest. Goody Cooley felt his skin. "His fever is very high. I've brought some willow bark tincture; we need to get him to swallow some." She rummaged through her basket and withdrew a small, amber-colored glass vial. "Mary, quickly, make an onion poultice, we can put it on his chest."

Mary rushed to the lean-to and gathered onions. She sliced them and set them over a pot to steam. When they were soft, she wrapped them in linen and place the hot onion poultice on his chest. Hugh returned to the hall after cleaning up his dishes. He had never felt so helpless as he watched the women work over Samuel.

A wave of nausea crashed into him; he fled out the door, making it just in time. Wiping the bile from his mouth, he staggered to the barn where he sat, hands over his face, on a rough bench. He needed something to take his mind off of Samuel. He picked up his scythe and walked out to Mary's flax patch and methodically cut the tall stalks. The repetitive swish of tool soothed his mind. Once cut, Hugh gathered the flax into bundles and tied rough twine around them, he would hang them in the barn rafters to finish drying.

Hugh looked up and saw Blanche approach. She brought him a cup of cider and asked if he was hungry. He took the cup, but the thought of food made him nauseous.

"How fares the child?" Hugh reached inside his waistcoat pocket for his pipe, filling it with tobacco.

"He does poorly, he has yet to wake from his fit. Goody Burt has come to help, I will see if I can get Mary to eat and rest a bit, she is exhausted."

Hugh watched as a steady stream of women came and went. Dying seemed to be women's work. Some brought food and drink, some came to give comfort and some were drawn by the morbid curiosity of death. Death stalked them all, none more so than the infant child. Hardly a mother in Springfield had not suffered the loss of at least one child. No mother lived without the specter of death hanging over her children.

Hugh felt unwanted in his own home. He shuffled over to the Bedortha's to check on Hannah. Poor wee mite, only three-years-old, she did not understand what was happening to her brother or why her mother had not come for her. Hugh reassured her that all was well, but she must stay at Auntie Blanche's house a little longer. He and Reice shared a cold supper, and given the circumstances, a few cups of rum. He made his way back home as night fell, sticking his head in the door to check on Samuel. Goody Burt said he was no better. Hugh grimaced and told her he would be in the barn, if he was needed.

Hugh lay on the hay, wrapped in a blanket. He thought to pray, but for what? A swift death for the sickly child or recovery and return to the constant illness that plagued him. It would be terrible for the child to die, but at least they could move on, pick up the pieces. They would have more children, God willing, and Samuel would be but a sad memory. Sweet Jesus, what sort of man am I, he thought, I wish for the death of my only son.

The next morning, Hugh checked on Samuel. Mary sat with him by the fire as Goody Lumbard prepared some food.

"Has he woken at all?"

Hugh accepted a cup of beer and took a sip. Mary shook her head. She looked haggard and worn. Her hair hung in greasy strands around her tear stained face. A sour, unpleasant odor wafted from her when she moved. Hugh thought she looked as if she had aged ten years overnight. As Hugh took a bite of bread, she mumbled something. Hugh strained to hear. "What say you, speak louder."

Mary raised her head and looked at Hugh. Her glazed eyes held a hint of madness. "Samuel is possessed, 'tis devil's work."

Hugh scoffed. "Your mind is overtired, Mary. You need to rest."

"Don't you dare tell me what I need. The Reverend Moxon is coming this morning to pray over him. His prayers will drive the demons out and Sam will be cured."

"Mary, the child is gravely ill, mayhap God is calling him home." Hugh reached out to touch her but she swung at his hand, batting him away.

Goody Cooley asked Hugh to fetch some water and then followed him outside.

"She made such speeches through the night, talking of witches."

Hugh bent to pick up a bucket. "She needs to rest; her mind is agitated. See if you can coax her to sleep a bit." He headed down to the river to get some water.

Later in the day, the Reverend Moxon arrived and in a booming voice prayed over Samuel as if the volume of his prayers could dislodge the sickness from the child's body. When the prayer was finished Mary spoke again of witchcraft. She insisted to Moxon that this was the devil's work. He tried to move away from her, his nose wrinkling in disgust at her smell. She snatched at his sleeve as he tried to depart.

"I have done my best, Goody Parsons, the child is in God's hands, but I fear you should prepare yourself for the worst." He plucked her hand from his garments, gave her a grim smile and a pat on her shoulder. "The Lord tells us that, 'Other physicians can only cure them that are sick, but Christ cures them that are dead.' If the child dies, he may one day be safe in the arms of his Savior, Goody

Parsons. We cannot grieve for that." With that he turned and left.

Once again, the house filled with women, making Hugh uncomfortable. Anthony left early to work in Henry Smith's fields, leaving others to tend to his wife. Hugh motioned to Goody Burt. "I am headed to Long Meadow. The wait is too difficult."

She nodded sympathetically. "Let me pack you some food, you must eat to keep your strength." She disappeared inside for a few minutes, returning with a linen cover basket.

"I will send Henry to you if anything happens."

Hugh spent the day in the Long Meadow, after a brief cool down the temperatures had risen, Indian Summer they call it. He brought his scythe and spent the day cutting and stacking hay. He planned to return with the wagon and load it up to use as fodder for the horse during the winter.

Hugh ate his meal in the late afternoon and smoked his pipe by the river. He thought about going home, but decided instead to sleep in the meadow under the stars. He lay there, lost in thought. He did not want to watch his son die. He would die, Hugh knew it in his heart. He could come to terms with death. He just did not want to watch the last breath slip from his son's body.

The next morning, Hugh woke from a dreamless sleep to the sound of his name. He sat up and watched Henry Burt cross the meadow as he called out for him. A sharp pain took him by surprise; he wiped a tear from his face. His prayers were answered. His son was dead.

# Funeral

October 1649

Mary could not believe her son was dead. She had fallen asleep in the chair, holding him in her arms. He died while she slept. She had not been watching over him in his last moments; she did not see him draw his last breath. She had not prayed as his soul took flight. What kind of mother was she, she thought? And where was Hugh while his son lay dying; off sleeping in the meadow.

Goody Burt, who spent the night in vigil with her, sent her husband Henry to find Hugh and get him home. Hugh had yet to show himself, coward, she thought. The other women who stayed the night had returned home to attend to their families. Only Blanche remained. She searched through Mary's chest in the parlor for a piece of linen to use as a winding sheet.

"Mary let us wash the babe and wrap him in this." Blanche held up a linen cloth.

Mary did not want to put her child down, somehow that would make it real, make it final. She clutched him tight against her breast but could feel his body grow colder by the moment.

"Mary, lay the child down. He is gone and there is naught we can do but see him properly laid out. Folk will be here soon to pay their respects."

A sharp rap rattled the door. Blanche set down the cloth on the table and went to open it. It was Reice, and with him was Hannah. "The child cries for her mother," he said, as he ushered her inside with a shrug of his shoulders. He spun on his heels, surveying the room and asked, "where is Hugh?"

"Hannah, my love, do not cry." Mary shushed her little girl. "Sit with your Auntie Blanche while I take care of Samuel."

Blanche sat down and drew Hannah onto her lap and tried to explain to the three-year-old what had happened to her little brother. Mary laid Samuel on the table and took her time removing the blanket which swaddled his body. Picking up a cloth, she dipped it into a bowl of water. The water was cold, 'twill give Samuel a chill, she thought, before she caught herself. Oh God, my babe is truly dead. The pain of her grief crashed over her in waves. She blinked away the tears and bit her lip to stop from crying out. Blanche offered to take over, but Mary shook her head with a low sniff. She took a deep breath, wrang out the cloth and began to carefully wash her boy.

His little face looked so peaceful, like an angel asleep. It made her smile. She let her eyes drift over his body. Shocked yet again by the sight of his lower torso. It painful to see. The skin was purple-red and swollen, dotted with open, ulcerous sores. Last evening, she showed it to George Coulton, he had drawn back in horror. None of the women had seen such an affliction. Mary Ashley and Sara Leonard agreed that it was a most mysterious ailment, as if the child's flesh was being consumed. An idea, dark and fleeting, slipped through her mind, witchcraft, this is witchcraft.

With tenderness, she washed and dried her son, then wrapped him in the linen Blanche had found, covering all but his face. She took the blanket and swaddled him in it, as if to warm him once again. She lay him in his cradle and gave it a little rock.

The door opened again and Hugh entered, followed by Anthony Dorchester. Her husband's sleep rumpled clothes were filthy and in need of a wash. He smelled of sweat and cows and needed to shave. Mary searched Hugh's face for signs of grief and thought she found none. As he came closer, she caught a whiff of tobacco.

"Good of you to come, Hugh. 'Tis only your child's death you've missed." Her voice quivered with emotion. "I see you took the time to take a pipe of tobacco afore you arrived home."

Hugh ignored her and crossed over to the cradle, he looked down on his son. He reached out and traced a finger lightly across his son's cheek and bent to place a kiss on his forehead. Then he turned away.

"Where's my Hannah? Come girl, let's go check our chickens?" He swept her up in her arms and headed out the door.

"Did ye see that Anthony, Reice, did ye see that?" Hugh's apparent lack of grief shocked Mary to her core. "Have ye ever seen a father react with such coldness to his child's death?"

"Come now, Mary, Hugh has never been one to show his tender feelings. Surely he grieves for the boy."

"Could he not show me, his own wife, some comfort or kindness. Yet he tends to his chickens with more concern than he gives a grieving mother."

Anthony and Reice stood quiet, they knew not what to say to this distraught woman. Anthony caught Reice's eye and nodded towards the door. With a slight lift of his chin, Reice signaled he understood. He turned to Blanche. "We will check on Hugh and see if he would like help with the casket."

The word casket cut through Mary's heart like a knife. She burst at once into tears, sinking to her knees. The men fled out the door. Blanche rose from her chair and embraced Mary, holding her while she sobbed. Mary grew quiet, her head rested on her friend's shoulder. At last, Blanche convinced her to lie down and rest for a while. Mary reluctantly agreed. She entered her room and sat on the bed. Blanche brought her a cup of strong cider with a shot of rum, and encouraged Mary to drink. Blanche knelt in front of her and removed her shoes. She took off Mary's cap and hung it on a peg. Gently, she undid the tight braid of Mary's hair, picking up a comb, she ran it through the tangles. Mary sighed, surprised to feel herself relax under Blanche's ministrations. She finished her cider and stretched out on the bed. Blanche assured her she would take care of food preparations if any neighbors arrived.

Mary's eyes fluttered open, stunned to find herself in bed. Someone had placed a quilt over her. By the light, she judged it was late morning or early afternoon. Her head felt fuzzy. She had slept, hard and deep, without dreams. Then she remembered and berated herself. How could she have slept; her child was dead. She lay there for a moment, listening to the murmur of voices coming from the hall. Neighbors come to gawk at her dead boy. Mary rose and braided her hair and replace her cap. She attempted to shake out the wrinkles in her gown, but knew it was useless. A deep breath steadied her mind, she entered the hall.

Anthony, Hugh and Jonathan Burt sat by the fire. Goody Burt helped Sarah Dorchester eat a bowl of soup. Mary heard female voices coming from the lean-to and recognized the voices of Goody Taylor and Goody Jones. Through the window she could see her daughter Hannah running in the dooryard with other children, they appeared to be chasing the chickens. She let her eyes drift over to the cradle, now placed in the center of the table. He son lay there, silent, untended and forgotten.

"Why have you left my boy alone, while you gossip by the fire?" She said aloud, to no one and everyone.

Hugh, hearing her voice, looked over at her. "Mary, you are awake, we were but planning for the funeral, 'tis all."

"You plan his funeral, 'tis all! He's dead but a few hours and you are ready to put him in the ground and have done with it." Hugh remained quiet.

"I shall sit by him." Her words were bitter. "You make your plans."

More neighbors arrived as news of the child's death spread through town. Hugh welcomed them in and led them to Mary. Busy with her neighbors, she did not notice Hugh and Anthony leave. When she asked, Goody Burt answered that he had gone with Anthony to dig the grave.

For the next few hours, Mary sat by the crib as a whirlwind of activity swirled around her. Her neighbors had come together to clean her house, cook food for the funeral meal, some had even taken clothing home with them to launder. Mr. Pynchon's man delivered a cask of sweet wine, a smaller cask of rum and a gallon of cider. Hugh returned home; she could hear him talking in the yard to other men. As evening drew on, the mourners drifted off home, leaving Mary alone in the house with Sarah and Hannah. Hugh and Anthony came inside, and everyone prepared for bed. Once again, Mary thought she would never sleep, but the effect of several cups of cider relaxed her mind, and she drifted off.

She woke in a state of terror. The room was pitch black, and she fought to remove the covers that smothered her. Mary's heart pounded in her chest; her skin slick with sweat. She was choking and gasped for air. As the fog in her mind cleared, she realized, it had been a dream. She lay still, her heart beat slowed as she listened to the familiar sounds of the house. Hugh, damn him, snored, sleeping as if nothing was amiss. A cock crowed somewhere up the street.

Mary rose, tiptoed her way through the house, slid out the door, and walked down to the river's edge. The water, flat and gray, sped past her. It was cold, Mary shivered and wrapped her cloak around her as she stared out across the river. She tried to puzzle together the pieces of her dream, like the shards of a dropped clay jug. Someone or something, a dark figure in the shadows, cast a spell on her. A supernatural hand wrapped around her throat, she couldn't breathe, just like the fit that had stopped Samuel's breath. The details of her dream became clearer; a witch had tried to kill her, just as it had killed her son.

The sun slid over the horizon and lit her path as she made her way back to the house. Anthony and Hugh were awake, she heard the privy door shut and someone talking in the barn. Her heart froze when she spied, leaning against the house, the town bier, used to carry the coffin to the burying grounds. Mary knew when she stepped inside, she would find the pall, a sheet of rich purple velvet, folded on her table, a stark reminder of what was to come. Somehow, she made it through the day.

The following morning dawned gray with low clouds that blocked the sun. Hugh was up early, as usual, to do his chores. Mary lay in bed, awake but loath to rise. If she got up, she would have to bury her son. She realized Hugh had not once spoken of the boy since his death, nor had he tried to comfort her, his wife. He is a cold-hearted brute, thought Mary. She heard Hannah calling for her, she got up and dressed. She put on her Sunday dress and her best apron, spotless, white and ironed by one of her neighbors. The house was full of food, so at least she would not have to cook.

In the early afternoon, the bell tolled, calling the town folk to the burial grounds near the river. Hugh carried Samuel's small casket outside and placed it on the bier. Blanche cover the simple pine box with the richly colored pall. Anthony Dorchester and Reice Bedortha shouldered the bier with ease and headed towards the road. Hugh, carrying Hannah, and Mary fell in behind them. As they made their way up the street in the direction of the meetinghouse, their neighbors joined the procession. Just past the house of Frances Ball, the mourners turned left down a narrow lane and made their way past the training ground. The graveyard lay close to the river. Anthony and Reice stopped next to a tiny grave.

Mary raised her head and glanced around. It appeared most of the town was in attendance. Mr. And Mrs. Pynchon were in Boston, but their daughter and her husband, Mr. Henry Smith were there. She noted another absence; Widow Marshfield. Blanche came to stand next to her. Mary whispered in her ear.

"I see the widow has kept away. I wonder at her reasons?"

"Do you?" asked Blanche, an incredulous look spread across her face. Mary ignored her.

"I fear she has been up to wickedness again, she hath cast the spell which has taken my son from me."

"Hush, Mary, do not speak so. Let us bury your son in peace without talk of witches."

The crowd quieted as Reverend Moxon, dressed in his black garb, arrived. He glanced at Hugh who nodded. The burying would begin. Mary, stared at the black hole and remembered the funerals of her childhood. Her mother's people had been Catholics who clung to the old ways of rituals and sacraments. The visual and spoken signs of God's love and forgiveness and the certainty of Heaven, were anathema to the puritans. She longed for their comfort. Instead, she watched as Hugh removed the pall and handed it to Goody Burt. She folded it and set it aside until needed again. Ignoring all else, she focused her attention on the little casket. Two men, lifted it from the bier, and lowered it into the ground. A shower of dirt startled her, she wept as the grave filled with earth. That was it, no words, no prayers, nothing. And now my son lies buried, and Reverend Moxon cannot assure me he is safe in the arms of the Lord.

The mourners made their way back to the Parsons' house. Scattered around the dooryard were trestle tables, laden with food and drink. Many brought their own cup which they filled with cider or wine. Someone handed Mary a cup of spiced rum, she took a sip, the warm liquid trickled down her throat. She spied Thomas Marshfield over by a food table. What is he doing here, she wondered, gloating over my loss? Has his witch of a mother sent him to spy on me? She refilled her cup and sidled over to him.

"Thomas Marshfield, I am all amazed that you show your face here today."

"What mean you, Goody Parsons? I am come, like everyone else, to show my respect to your family for your loss."

"I suppose your mother is gloating over this; she has got her revenge on the Parsons."

"I'm not sure I follow your meaning, Goody Parsons."

"Your mother has cast a spell on my Samuel, taking him from me."

"Goody Parsons, I caution you, do not make the same mistake again. My mother is gone to Boston with the Pynchons. I dare say, she will not know of your son's death until she returns next month." Thomas put down his cup and prepared to leave. "If you need someone to blame for your loss, look elsewhere for your witch, for it is not my mother."

He strode off, leaving Mary confused. *I know 'twas witchcraft that took my son.* The sound of raucous male laughter interrupted her musing. Mary turned with a frown and searched the crowded yard for the offenders. The sight of her husband, cup in hand, laughing with Griffith Jones and William Stebbings shocked her to her core. *He laughs,* she thought, *my husband laughs on the day I bury my child.* As she studied him, a thought unfurled in her mind, *he is happy, he is happy the child is dead.* Mary covered her mouth with her hand to suppress a gasp of horror. Suspicion crystallized in her mind. *He wanted the child to die. Hugh wanted Samuel dead.*

As Mary watched her husband, he lifted his head and look straight at her, their eyes locked. His face dark and unreadable. *He knows my thoughts; he reads my mind. My God, 'tis him, Hugh is the witch.*

# Darkness

October brought the return of cool autumn days as the year marched towards winter. Springfield's farm families felt the pressure to complete their harvest work. There were pumpkins to pick and store in cold cellars with the turnips, onions and cabbages. Goodwives preserved and pickled the last of the summer crop of cucumbers, peppers and other soft vegetables. They would bring a bright bit of summer to savor on cold winter days. Apples and pears needed picking, the least blemished stored in barrels. The majority of the fruit would give up its juice to the cider press, its golden liquid filling oak barrels. With the addition of a little sugar and a period of fermentation, the bubbly concoction would turn into a pleasant, mildly alcoholic libation that helped take the edge off their difficult life.

It had been three weeks since Samuel died. Mary had done little work. Or at least very little profitable work, thought Hugh. He came home tired and hungry after a long day, looking forward to some supper. Hannah was sitting by Sarah's pallet, singing to her.

"Where's your Mam?" Hugh tousled her fair hair, smiling at her.

Hannah pointed to the parlor. "Mam's asleep."

Hugh's smile faded. He strode across the hall and opened the parlor door. Mary was asleep on the bed. He leaned over and shook her awake. She moaned but did not open her eyes. Hugh, in a hunger fueled rage, grabbed a corner of the bed cover and pulled it off of her. "Get up, Get up this instant."

He dropped the cover to the floor and shook her. She opened her eyes, glazed and unfocused. "Why did you wake me?" she said, with a whimper.

He sat on the edge of the bed and slapped her face until she awoke. "Stop it, Hugh, leave me be." She struggled to sit up, running her hands through her loose tangled hair. "Why are you home so early?" She glanced around the room.

"Early?" Hugh was incredulous. "'Tis nigh on dark. I'm home for my supper."

Mary struggled to rise. "I only meant to lay down for a minute." She rubbed the sleep from her eyes.

"I guess there is no supper prepared." Hugh looked at her in disgust.

Mary hung her head and made no reply.

"I'm taking Hannah up to Blanche to see if she can feed us, since you seem to be unable to care for your family." He turned and stalked from the room.

When Hugh returned, he found Mary spoon-feeding Sarah Dorchester a thin gruel. The woman's health was failing. Hugh guessed she did not have long to live. Hugh glanced at Mary, she had dark circles under her eyes, and her hair hung in a dirty tangle. She needs to bathe, thought Hugh, wrinkling up his nose at her smell.

"The pigs need butchering." He fixed his gaze on her, hoping for something of a response.

She slid her eyes over to him, shaking her head. "I can't Hugh, the blood.... 'tis too soon...."

"Mary I cannot do all this alone, you need to snap out of your doldrums."

The next morning dawned clear and bright. Hugh stepped outside, and the pigs trotted up to him, rootling at his feet for food. He decided to butcher the pigs, rather than wait for Mary to come to her senses.

Hugh assembled the tripod over the dooryard fire pit and hung his largest iron kettle from the hook. After filling the kettle with river water, he piled kindling underneath and lit the fire. Hannah threw pine cones on the flames and soon they had enough heat to bring the pot to a boil. Hannah wanted to stay outside, but Hugh did not want her to watch. He sent her inside, telling her to stay with her mother while he took care of the pigs.

Hugh caught the animals, one at a time. He would keep the female who would breed come spring. He dispatched the two males in the blink of an eye, slitting their throats to prevent any squealing and suspended them over a tub until they bled dry. Then, he slid the carcasses into the kettle of boiling water to scald the skin and hair. To remove the hair, Hugh rubbed the body with rosin, the sticky, amber byproduct of turpentine. When the carcasses were ready, it was time to butcher the meat.

His knives honed to a fine edge, Hugh carved them into slabs and joints of pork which he rubbed with salt and layered in a large wooden tub. He moved the tub to the lean-to, where the salt would leach the water from the meat and begin the curing process. He would check it daily for nine days. On the ninth day, he would rub it with hot salt, saltpeter and pennyworth and let it cure for another nine days. Finally, the meat went into the smoking closet, built into the chimney. There, the smoke and low heat would do its work. It would take about three weeks for the bacon to cure. This was woman's work and Hugh resented having to do it.

Hugh decided to speak with Mary, thrash out his concerns. She should be the one taking care of this chore.

He needed her help to ensure that, not only did they have enough food to make it through the winter, but excess corn and wheat to trade come spring. As he worked, he imagined what he would say. He would stay calm, he told himself, no matter what she said. He would not lose control. He would explain their needs and how his patience had run out. It was time to set aside her pain and get on with life.

It was late afternoon when Hugh put the last of the pork in the tub, covering it with a thick layer of salt. He cleaned up the dooryard, throwing straw over the blood that had spilled onto the ground. It was already attracting flies. Hugh took his time, sluicing the blood from his hands and arms. He dunked his head into a bucket of water, enjoying the cooling sensation as the water ran in rivulets down his back. He was hungry but still reticent to face Mary. With a sigh, he pulled open the door and entered his house. Hannah was content, playing with a corn doll in the corner. Sarah and Anthony were eating their dinner. Sarah gave Hugh a weak smile and said, "Don't worry Hugh, we have fed Hannah, she is such a good child."

"I thank you, Anthony. Where is Mary?" Hugh looked around and saw her cloak hanging on the peg. She would not go out without it.

Anthony pointed to the parlor. "She has been in there all afternoon."

Hugh crossed the room and flung open the door. He was angry to see his wife asleep on their bed. Sleeping, damn her! He thought, here I am working like a mad-man and she is asleep. Hugh marched over to the bed and shook her awake. She's been at the cider, thought Hugh, smelling her breath. He grabbed the coverlet and yanked it off her body, then took a hold of her by the arms pulled her into a sitting position.

"Wake up, Mary."

"Leave me be, Hugh, I've had a difficult day." Her voice had a brittle edge, and tears welled in her eyes.

Her words ignited Hugh's temper. The white-hot anger rose and could not be suppressed any longer. "You've had a difficult day!" Hugh was incredulous. "You've not done a damn bit of work, not even fed or cared for your own child and it appears you've had more than a cup or two of cider." His voice rose to a crescendo, he shouted, red-faced, in her ear. "Now, get up this instant." Hugh paced around the room. "I've worked my fingers to the bone today while you loll about. Get your arse out of bed and put supper on the table." Hugh's anger punctuated every word.

"How can you be so cruel? My son is dead, you may not grieve for him, but allow me to."

"Grieve all you want, cry all you want, but do your work while you're at it."

Mary swiped at the snot running from her nose and the tears from her eyes. "You're a heartless devil, Hugh Parsons, and I rue the day we married." She spat at him.

Hugh found he did not care what she thought of him. He did not respond. They were stuck with each other, and by God he would not tolerate a lazy wife. Bending over her, he lifted her face to his and in a voice as soft as it was threatening, he said, "Get up now."

They stared, unblinking, at each other. Mary, perhaps sensing the real threat behind his words, broke away first. Hugh released her and backed away from the bed. With a loud sniff and a final swipe at her tears, Mary stood, shook out her gown and walked out of the room. Hugh sighed and sat, bone tired, on the edge of the bed, and rubbed his hand over his face. God how that woman tried his patience. Why can't she see he only wanted what was best for his family? She exasperated him. He could hear her now slamming pottery down on the table. If she broke anything, he would wring her neck.

They ate their dinner in stony silence, only the quiet whispers of the Dorchesters echoed around the room. Hugh was hungry. He kept his head bent down over his plate as he wolfed down the simple meal of bread and cheese with cold sliced beef. With food in his belly and a few mugs of ale he felt his anger dissipate. He belched, wiping his chin on his linen.

He glanced over at Anthony. "I hear Mr. Smith has organized a work party for the morrow. Going to cut timber. Are you going?"

"Aye," said Anthony, "Mr. Holyoke is wanting lumber for his new barn. Will you saw the boards?"

"Aye," Hugh poured himself a third cup of ale. "I spoke with Holyoke last week and agreed to the work. I'll need help though." He turned to Mary. "Since you spent your day in bed, mayhap you can run up to the Taylor's and tell Jonathan I need his help tomorrow with the boards."

Mary bristled at his tone, pursed her lips saying, "I need to put Hannah to bed, you go."

A muscle twitched in his jaw. He would not fight with her again. With a cold, unblinking smile, he said, "I say you will go, Mary."

"'Tis almost dark."

"Then you best be going." He heard Sarah Dorchester draw in her breath, but he was beyond caring what the Dorchesters thought.

Mary tossed her head, throwing him a dark look, which he ignored, but she grabbed her cloak and headed out the door. The tension in the room eased with her departure. Hugh let out a sigh of relief and pulled out his pipe. He asked Anthony to join him outside for a smoke but he declined. Hugh went out by himself, there was a slight chill in the air, so he pulled the door closed behind him, lest it get too cool in the house. He walked over to the barn before lighting his pipe. He sat on a stump, enjoying the tobacco. The remaining pig snuffled around him, no doubt missing her siblings.

Hugh stayed outside until Mary returned from the Taylors. Although cool, it felt good to him and he enjoyed the solitude. The sky had turned a pinkish purple as the sun made its way below the horizon. It would be full dark soon. He could hear Sarah coughing in the house, the sound carried on the dry air. It was easier to ignore during the day, but seemed to grow louder as the night progressed. He thought he would have a tot of rum to help him sleep, not that he wasn't bone tired, but his mind seemed to never still.

The sound of someone coming up the path from the river distracted him from his thoughts. Mary was returning. She had taken the river path and was in a hurry. She'll turn an ankle at that rate, he mused. As she rushed past him, he spoke. "Is aught amiss?"

Startled, Mary cried out. She was out of breath, chest heaving. She stopped and placed a hand over her heart. "By God Hugh, you frightened me near to death."

"What made you hurry so? 'Tis too dark for rushing about, you might trip and hurt yourself."

"Humph, as if you care," she muttered. "I've just had a fright 'tis all. I thought I spied a dog on the river path."

"A dog, loose?" he asked, "whose was it, could ye tell?"

"Nay, it was a great shaggy thing. It stood there, not making a sound or a move."

"Where about?"

"Near to the Bedortha's. 'Twas standing just off the path."

"Mayhap it was a shrub, or one of those shape shifting hobgoblins you tell Hannah of." His voice dripped with sarcasm. They walked towards the house. It was full dark with little moon to see by.

"Mayhap it was the Bwca, shifted into the shape of a great dog or mayhap it was a witch, Hugh."

He noted a hard edge to her voice. "A witch can change his shape," she said.

Hugh held the door open for her. "So, your witch is a man now, is it? Don't go accusing anyone. I've not the money to pay your fine and I don't think you'd like the whipping it will cost you."

"When I'm ready, Hugh Parsons, I will make the truth known!"

Hugh ignored the veiled threat in her voice.

# Suspicion

November blew into Springfield on a strong north wind, followed by a hard frost, three nights running. Autumn was at an end. Only the most winter hardy crops remained in the ground. With the harvest behind them, Hugh and Anthony spent many hours, chopping wood for winter fuel. While the men swung their axes, Mary picked up the pieces and piled them into neat stacks, a hand's reach from the door. As the seasons transitioned from fall to winter, the pace of work ramped up to finish preparations for the frigid months ahead.

November brought a more painful transition for Anthony Dorchester. On the 9th, a bright, clear, cold day, Sarah breathed her last. She had rallied in late October, but within the past few days, she coughed up bright red blood. The day before she died, she lapsed into unconsciousness. Anthony and Mary kept vigil, listening to her death rattle, watching the life slip from her body. Hugh went to the Bedortha's telling Blanche that the end was near. She would want to be with her childhood friend when she passed.

Anthony sat on one side of Sarah holding her pale, cool hand. Mary sat opposite. Together, they watched her breathing grow ever more shallow. Mary thought each one her last. Her mood was pensive, and she spoke of their childhood in Llanvaches. The three of them, Mary, Blanche and Sarah were carefree and happy, or so it seemed looking back through the prism of nostalgic memories. "We ought never to have come here. We should have stayed in Wales." A wistful yearning filled her voice.

Anthony turned to look at her. The edges of his mouth lifted in a sad smile. "Ah, Mary, there was naught for us there; no future."

"Humph, what future is there here? My son gone, and your wife lies on her deathbed." Mary looked down at her hands, curled in anger and resentment. "'Tis a cursed place."

"'Tis true we suffer now, but better times are ahead, Mary, we must make the most of this opportunity." Anthony spoke in a hopeful tone. "Mr. Pynchon promised that I shall receive my house lot and planting fields at the next town meeting. This would never happen back home."

Mary stared at him, shaking her head in disbelief. "You sound just like Hugh; your wife is near death and yet you speak of land. Land she will never see." Bitterness crept into her voice. "You should be careful lest you become too much like him."

Anthony did not respond. They sat in silence, listening to Sarah's ragged breath. "Anthony, can I tell you something?"

Anthony glanced over at Mary, she was staring at Sarah. "Of course, Mary. What is it?"

Mary leaned across Sarah's body and spoke in a whisper. "I suspect Hugh is a witch." She watched as Anthony's jaw dropped in surprise. He opened his mouth to speak, but no words came out. "I know, I know, it sounds mad, but I know 'twas him what caused Samuel's death. He tired of the child and his sickness. He wanted him gone."

"Mary, I caution you, a wife should not make such evil speeches against her husband. I grant you, Hugh is a hard man. But he is ambitious, and he is a good provider." He reached out for her hand and gave it a gentle squeeze.

"Hugh may not grieve like you but that hardly makes him a witch."

"But, Anthony, what if he is and what if he is doing the same to Sarah, wishing her dead?"

"Hush now, Mary. Caring for Sarah has exhausted you; you're not in your right mind. Sarah has been sick a long time, 'tis not Hugh's doing. This is dangerous talk. I'll hear no more of it." He pulled his hand away and turned his attention back to his wife.

Mary, not wanting to drop the subject, opened her mouth to say more. But the door flew open and a blast of cold air ushered in Blanche and Hugh. Hugh strode over to the fire, holding out his hand to warm them. He glanced over at Mary and caught her eye. Mary paled at the sight of him.

"Mary, are you unwell?" Hugh's eyes bored into her as if to penetrate her mind. He knows, she thought, as panic welled up inside her. He knows I spoke about him to Anthony. "Nay, I am not unwell." She turned to Anthony, desperation written in her eyes. "We were speaking about..." Her voice trailed off. Oh God, think of something, her mind was frantic, why cannot I think of something.

Hugh frowned at her. "Speaking about what?"

Mary looked wild-eyed at Anthony, her face fraught with fear. Anthony jumped in, saving her. "We were just talking about Wales, and our home village of Llanvaches."

"Ah, Wales, how I miss it." Blanche scooted a stool close to the fire near Sarah.

Hugh, still in his cloak, glanced back at Mary. "Well, if you're sure you're fine, I will leave you to your reminiscing. I left bricks in the kiln that need tending." He turned to go, but halted, stopping to take a last look at

Sarah. Without a word, he slapped his hat on his head and walked out the door. Again, a blast of cold air filled the room. Mary shivered, a chill from the cold or something sinister she did not know.

Mary turned her attention back to Sarah and studied the labored rise and fall of her chest. Her breathing slowed. It will not be long, she decided. Sarah died less than an hour later. Tears slide down Mary's face, it was almost too much to bear. She and Anthony embraced, he shook with grief, trying not to cry.

They buried Sarah two days later. Once again, town folk crowded into the Parsons' home for food and drink. Few knew Sarah, but a death was a death, and she deserved a proper send-off. Mary felt wooden and numb throughout the proceedings. She tried hard not to relive the emotions of burying her son. Hugh was Hugh, making deals and bargains all the while drinking rum and eating meat pies. He appeared unaffected by Sarah's passing.

The year crawled to an end. A December snow storm left a thick blanket that drifted against the door. It kept them housebound until Hugh could clamber out a window and shovel the snow away. January was cold, but in between bouts of bad weather they could get out and about. Hugh came and went as he pleased, not bothering to tell Mary where he was going. It suited her fine. She hated when he spent the day indoors with her and Hannah. When he did, they either argued or ignored each other. Poor Anthony was their go between. He too stayed away if possible.

Only at night did Hugh remember he had a wife. Mary endured his conjugal needs, what choice did she have? One night, Hugh rolled off her and as usual, pulled the coverlet over himself and fell to sleep. Within minutes his snore reverberated around the room. A candle burned on the table. Mary sighed; she would have to get out of bed to extinguish the light. She cupped her hand around the flame and bent to blow it out when she stopped. This may be my chance, she thought.

She picked up the candlestick and crept towards her husband's side of the bed. Hugh moaned and muttered a string of garbled words, but remained asleep. Mary strained to decipher the words to no avail. She held the candle over the bed and pulled back the cover, praying that Hugh would not wake. Mary searched his body for a witch's mark. She held her breath as she waved the candle back and forth, not sure if she wanted to find a telltale mark. But she saw nothing to confirm her suspicions. Disappointed she blew out the candle and slid under the covers.

The next morning Hugh was garrulous. "I had the strangest dream last night. I was fighting with the Devil."

"The Devil!" Mary's eyes widened in surprise. She fought the urge to make the Sign of the Cross.

"Aye, I was fighting, and the Devil was about to overcome me, but I got the mastery of him at last." "What do you think it signifies?" Mary's brow narrowed as she attempted to puzzle out the meaning of his dream.

Hugh stood, wiping crumbs from his shirt. "Why should it mean anything, 'twas but a dream? I am going up to Mr. Pynchon's this morn, I hope to get leather to repair my flail. I'll need it for the next wheat harvest." He threw his cloak around his shoulders and pulled on his linden cap. "I should be home for my dinner." He was out the door, leaving Mary with unanswered questions and much to stew on.

The day was bright and sunny, but cold, bitter cold. Hugh stepped up his pace, attempting to keep warm. Few people were about, Hugh suspected they were home warming themselves before their fires. It was a fair walk up the road to Mr. Pynchon's warehouse, maybe he should have taken his horse, he thought. But he hadn't wanted to bother with saddling it up. He pulled his linden cap down over his ears to keep them warm.

Arriving at the warehouse, he yanked open the door and stepped inside. No one was about so he shouted a loud 'hallo.' Hugh smirked when Simon Beamon popped up from behind a pile of crates. Sleeping, thought Hugh. Simon's bulbous nose, red at the best of times, was even more so. He pulled a dirty linen from his pocket and gave it a tremendous blow. He stank of alcohol. Hugh guessed he had been into Mr. Pynchon's rum, trying to stay warm.

"Ah, Goodman Parsons, what can I do for you?" He inquired, followed by a loud burp.

Hugh's eyes narrowed as he stared at Simon, with a grim smile he asked, "Staying warm are ye, Simon?" Simon glared back at Hugh, but did not respond to his comment.

"Humph, I broke my best flail threshing wheat after the harvest and am in need of some whit-leather to repair it, do you have some?"

"Oh, indeed I do, but unfortunately for you, I'm in a hurry to leave. You will have to return another day." His officious manner set Hugh's teeth on edge.

"Come now, Simon, you can fetch me a piece of leather and still be on your way." Hugh was getting angry. I walked all this way in the bitter cold for this single errand. I'll be damned if I leave without my leather, he fumed silently.

"Nay, Nay," the little man insisted. "I've the horses hitched to the cart, and I'm headed to the woods to load

206

lumber for Mr. Pynchon." He gave Hugh a nasty smile. "Now if you will step aside, I'll be on my way."

Hugh's hands curled into fists as his anger flared. Simon would give him no leather. What an ass, he groused. Hugh reached out and poked Simon in his chest with enough force to make his step back. In a threatening tone, he said, "I will return, but I wish you no good in your current errand." He turned and walked to the door, slamming it as he left.

Hugh arrived home in a foul temper. Jonathan Taylor was sitting before his fire talking with Mary. He greeted him and then asked Mary to get him a cup of rum.

"I'm froze near through." He said, teeth still chattering.

"Did you get your bit of leather?" Mary poured him a generous measure, then offered Jonathan a cup.

"Nay, that ass of a man, Beamon, refused me. He claimed he was off on an errand."

Mary and Jonathan murmured noises of commiseration before Hugh continued with his story. "But I gave him a great thump on his chest and wished him ill on his errand."

Mary glanced over at Jonathan, who rolled his eyes at her. Hugh noticed the exchange and shot his friend a black look. "Husband, why do you threaten that man? Mayhap he was busy and could not stop."

"Oh please, if it were Goodman Cooley or any other man, he would have gotten the leather. But mark my words, I'll not forget this slight." Hugh drank his rum in grumpy silence. He glanced over at Jonathan. "What's new with you, Jonathan?"

"Ah, nothing new." Jonathan shook his head. "My wife is with child and is retching without stop. The noise of her was making me ill, so I came out for a visit."

Mary gave a harsh laugh. "Soon enough, twill be Hugh knocking on your door, Jonathan."

Hugh turned his attention to her. "What mean you, wife?"

"I too, am with child."

# Trowel

Spring was a time of anticipation, like the promise of a young lover's kiss. Summer, a season of fecund indolence, was ripe with consummation, swelling with new life. Evidence of summer's fertility was on display everywhere one looked. It was the season most feared by the puritan who recalled the pagan festivals with abject horror. The primal call of ancient tradition was strongest in the warm summer months. Grievances, which festered and grew in the smoky, dark isolation of winter, withered away; lanced by the rays of the hot sun. Along with heavy garments, housewives packed away the slights and insults of winter that would be aired, once again, come the first frost of fall.

Hugh and Mary reached an unspoken accord and were civil to each other. The temperate weather afforded them long hours apart. Hugh spent the majority of the day working in the fields or at his kiln, and many nights he slept at Long Meadow. The warm days enabled Mary to move about, despite her belly, which swelled in rhythm with the season. Anthony remained with them while he awaited his land grant or the hand of a bereaved widow, either would make him happy.

On a warm evening, after supper, Hugh sauntered down to the river's edge to smoke. It felt cooler near the water. The river ran low this time of year. Mossy boulders broke the surface, and a small spit of gravel was exposed. Hugh enjoyed the peaceful sound of water as it burbled around rocks; a loon called in the distance. He settled on his favorite tree stump, his head bent over his pipe, when a man called out his name. Hugh looked up. Through a haze of smoke, he spotted John Lumbard as he walked up the river path towards him. Hugh raised his pipe and beckoned his neighbor to join him. "Well then, John, what news have you?"

John dropped himself down on a nearby stump and pulled his pipe from his pocket. "I beg a favor."

"Oh, what need have you?"

"Might I borrow your trowel?"

"Humph, did you not just borrow one from Goodman Lankton a day ago? And now you want mine. What are you up too?" Hugh chuckled at his neighbor.

John sighed, and explained how he lost the trowel. He was, he said, at work in the dooryard, daubing mud into the chinks of the house, when the sudden appearance of two unfamiliar, male Indians startled him. "They're quiet devils you know. They can sneak up on folks and not make a sound!" He continued his story. The Indians asked him for some food, and without his consent walked straight into the house. His wife, who was at work in the hall, got such fright from their sudden appearance, she dropped her second-best bowl and broke it. John said he followed them in and offered them some meat and cornbread. After they had eaten, John shooed them out and sent them on their way. "When I went to resume me daubing, the trowel had vanished. The wife and I searched high and low for it, but to no avail. Those scoundrels must have picked it up and taken it away with them!"

Hugh commiserated with his neighbor. "Ah, I know the very pair you speak of. I heard just today that Benjamin Cooley ran them out of his workshop, two day ago." He added, "they're not from Agawam or Long Hill Town, perhaps somewhere further north of here."

When Hugh finished his pipe, he knocked out the ashes and re-pocketed it. With a last look around, he got to his feet and motioned to John to follow him. "I've only the one trowel, so keep an eye on it."

They walked up to the barn where Hugh pulled the trowel from its peg, handing it to John.

"Thank you, Hugh. I should finish tomorrow." Tool in hand, John made his way home.

The next morning, Hugh wanted to visit Long Meadow, but Mary's announcement that the cornmeal barrel was all but empty, quashed his plan. She added that her back ached, her feet were swollen, and the corn was too heavy for her to carry. Hugh had to go to the mill. Disappointed, he saddled his horse and set off, a bag of dried corn perched in front of him. The day was warm and fine; small white clouds scudded overhead. His mood improved. He reckoned he might still make it down to the meadow if he could get someone to deliver the cornmeal to Mary.

The mill, located a bit south of John Lumbard's place, sat on a small stream that flowed into the Connecticut River. The mill stream, like the river, was low, but the current remained strong enough to move the water wheel. As he drew near, Hugh heard the sound of the great millstones grind against each other as they turned.

Hugh carried his corn into the mill house and hailed Ezra Potts, the miller, who was scooping cornmeal into a burlap sack. There were several orders ahead of him explained Ezra, he would have to wait. Hugh set down his heavy bag of grain and stood watching the great stones turn. Hearing someone else arrive, he turned to see Simon Beamon enter the building. Hugh ignored him. Potts gave Simon the same story, he would have to wait his turn.

"No matter," said Beamon, "I'm on Mr. Pynchon's time, so I've naught to do but wait." He pointed to a shady tree, "And I'll have me a little nap whilst I do." He tossed his head back and emitted a loud cackle as he slapped Ezra, a little too hard, on the back. His breath stank of liquor. Hugh and the Miller exchanged glances. Potts rolled his eyes in disgust, which sent Simon into gales of laughter. The man was dead drunk, Hugh decided.

"You'll not be on the magistrate's payroll for long if you do not stay out of his rum." Ezra warned him. Simon shot him a dirty look. Hugh took advantage of the situation and asked Simon if he would carry home his corn to Mary.

Beamon seemed surprised by the request; he scratched his unshaven chin and pretended to consider it for a moment. "Nay, Hugh Parsons, carry your own corn home. I'll not do it."

Hugh's blood boiled. Why was this man so damn difficult, he wondered? "Come Simon, 'tis not a burden on you, and you go right past my door."

Simon gave Hugh a sneering, black-toothed smile and shook his head. "Miller, wake me when Mr. Pynchon's corn is ground." Beamon stumbled over to the oak tree.

Disgusted, Hugh, shot back, "Beamon, we'll see what Mr. Pynchon has to say when I tell him that ye go about his business a drunken fool!" Without waiting for a reply, he mounted his horse and rode back home.

For the next few hours, Hugh mended the fence betwixt him and Jonathan Burt. His pigs had thought they liked the look of Jonathan's field and had knocked a section down before they decided they were better off on Hugh's side and returned home. After a quick dinner he judged it time to retrieve his cornmeal. It was just past midday and was quiet on the street. Hugh spotted a lone man, William Branch, who ambled past, headed for his noon meal. Humph, he thought with a tinge of jealousy, Branch has been to the Long Meadow.

Ezra Potts, tying a sack of meal, laughed when Hugh stuck his head through the door. Hugh stood bemused as the Miller chortled. "What amuses ye so?"

"Ah Hugh, did ye not see Simon Beamon as he rode past yer house?" Potts' belly shook with laughter.

"Nay, the only man I saw was Goodman Branch." Hugh stood with slight smile on his face, unsure what direction the Miller's tale would take.

"Well then, ye missed quite the sight." He laughed even louder; tears streamed from his eyes.

"Come now, ye keep me in suspense." Hugh tapped his foot in mock impatience.

Potts composed himself at last. "Oh, my Lord, the man must have had a flask of rum with him. He was dead drunk when I went to rouse him. He could barely walk to his horse. My boy and I had to help him mount before we handed him up the bag of meal." Again, he laughed at the memory.

Hugh, rolled his eyes, waiting for him to continue.

"Ah, sorry, just 'twas so funny." The miller wiped his streaming eyes. "So, Simon mounted his horse and turned for home. He got but a rod up the path when he fell off the horse. He landed sprawled on his back in the dirt the bag of corn atop him."

Hugh howled with laughter. "Serves him right, I...."

The Miller waved his hands and stopped him before he could say more. "Wait, wait, till I tell all," he continued, "I sent me boy to run after him and help him back in the saddle. Again, he traveled about a rod and again he fell. Ah 'twas quite the sight, Hugh, I wished ye had been here to see."

Hugh laughed, "Truly, I am sorry to have missed it. 'Tis a wonder he made it past me house at all."

Well, Hugh thought, as Ezra fetched his order, maybe 'tis best that Simon refused me, he might have spilt my meal in the street. Hugh untied his horse and mounted it. The Miller's boy handed him up his burlap bag. It was a short walk home. Hugh enjoyed the warm afternoon sun and the easy rolling gait of the horse relaxed him. He smiled again at the thought of Simon on his arse-end in the road, with Mr. Pynchon's grain perched atop him.

Two figures darted out of the wet meadows and crossed the road about a quarter-mile in front of him. He shaded his eyes with the brim of his hat, hoping to get a better view. He spotted the pair making their way towards Lumbard's house. Aha, he thought, 'tis the trowel thieves. With a flick of his switch, he sent his horse into a trot trying to close the distance between them. Hugh dismounted at the house and flung his reins around a fence post. He scanned the dooryard but saw no one. Hearing John and Goody Lumbard though the open window, Hugh pounded on the door. A moment later a musket barrel, followed by John's head, poked out the window.

"Ah, Hugh, 'tis you. I'm keeping my door closed. I'll not take a chance again. Have you come for your trowel?" John's head disappeared and Hugh heard him open the door. A moment later, he stepped out. "'Tis hot as blazes in there, but the thought of their return terrifies me wife. If I ever lay eyes on those blackguards again," he said as he picked up a stout stick that leaned against the house, "I shall thrash them till they beg for mercy."

Hugh gave him a grim smile. "'Tis why I've come. They are here about somewhere. I saw them, not five minutes ago, headed this way."

At that moment, a young Indian male appeared at the edge of the house. John gave a shout and raised his stick, waving it about like a cudgel. "Thieves, rogues, where is me trowel?"

George Lankton's trowel, thought Hugh, but no matter. The startled Indian turned and fled. Hugh watched in amusement as John gave chase, he knew his portly neighbor would not catch the lithe figure as he sprinted away. Her husband's shouts roused Goody Lumbard who rushed out of the house. "Oh, my Lord, help us! What's amiss, Hugh, what has happened?" Her face a map of worry, she clutched a butcher knife in her hands.

Hugh laughed. "Your husband has given chase to the Indians."

"Oh, Lord preserve him!" Her voice trembled with fear.

"He'll be fine Goody Lumbard. Don't you fret." Hugh regretted his flippant remark and moved to put a calming arm around her, when they heard footsteps, moans and groans.

"He escaped!" John reappeared, red-faced and out of breath. "The blackguard got away. But I shall complain of them on the morrow, mark my words."

Goody Lumbard rushed to his side, and after reassuring herself that he was unharmed, upbraided him for chasing the Indian. Hugh smiled at the pair. As he turned to leave a shaft of late afternoon sun struck an object near a bush, causing it to shine with reflected light. Without a word, he walked over, bent and picked it up.

"What's this then?" He held a trowel by the handle. "I believe 'tis Goodman Lankton's trowel, is it not?" With a loud guffaw, he handed Lankton's tool to a now flabbergasted John.

Goody Lumbard, slack jawed, was astonished to see the tool. "I swear by the Almighty, we looked everywhere for that thing. I swear 'twas not there yesterday. Did I not hang my laundry on that very bush this morn?"

John gaped at the tool, then turned to his wife, his brow furrowed. "'Tis some devilish magic at work here."

Together, they turned wide-eyed and looked at Hugh.

# Dog

The languid days of summer passed; July melted into August. Mary's belly swelled as the child inside her grew. The heat sapped her energy, and her torpid movements gave her the appearance of calmness which belied her inner turmoil. Although Hugh's mood moderated with the season, she remained wary of him. She feared, with good reason, that come harvest time her pregnancy would cause her grief.

Mary sat in the hall, the window and door thrown open to entice in an early morning breeze. A basket of torn and frayed clothing perched at her feet. How does that man rip all his garments, she wondered, as she mended a tear in one of Hugh's linen shirts? Hannah entertained herself chasing chickens out of the house, squealing with laughter each time a bird followed her back in.

Despite the early hour, sweat trickled down Mary's back. She lifted her head when the sound of laughter floated in the open window. Hannah flew inside. "Mam, Auntie Blanche is here!" She raced back outside.

Mary looked out and saw Blanche, accompanied by Sarah Ashley and Abigail Munn.

"We're off to forage for mushrooms. Are you well enough to join us?" Blanche looked at Mary's bare swollen feet and grimaced.

"Aye, I'll come." Mary folded away her mending and sent Hannah to fetch a basket.

It was a typical August morning, humid and airless. Mary spied thunderclouds building off to the east. If they were lucky, they would see rain by late afternoon or early evening. The women and children meandered through the now dry meadow. The once green grass was waist high, brown and brittle. It snagged their clothing as they slid past. Blanche led them towards the trees, picking the last of the summer berries. To their surprise, they discovered a patch of blueberry bushes and feasted on the ripe purple fruit.

Mary clapped with delight when she stumbled upon a clump of yellow primrose. In a breathless voice, she beguiled the children with tales of Druids, priests of the old religion, who used the plant to brew magical potions and fairies who slept in the bright yellow blossoms. Laughter pealed as mothers watched their children search the blossoms for fairy folk.

Wading through tall grass, they drew nearer the tree line. The incessant buzz of cicadas filled the air as jeweled dragonflies flitted around their heads like crowns. A sudden scream ripped through the meadow. Blanche, arms flailing, staggered backward, almost knocking Abigail Munn to the ground. Mary and the others turned to flee the unseen foe when a group of Indian women materialized around them, as if out of thin air.

They too carried woven baskets; seeking the last of summer's bounty. The rival bands had a momentary standoff before the native women melted away into the trees. The Springfield women stared, slack jawed, at each other without speaking before breaking into nervous giggles, relieved that the others were gone. Sarah Ashley giggled and said they had found the fairy folk after all. Mary shuddered. She had never gotten accustomed to the constant presence of the natives, even the females intimidated her.

"Did you hear how Thomas Miller attacked that old Indian, oh, what's his name?" Sarah waved a hand around in frustration. "You know!"

"Oh aye, old Reippumsink," said Blanche, nodding her head. "Reice says his two sons complained to Mr. Pynchon. Said Thomas hit him with the butt of his gun."

"My Robert says Pynchon has a soft spot for the Indians, he indulges them," said Ashley, in a tone that implied she agreed with her husband.

"Reice says 'tis why they are so bold," said Blanche. She glanced around at the other women. "He told me that one broke into Rowland's place and stole his wife's best red petticoat!"

The women sniggered and a raucous debate ensued. What use would an Indian make of a red petticoat! They all agreed however, if an Indian burst into their house whilst they were home alone, they would be terrified.

"Well," said Mary, in a saucy voice, "what would scare you more, Indians sneaking into your house, or--," she paused, a twinkle in her eye and a mischievous smile on her face, "--or the sight of Samuel Terry rubbing his secret parts against the meetinghouse wall!"

Her question sent the women into gales of laughter. They had all heard the story of how Hugh and John Lumbard, on watch duty last Sunday, had caught Samuel masturbating outside the meeting house, while Reverend Moxon and his congregation were inside at prayer. Pynchon had the amorous, young servant whipped for his crime. Perhaps the knowledge that the entire town knew and laughed behind his back, might be the worst punishment.

By noon, the heat grew oppressive, even in the deep shade of the trees. The air was still, save the drone of insects and the occasional call of an unseen bird. Mary sat with the children while the other women filled baskets with mushrooms and other wild edibles.

Pleased with their bounty, the group made their way home. Mary decided her swollen, painful feet were worth the effort.  How lovely it will be, she thought, to have a few fresh mushrooms with their supper tonight and juicy berries for breakfast. The rest she would dry, a taste of summer in the cold months to come.  The thunderheads had grown while they worked in the forest, there would be rain by afternoon.

August segued into September, and in the blink of an eye, the final days of summer slipped past. The seasons turned, and harvest time was upon them. Hugh, as Mary knew, complained of her inability to help reap and stack the wheat.  But even he had to admit, that she, in her pregnant state, was of little use to him. Anthony remained with them, so it was not as if Hugh was without help. Between the two and with occasional help from Jonathan Taylor, the Parsons' crops were harvested and stored away for winter.

After a brief cool down in mid-September, the days grew warm again, the English called it Indian Summer. The fleeting interlude was welcome by many, a last chance to complete preparations for winter. Mary, however, was not enjoying it. She was hot, tired and swollen. Her feet and ankles ached, her back ached. Her temper frayed, she sat outside in the shade, watching Hannah play, while she mended linens. Her mood improved when Reice and Blanche arrived. Reice stopped only to say hello and then headed to the mill. He would stop back to collect his family on his return.

Mary, unable to attend lecture the past two Sundays, was glad of any tidbit of gossip. Blanche regaled her with the activities of their neighbors.

"Here is something strange," said Blanche, as she ran her fingers through her son's curly locks.

"Humm." Mary glanced up from her sewing.

"The other night, Joshua ran to Reice and tried to get on his knee. Reice asked what was amiss, and the boy said the dog scared him."

"What dog?"

"Exactly, there was no dog we could see, but Josh insisted, quite earnestly, there was a dog under the bed."

"Well, 'tis strange indeed," said Mary, pulling on her bottom lip.

"'Tis, and the strangest part is that he insists the dog is the Parsons' dog." Blanche laughed at her son's vivid imagination.

"What!" Mary reacted with surprise. "We have no dog, nor have we ever had a dog!"

Blanche nodded her head. "I know. 'Tis why it's so strange, but the child insists."

At that moment, Reice ambled up, a large bag of cornmeal slung over his shoulder.

"Ah Reice, I was just telling Mary about Joshua and the dog, tell her." Blanche looked up at Reice.

"Tell her what?" Brows drawn, he studied his wife's face, confused by the request.

"About the dog." Blanche glared at him.

"But you said you told her." He stared as his wife a moment longer before deciding he'd better say whatever she wanted. "Joshua says there is a dog under his cradle or under the stool and it's your dog."

Mary mulled over the story before asking Blanche, "When did Joshua last see the dog?"

"Yesterday afternoon, I believe." She nodded her head in confirmation.

Mary stared into the distance; eyes unfocused. "Hugh was not at home then."

"What has Hugh got to do with the dog?" Reice and Blanche exchanged glances, puzzled by her statement.

"A witch can change his shape, can he not?" said Mary, as if to herself.

Blanche shot Reice a look, eyebrows raised, and jerked her head toward home. "I'm sure I do not understand your meaning, Mary. Oh Lord, Reice, think of the time, we must be away home if we are to eat supper tonight."

With a sigh of relief, he helped Blanche to her feet and hoisted the heavy bag of cornmeal. They said a quick goodbye to Mary and hurried away.

"I think Hugh is a witch," said Mary aloud, to no one.

Two weeks later, Mary woke with a nagging backache. She rubbed it as she prepared breakfast. As she set Anthony's trencher in front of him, Mary felt warm liquid run down her legs. It made a little puddle on the floor between her bare feet. Her water had broken. Anthony glanced from her face to the puddle and back. He broke into a sheepish grin and without a word rose to find Hugh.

Hugh alerted Blanche who rallied the neighbor women. Grateful for a break in their harvest labors, they looked forward to day of rest and gossip, at least for them. Mary's labor lasted about twelve hours; the birth easy. The child, a boy, gave a lusty cry and pinked up within seconds. Goody Cooley tied the still pulsing cord with string and cut it with the sharpest knife, severing the physical connection between mother and child.

The Sunday after the birth, Hugh carried his son, Joshua, to the meetinghouse for his baptism, an act which saved his immortal soul from the clutches of Satan. Mary, home abed as she recovered from the birth, did not attend. Reverend Moxon performed the ritual after the day's lecture. Blanche and Reice stood as godparents. The baby remained quiet as Blanche unswaddled him. She passed him, naked, to Moxon who immersed the child in a basin of cold water. Still, he did not cry.

"'Tis a not a good sign," said Reice, shaking his head as he muttered.

Hugh made a rude comment under his breath and gave Blanche a pleading look. Reice appeared startled as if he had not realized he had spoken aloud. He blushed, and said, "The child is supposed to cry."

Hugh, eyes narrowed, frowned at him. "What mean you?"

Blanche glared at her husband, her wifely signal to keep his mouth shut went unheeded.

"The child cries when the Devil flees its soul."

Reverend Moxon harrumphed and looked down his nose at Reice, displeased by the interruption. Reice had the good grace to look sheepish as he mumbled, "Well 'tis what my Gran always said."

"For Christ's sake, Reice, shut up!" Blanche turned to Hugh and apologized.

Mary lay abed awaiting their return. She and Hugh had fought over the name of the child. She wanted to call him Samuel in memory of his older brother, but Hugh refused. He chose the name Joshua. He claimed to dislike the current tradition of recycling names of dead children, saying he found it downright morbid. The boys were different and Joshua deserved his own name.

He's right about one thing, the two boys were nothing alike. Samuel had been a pale golden child, Joshua was dark, his abundant hair jet-black. He was almost silent. Samuel, always sick, cried constantly, but this child rarely fussed. He seemed to study the world with wide, solemn eyes. Mary had adored Samuel from the moment she laid eyes on him, but she found this silent child intimidating, if not downright frightening. She kept her feelings to herself, but day by day, her sense of unease about the child grew.

# Boy

December 1650

On a cold December afternoon, Hugh rode to Long Meadow to check on his new milk cow and her calf. He bought the pair from Elizur Holyoke three weeks ago. The calf was a robust male with a soft, brown and white spotted hide, and long fringed, liquid black eyes. Hannah fell in love with it at first sight. At six months old, the calf was still nursing and did not venture far from its mother. Hugh wanted to reassure himself that they were well.

He saw no one on his journey to the meadow; it was quiet, just the rustle of dried grass and the occasional bird call. The sky was a clear, deep blue, but a biting wind stung his face and hands. He wished he'd worn his scarf. I'll see to the cows and head straight back, he thought, with a shiver. Hugh loosened the reins and encouraged his horse to walk faster.

As they crested a slight rise in the path, Hugh had a good view of the meadow and his own division, enclosed with a new picket fence. At the near end, he had built a sturdy oak timbered shed to shelter his animals during the coldest months of the year. The building included three stalls for cattle and a loft to store the hay he cut and baled in late August. Someday, he would build a great barn, like the one back home on the Parsons' farm in England.

As Hugh drew nearer, his calf shot out from the side of the shed. A small figure followed; a boy wielding a large stick. What the blazes is going on here, he wondered? It took him a moment to assess the situation. Jesus, he realized, that idiot is beating my calf. He kicked his horse into a gallop, closing the distance to the shed. The boy, intent on chasing the animal, did not hear his approach.

When Hugh reached the building, he flung himself from the saddle and gave chase on foot. The boy had the calf trapped in a corner of the fence line. He raised the stick high over his head intending to strike the calf. Hugh, enraged, shouted for him to stop. The boy, hearing him, whipped around. His mouth fell open as his eyes widened in fright at the sight of a furious man charging towards him. He dropped the stick, ducked under the fence, and sprinted across the meadow.

Hugh stared after him. 'Twas Cooley's boy, he realized, watching him disappear. He turned his attention to his calf. Wild-eyed with fear, the animal bleated for its mother; she bellowed for her calf from the shed. Murmuring in a low gentle voice, Hugh calmed the animal as he ran his hands over its back and haunches. He was angry to see flecks of blood where the stick had scratched the soft hide, but found no serious injuries. Hugh led the calf back to the shed, untied its mother and let the pair comfort each other. I don't know what that boy was up to, Hugh fumed, but I will thrash his hide when I catch him! Assured of the animal's safety, Hugh remounted his horse and cantered back towards Springfield. He wanted to catch Cooley's boy before he made it home.

Daylight was fading fast as Hugh rode past the mill, the first stars twinkled in the darkening sky. As the weak winter sun slide over the horizon, the temperature plummeted. Fueled by his anger, Hugh did not notice the cold. When he came abreast of his house, it was full dark, but a bright quarter moon lit the landscape. Hugh scanned the sides of the road looking for Cooley's boy. A sudden movement caught his attention. Aha, he thought, with a grim smile, there he is. Hugh dismounted and raced after him. The boy had run the distance from Long Meadow; his breath came in ragged painful gasps, and he limped from a twisted ankle. Hugh caught him with little effort.

"So, you think you can beat my calf and run from me, you scoundrel!" Hugh held him by the scruff of his thin coat, both of them winded and puffing. He raised his hand as if to strike a blow; the boy covered his tear-streaked face with dirty hands.

"Don't hurt me, don't hurt me, Goodman Parsons, I beg you, forgive me!" The boy mewled.

Hugh lower his arm, unable to bring himself to deliver the blow, but determined to teach the boy a lesson, he had an idea. Twisting the youth's arm while warning him not to cry out, Hugh dragged him to the side of the house and yanked open the cellar door. Grabbing him again by the neck, Hugh tried to force the boy down the stairs. Despite his pitiful size, the boy fought back.

"Stop fighting you damned little rogue!" Hugh struggled to maintain his balance but their legs became entangled, and the two fell headlong down the steps. Hugh landed with a grunt a split second before the boy landed atop him. The pair grappled with each other on the cellar floor before Hugh pushed the boy aside and hobbled up the stairs. He slammed the door shut behind him then bolted it from the outside. A pitiful wail rose from the cellar. Hugh dusted himself off. He collected his horse and led it to the barn, giving it some oats. He wasn't sure how long he'd leave the boy trapped in the cellar. Perhaps a few hours. he decided, that will scare him.

Hugh stepped inside the house as if nothing had happened. Mary, with a wary look on her face, stared out the door a moment before Hugh closed it tight.

"Did you hear a scream a moment ago?" she asked.

"A scream? Nay, I heard naught, but the wind kicked up on my ride home, mayhap that is what you heard." Hugh removed his outer clothes and hung them on a peg. He did not want her to find out about his little prisoner, she would make him let the boy go. He gave her an innocent smile. "Or maybe 'twas the owl that roosts in the chestnut tree."

Mary stared at him a moment longer, then headed for the larder. "'Twas no owl," she said, muttering to herself.

Hugh rocked Joshua and sang a silly song with Hannah while Mary prepared supper. He ate with gusto and even complimented her on the pottage, which surprised her. When he finished his meal he sat back, a satisfied expression on his face. "I've got to go out for a bit. I need to talk to Jonathan Taylor about work tomorrow."

He pulled his cloak of the peg and threw it around his shoulders. Mary noticed a large tear in the material and stuck her hand threw it.

"I thought you went to check on the calf, how did you get such a great rent in your coat?" Mary gave him a shrewd look.

Hugh laughed. "I was chasing a sprite through the meadow!"

"Da, what's a sprite?" Hannah looked up at him with curious expectation, her large eyes shining.

"A sprite is… someone like you!" Hugh chased after Hannah who squealed with delight when he caught and tossed her in the air. "Now, I'm off. You can mend the coat tomorrow."

The night was frigid, his breath crystallized with each exhalation. He yanked his hat down around his ears and hurried towards the Taylor's place. As he approached the house, he spied a hunched figure in the gloom. It scurried around the corner of the building and drew close to the door. Hugh crept forward, trying not to make a sound. He put his hand out and grabbed a handful of wool cloak and yanked backward.

"Gaaa...." The man swung around. It was Jonathan. "Jesus man, you scared me half to death." Jonathan clutched his chest.

Hugh doubled over in laughter, slapping his thighs. "Oh Lord Jonathan, you should have seen your face."

"Shut up Hugh." Embarrassed, Jonathan opened the door and waved Hugh inside.

Hugh moved to stand by the fire, rubbing his hands to warm them. "What were you doing out in the cold, anyway?"

"A loud noise startled me and I stepped out to investigate. 'Twas only two of Mr. Matthews pails, what fell down, probably blown down in this wind." He pulled two stools near the fire and sat on one. "What brings you out?"

"Do you want to help me saw lumber on the morrow?"

"Aye, sure. Do you want a mug of ale?" He rose not waiting for an answer.

Hugh sat and stretched his legs out towards the hearth. He said over his shoulder, "Do you know the Cooley boy?"

Jonathan grunted an affirmative as he handed Hugh his ale. He took a long sip and sighed, wiping his lip with his sleeve. "He nothing but beat my calf today, up at Long Meadow. His master will take no order with him, but I will." He laughed to himself.

Jonathan opened his mouth to ask a question when the door swung open, and Goody Taylor rushed in. Hugh was not fond of her, nor she of him. He finished his ale and returned home. Before he entered his house, he unbolted the cellar door and held it open.

"Get you gone you rascal, and if you ever raise a stick to my animals again, you'll get worse than this."

He felt the body of the boy rush past him and heard him run up the road. The house was dark when he slid inside. Mary was already abed. He chuckled to himself as he prepared for sleep, thinking of the Cooley boy. I hope he's learned his lesson tonight.

The next morning, Hugh left early to meet up with Jonathan Taylor to saw lumber. Anthony sat at the table holding Joshua while Mary cleared the breakfast dishes. "I'll be leaving soon."

Mary looked up from her work. "Where are you off to today?" She dragged a rag across the table surface, wiping up crumbs.

"I mean to say, I will move out of your house soon. I have my lot at last and plan to start construction on a house next week." He gave Mary a smile. He was courting a widow and hoped to marry her. "You will be happy to have me out of your house. I've been here too long."

"Nay Anthony, 'tis a comfort having you here." She stopped working. "In fact, I feel safer with you in the house."

"Safer?" He looked at her, a slight frown on his face, not understanding her meaning.

"Have you been kept awake by the banging noises without the house?"

Anthony shook his head without reply.

"Strange they only occur when Hugh is gone from home in the night?" Mary's voice rose as she spoke. She ignored the warning look in Anthony's eye. He handed Joshua to her. "Well, have you?"

"Nay, I cannot say I have heard any noises, but then I am so tired it would take a tempest to wake me." He chuckled at his jest in an attempt to change the subject.

His attitude annoyed her, but she persisted. "'Tis probably Hugh himself what makes the noises. He wants to scare me."

Anthony sighed and sat back in chair with arms crossed. He tilted his head and looked at her, eyes narrowed and a deep furrow forming between his brows. "What do you mean? Hugh can hardly be in the planting grounds and banging around outside your house at the same time."

"He can if he is a witch."

# Pudding

Hugh disliked February more than any other month; the last few weeks of winter were the hardest to bear. Foul weather and frequent snowstorms kept them trapped inside a house that stank of baby shit and cabbage. He longed for spring and was eager for planting season to begin. Hugh spent the slow, dark days dreaming of the future. Therein lay the real problem with February, too much time to think.

Hugh was pleased with last year's harvest. The weather had cooperated and the yield of corn and wheat was plentiful. He had a surplus of each which he planned to sell. There were rumors that Pynchon expected several new families to settle in Springfield by springtime; potential customers. Or, he thought, he could trade it to Mr. Pynchon, who would ship it to Boston, to sell for a large profit.

He had to admit, he was behind on the bricks. But with Mary back on her feet, he could catch up on back orders. Anthony had moved out. Hugh would miss the extra pair of hands, but he was glad to have his house to himself, and there were men who needed extra work. Men like Jonathan Taylor, who would work for daily wages.

Although pleased with his progress, he was hungry for more land, more profit, and more sons. He decided to take on an apprentice come spring. A lad who could learn the trade of brick making and help him until he had grown sons to work the land and kiln. He would find an ambitious boy, eager to get ahead. A boy like me, he grinned, not like that idiot Cooley boy.

"Hugh!" Mary's sharp voice pierced his reverie. Ugh, he thought, she's the one dark spot in my fine future, but there's naught I can do about it. His wife was working in the parlor, sewing a new dress for Hannah, but she stepped into the hall.

He glanced over at her, from his seat by the fire, where he rocked Joshua's cradle with his stockinged foot. "What do you want?"

Mary gave him a sour look but ignored the abruptness of his question. "I forgot to tell you, Robert Ashley stopped in and asked for you. Can you stop by his house, he wondered?"

"When was this?" He frowned at her, he had been at home all morning.

"When you were perched on your throne." She pointed in the direction of the outhouse. "He did not want to wait."

Hugh rolled his eyes at her, but was thankful for an excuse to stretch his legs and leave the house. He pulled on his boots, grabbed his cloak, and fled out the door. Hugh arrived at the Ashley's house in good spirits after his brisk walk. Robert opened the door and ushered him into the hall. A fire roared in the hearth; the room toasty warm.

Robert poured them each a mug of ale, and they settled at the table. He'd gotten word, he said, from Simon Beamon that twenty acres of land was up for sale. Robert could not afford to buy the entire parcel. He suggested to Hugh that they purchase it together, split the lot and the cost. Hugh said he would think it over and give him a decision after lecture on the morrow. He mulled it over in his mind on his walk home. Mayhap I can buy the entire lot myself, no need to split the land with anyone.

Over supper that evening, Hugh recalled a snippet of gossip he'd heard from Sarah Ashley. He glanced over at Mary. "Have you ever heard of the Carringtons? I believe Goody Ashley said it was John and Jane — nay wait, John and Joan Carrington."

Mary pursed her lips, thinking, she shook her head. "Nay, I cannot say I've ever heard their names. Where do they bide?"

"Down in Wethersfield, in Connecticut." Hugh took a bite of bread and chewed while Mary waited for an explanation. At last, he swallowed and said, "The constable arrested them both, on Monday last."

Mary frowned, unsure of the point of the conversation. "What are they charged with?"

Hugh held Mary's gaze, watching for her reaction as said the word, "Witchcraft."

Her jaw fell, and her eyes glittered with excitement. "Witchcraft," she said, her voice dropped to an excited whisper. "What did they do?"

"Don't know. Undoubtedly 'twas a busybody making false claims against them." His point flew right over her head.

"I hope that God will find out all such wicked persons and purge New England of all witches before long."

"Mary....," Hugh shook his head and sighed at her, "Never mind."

After lecture, the Parsons and the Millers joined the Ashleys at their home. The men gathered around the table sharing a warm mug of spiced ale while Mary, Margaret Miller, and Sarah Ashley sat by the fire. The men discussed the land purchase and argued over how to finance the sale. Hugh thought the lot overpriced and bowed out of the deal. The women's conversation drew his attention when he overheard Margaret Miller utter the word, witch. He stepped over to the hearth standing opposite his wife.

"You speak of the Carringtons of Wethersfield?" He looked at Mary.

"Aye," said Sarah. "We wonder what crimes they committed."

Mary looked straight at Hugh. "The Court in Boston will know how to deal with them. I hope they hang."

"Enough talk of witches. For all we know the Carringtons are naught but innocent victims, not unlike Widow Marshfield." Hugh gave the women a grim smile.

"Innocent victims. Pshaw, they should be run out of the Colony." Mary latched onto the subject and did not notice her husband's scowl.

"Mary, enough." Hugh glared at her, his patience lost.

"Don't you tell me.... Hugh!" Mary screeched then covered her head with her hands as Hugh picked up a rock from the side of the hearth and made to throw it at her. Sarah Ashley gasped aloud, even the men stopped their talk to see what happened. Hugh threw the rock into the fireplace and bent down next to his wife. "No more talk of witches." He walked away.

The following afternoon, Hugh and John Lumbard trudged home from the northern end of the tree lots. They had spent the day swinging axes, their arms ached, and their hands were raw. The arduous work was dangerous, but it was highly profitable. They left the trees where they fell and would return later in the week to strip the limbs; turning trees into logs. Horses and carts would haul the logs out of the woods and drop them at the saw pits, where he would saw them into individual boards. Hugh had plans to sell his share. As he walked, he mulled over how best to spend it. Maybe I'll purchase another cow or two. Mary can learn to make cheese.

As he and John made their way through town, they spied George Lankton enter Francis Pepper's ordinary.

"Appears George worked up a thirst today." John snickered. "Shall we join him?"

"Ah, I dearly want to, but I must check on my cattle and see how they fare." Hugh cast a longing eye at Pepper's door. He'd love a mug of ale. "But I need to speak to Lankton about buying some of his hay. Those cattle eat more than I knew."

"Well, you'll have no luck with him. I heard Goodman Herman has already bought up all of George's spare hay. He'll have none to sell you."

"Damn. Well, you never know with Herman, he may have more squirreled away. It cannot hurt to ask."

As they approached the Pepper's place, John stopped to have a drink. Hugh said goodbye and walked on, passing his house on the way to the Long Meadow. His livestock appeared healthy, but the pile of hay in his loft grew short. It would be another two months until the spring grass could support the animals.

The day grew late, and the temperature dipped as Hugh plodded home. His stomach rumbled and his feet were like stone weights. Too tired to go anywhere but home, he decided to call on George another day.

Just after mid-morning, Hugh rapped on Lankton's door, no one answered. Stepping back from the house, he saw smoke streaming from the chimney. Someone's bound to be home. He knocked again, this time he yelled in hopes someone would hear him. As he was about to turn away, Goody Sewell cracked open the door. He heard others talking in the hall.

"Is Goodman Lankton here, I need to speak with him?"

"Nay, he is not at home." Without another word, she closed the door.

"Damnation," he muttered, as he slogged home. Well, he thought, I shall just have to be more economical with the hay I have and make it stretch. Mayhap we will have an early spring, and the cattle will have fresh grass to eat. He returned to an empty house. Mary had taken the children out visiting. Hugh, happy to be alone, busied himself in the kiln house, working on a brick order.

Mary was quiet when she returned. Typically, she burst through the door, gossip spilling from her mouth. Not until they were eating supper did she mention her visit. "We stopped in to visit Goody Sewell this morning." She peered up from her trencher, a brittle smile on her face.

"And." Hugh waited for her to continue.

"Goody Sewell said she visited the Lankton's house earlier this morn." Again, she paused and studied Hugh, a strange half-smile on her face. She seemed to want him to say something, but he kept quiet.

"She said Goody Lankton made a pudding, today." Again, she paused. "What do you think she found when she flipped the pudding out of the bag?" she asked. Her voice vibrated with excitement.

Hugh's eyes narrowed as he tried to decipher what game she played. "A pudding," he said.

"That's right, a pudding, sliced down the middle as if cut with a knife." She raised her hand in the air and made a cutting motion.

"And?" He thrummed his fingers on the table top, not caring about spoiled puddings.

"'Twas not done by human hand." Mary leaned forward, a strange, wild look in her eye. "'Twas done by magic!"

Hugh sat back and groaned. The witchcraft case in Wethersfield has gone to her head. She was obsessed.

"Can you guess who called at the house not an hour later?" Her voice rose, becoming louder and her face grew animated.

"Who?" What now, he wondered.

"You!" she shouted.

"Me!" He raked his fingers through his hair, trying to puzzle out her meaning. His eyes widened in horror and his mouth fell open as he realized her intent. A coil of fear unfurled in his gut. "You think I am the witch." Bile rose in his throat as he pounded his fists on the table, sending pottery crashing to the ground.

He leapt up from the table. "What the Devil do I care about the Lanktons or their damn pudding! Have you lost your mind, woman?" He roared in fury.

Mary, mouth agape, stood trembling. She stretched out her arm, shaking a finger at him. "You call on the Devil, your master." Her eyes wild; she stalked around the table after him. "Admit it husband. If you are the witch, admit it now! It's not too late to save your immortal soul!"

Out of control, she screeched at him, spit flew from her mouth. Hannah wailed, terrified by the sight of her parents fighting. Joshua, startled awake, reacted with a squall of his own, adding to the cacophony. Mary ignored her children and lashed out at Hugh with her fists. Arms flailing, she struck him several times in the chest before he grabbed her by the shoulders. He shook her hard; her head whipped back and forth.

"What have you done? What the hell have you done? Are you trying to destroy me? Destroy our family?"

Hugh flung his wife away from him. His utter disgust for her written across his face, staggered by her betrayal. She landed, splayed out on the floor, sobbing. The children's wails grew louder, adding to the crescendo. His chest heaving, Hugh rubbed his hands over his eyes. God, he prayed, let me wake from this nightmare.

He strode over to Hannah and lifted her into his arms. Cradling her head against his chest, he murmured words of comfort in her ear. Joshua's cries were pitiful, but Hugh's hands were full with his daughter.

"Mary, get up and see to Joshua." He spoke with a calmness he did not feel. When Mary failed to move, he growled, "See to the child - now!"

# Cut

Morning dawned cold and gray with a spitting rain. His thoughts in turmoil, Hugh decided to speak to Mr. Pynchon about Mary. He headed out early, his boots squelched along the muddy road. He hoped Pynchon could provide counsel to help him rein in Mary and her wild accusations. Hugh's errand was in vain. The magistrate was in Hartford, Connecticut. There was naught to do, save return on the morrow. The rain turned to icy pellets as if to mirror his mood. He trudged back home; his collar turned up to the wet cold.

As he drew near the Lankton's house, he spotted George and Thomas Sewell conversing under the cover of the doorway. Good, he thought, maybe they know when we resume work in the tree lots. Both men stiffened as he approached. Hugh watched a wary look passed between them. Mary's foolish talk has spread. Act normal, he told himself, this will all blow away in a few days.

"George, Thomas, good day to you." Hugh stamped his feet to keep them warm, his hands jammed in his coat pockets.

"Goodman Parsons, what brings you out on this foul day?" George Lankton stood, legs spread and arms crossed, in a defensive posture, as if to guard the entrance to his house.

"I was on an errand to Pynchon's, but he is not home. Has he decided on the date of the next workday?" Breathe Hugh, breathe, he repeated to himself.

"Friday, if the weather clears." George turned to Thomas Sewell, ignoring Hugh. "Thomas come inside, 'tis too cold to stand out here."

The door slammed shut in Hugh's face. He made a rude gesture, unseen by the occupants, and resumed his journey home. The street was quiet, the rain and sleet kept everyone inside. Hugh saw Reice step outside his door, but did not stop. He was wet through and chilled to the bone. Images of throttling his wife kept him warm. How on God's earth could she think him a witch? If I was a witch, he thought grimly, I'd do a hell of a lot worse than split a blasted pudding.

Friday morning, a weak sun rose; it was cold but clear. Hugh packed food for dinner and filled a jar with ale, stoppering it with a wooden plug. He called in at the Lumbard's to collect John and the two walked in companionable silence to the tree lots. Hugh sunk his ax deep into an oak tree, John stood nearby.

"Did ye see George Lankton about the hay?"

Hugh, concentrating on his aim, shook his head.

"It's just as well," said John. "He has none to sell."

Hugh swung again. The thwack of axes echoed around them as other teams worked nearby. Felling trees was a dangerous business. The crushing injuries from a falling tree could maim a man for life, if not outright kill him. For safety, they worked in pairs, alerting others when a tree was about to crash to earth. Hugh and John paired up; each took a turn with the ax.

By the dinner hour, Hugh was ravenous. He had skipped breakfast in his haste to get away from Mary. He perched on a fallen tree, away from the others who gathered around a group of fresh stumps. Hugh's disposition remained dark, he had yet to speak to Mr. Pynchon, who had only just returned from Hartford. He had no stomach for the raucous mealtime banter of the work party. Hugh unwrapped his food and ate his simple meal. Snatches of conversation and laughter drifted over to him.

"Why does Hugh Parsons sit so far from us?" Thomas Cooper spoke in a booming voice, meant for Hugh.

"To see what we know," replied Thomas Miller, in a conspiratorial tone. "Goodman Pritchard, did you hear of the cut pudding at Lankton's house?"

Cooper and the others laughed. Hugh's jaw tightened in anger as he listened to them banter about the damn pudding. They are worse than women with their gossip, he groused to himself.

"Goody Lankton made another this morning and the same thing happened, 'twas cut in half as if with a knife."

"Mayhap Goody Lankton cannot make a decent pudding is all."

"Nay, nay she is a fine pudding maker, so her husband says. 'Twas witchcraft that caused her pudding to split, not the hand of man."

Robert Ashley, who sat farthest away from Hugh, spoke next. Hugh caught only part of his speech. "My wife...... Mary Parsons said.... is a witch!"

Damn that woman, he cursed under his breath, she has spread her nonsense all over town. I am the laughingstock of Springfield. His appetite gone, he threw down his food and picked up his ax. He attacked a tree with a ferocity that caused a smirking discomfort in the other men. Soon, they too returned to their work.

About twenty minutes later, a cry of pain echoed through the forest. Axes dropped, everyone hurried towards the injured man, Thomas Miller. Blood oozed between his fingers as he gripped the lower part of his right leg, making bright red drops in the snow. "How bad is it?" Someone asked. Thomas grimaced in pain as he removed his hands from the wound. Robert Ashley peeled away the torn stocking revealing a long gash on his calf.

"You're in luck Thomas, it does not appear to have gone to the bone. 'Tis a nasty cut, all the same." Robert Ashley reached into his pack and removed a roll of clean linen. He tore it into strips and wound it around the injured leg to stop the bleeding. "How did you do it?"

Thomas Miller's eyes flicked over to Hugh then back again. "'Twas if some unseen hand made me swing the ax at my own leg. 'Twas the work of the Devil."

Thomas Cooper gasped aloud; the surrounding men exchanged fearful glances. Hugh glanced at John Lumbard and flinched when his friend made a not-so-subtle move to distance himself from him. Not knowing what to say, Hugh remained alone, tight lipped and quiet. This is a nightmare, he thought. Mary has the whole town convinced I am a creature of the Devil.

Two men helped Thomas Miller into a wagon, laying him in the bed with his leg propped. Hugh watched as the wagon rolled back towards town. The mood among the work party grew tense, the men muttered amongst themselves. Evening approached, and it would soon grow dark in the forest. A chill ran down Hugh's spine as a wolf howl echoed in the distance. The forest had a sinister feel after dark, the events of the day heightened the sensation. Gathered in nervous groups, the men agreed to disband, eager to get home.

As he made his way alone through town, Hugh stopped at Francis Pepper's for a drink. If he went straight home, he feared he might do physical harm to his wife. He ducked under the sill and entered the darkened building. The crowded room fell quiet. Word of the accident had reached those drinking inside. Hugh scanned the chamber for a friendly face but saw only suspicion and fear. He scowled and ignored them as he asked Francis for hot rum. He took his drink and sat on a stool by the fireplace. Despite the fire, he shivered, his heart a frozen block in his chest.

The evening was upon them; the light of the blaze and several oil lamps did little to cut the gloom. Hugh raked his eyes around the darkening room and spotted William Warrener and his wife Joanne and Goodman Munn and his wife Abigail. Seated nearest to Hugh was a newcomer to Springfield. Thomas Burnham was a large man who spoke in a loud booming voice. He had introduced himself to Hugh after Sunday's lecture, but Hugh knew little about him.

Hugh's mind drifted back to the afternoon's events. If anyone is to blame for Miller's accident, it was the man himself and the bottle of cider he drank with his dinner. It dismayed him to see how quick his friends were to abandon common-sense in favor of the sensational.

"Goodman Parsons, ahem, Goodman Parsons." A voice disrupted his musings.

Hugh lifted his head and looked around before realizing that Burnham was speaking to him. Hugh glanced over at him. "What?"

Burnham leaned in as if to speak in confidence, but instead spoke in a loud voice. "Here is strange doing in town about cutting of puddings and whetting of saws in the nighttime."

There was a moment of stunned silence, everyone waited for Hugh's reply. Hugh's expression froze, he did not respond. His head spun with images of puddings. He did not understand the reference to whet saws in the night.

The room buzzed like a swarm of angry bees; Hugh felt the sting of their gaze.

Burnham, sensing Hugh's discomfort, needled him further. "That is strange you should not know of these things and I, but a stranger in town, hear of it in all places, wherever I go."

Hugh remained silent, staring into his rum as if the cup held the answer to his predicament. The women behind him talked about the pudding while the men discussed the saws.

Goodman Munn spoke in a pious tone. "I would that those that whet saws in the night time and on the Lord's Day were found out."

The other drinkers nodded in agreement. Burnham jumped in saying, "You sawyers need to look at it."

Hugh drank two more cups of hot rum before he staggered home. Despite the alcohol, his mind was clear. He was furious. When got home he would give Mary such a clout on her head she would never speak of witches again. This had gone on for too long. It was time to end this foolishness.

The house was quiet as he approached, no light shone through the windows. He unlatched the door and entered a cold empty house. The fire extinguished; no candles lit. Mary and the children had gone. Hugh frowned. What game did she play, he wondered? He rekindled the fire, and was feeding it pieces of fatwood when someone banged on the door. Aha, he thought, she has returned. To his surprise, he found not his wife, but the constable, Thomas Merrick, standing on his doorstep.

"Ah Goodman Merrick, what brings you out on this cold night?"

"Official business, I fear." Hugh's heart sank. God help me, here it comes.

Merrick, unable to meet Hugh's eyes, cleared his throat. "Hugh Parsons, I hereby notify you that you are to appear before Magistrate Pynchon on the first of March, Wednesday next." He looked down at a scrap of paper, studying it for a moment, "you stand accused of the offense of witchcraft."

# Deposition

Hugh spent the next day home alone, he was not yet under arrest, but Merrick gave him strict orders not to leave town. The constable would not divulge the whereabouts of Mary and his children. He figured they would be with Blanche. His mood was brooding and dark, alternating between anger and despair. Why had Mary turned on him? He was a good husband and father. What had he done other than improve her life? Were they not working on a common goal of prosperity? Was it her wish to be poor? His mind was awash with unanswerable questions.

A jury would acquit him. Who would believe Mary after her incident with Widow Marshfield? But why charge him? It must be that the Carrington case has everyone spooked, seeing a witch behind every bush. Mayhap Pynchon wanted to have a public hearing so he could censor Mary and any other accusers for their wild tales.

Hugh spent the morning at work around his house and barn. He wished he could walk to the Long Meadow. He decided he needed to stretch his legs and undertook a walk to the Taylor's house. He would question Jonathan; find out what he knew. Goody Taylor cracked open her door to his knock. With a look of fear on her face, she told him her husband was not at home but at Merrick's barn, doing work for Thomas. The door slammed in his face before he could thank her.

Hugh continue up the street and found Jonathan mucking out the horse stall. Hugh hailed him as he entered the barn. Jonathan stopped his work, he looked surprised to see him. "Good day, Hugh. How are you faring?"

Not waiting for an answer, Jonathan put the pitchfork down and the men stepped outside. Jonathan lit his pipe, Hugh did likewise, finally answering, "Not so well. I am anxious to get this over with and get on with me work." Hugh paused and then asked, "Can you tell me who my accusers be?"

Jonathan blushed and looked uncomfortable. He stammered, "I cannot tell you."

"What do you mean, 'I cannot tell', of course you can tell. 'Tis not fair that I do not know who accuses me of this crime." Hugh found himself getting angry and tried to remain calm.

Jonathan reacted to Hugh's abrasive tone by getting angry himself. "I cannot tell you anything." He pointed to the street with his pipe. "But I believe your biggest accuser goes now to testify."

Hugh whipped around and caught sight of Mary scurrying up the street with Thomas Merrick at her side. God help me, he thought, she is on her way to see Mr. Pynchon. Hugh mused out loud. "I shall be examined soon, I suspect." Jonathan said nothing and Hugh returned home, none the wiser.

On Wednesday, the first day of March, Thomas Merrick escorted Hugh to the meetinghouse. He was unsure of the process, but was confident that once he testified, he would be cleared. Thomas was terse, communicating only what was necessary. Hugh followed along behind him, shoulders back and head held high, he would not allow his neighbors to see his shame.

A hush fell over the crowded meeting room as he entered. A quick glance confirmed that all the town was present. Come to gape at the spectacle, Hugh thought. We shall see who is in the dock next. I will have them all in for slander.

William Pynchon made his entrance a little before ten, he was a very punctual man. Dressed in his usual black garb, he looked every inch the part, his expression serious and unsmiling. He stood facing the crowd, not looking at Hugh. He reached for his gavel, the sound, as it hit the table, reverberated around the room. Hugh felt a shiver run up his spine. Pynchon turned and raked his cold gaze over Hugh; it was as if he was looking at a stranger, not a man he had known and worked with for the better part of ten years.

"Hugh Parsons, you are attached upon suspicion of witchcraft. You are not charged as yet, but a decision will be made when all testimony has been taken. Do you understand?"

"Aye, sir."

Hugh felt a ripple of tension flow through the room. He glanced around looking for Mary. She did not appear to be present. Good, he thought with relief, I'd be tempted to throttle her.

William Pynchon turned to his clerk. "Call your first witness if you please, Goodman Burt."

Henry Burt rose and called George and Hannah Lankton. The couple made their way to the front and faced the magistrate. Henry read their testimony taken at their deposition:

*Testimony of Goodman Lankton and Goody Lankton: Deposed in Court 25 February 1651*

*George Lankton and Hannah his wife do jointly testify upon oath; that on Friday last, being the 21 February, they had a pudding in a bag, and that as soon as it was flipped out of the bag, it was cut lengthwise like the former pudding, and like another on the 23 February, as smooth as any knife could cut it, namely one slice along, wanting but very little, from end to end.*

*Also Hannah the wife of George Lankton saith upon oath, that a neighbor came into, and she showed it to him, and that neighbor took a piece of it and threw it into the fire: and she saith that about an hour after, perhaps a little more, she heard one mutter and mumble at the door; then she asked Goody Sewell who was then at her house (and near the door) who it was, she said it was Hugh Parsons, and that he asked whether Goodman Lankton were at home or no. I said no, and so he went away, but left not his errand, neither did he ever since come to signify his errand.*

The courtroom buzzed when the testimony finished. Incensed, Hugh could not believe William Pynchon was falling for this pudding business. What did he care about the Lanktons or their puddings, for God's sake?

Pynchon turned and asked Hugh, "Goodman Parsons, you will please tell the court what your errand was in seeking out Goodman Lankton."

"Sir, this accusation is ridiculous, I am no witch, and -." Pynchon cut him off and again asked his errand.

"I am no witch. I will sue you all for slander, when this business is finished." Hugh muttered.

Pynchon looked displeased with Hugh, banged his gavel again. "Hugh Parsons, you will give a direct answer; what was your errand?"

Hugh bit back a sharp retort, and said instead through gritted teeth, "I went to get some hay off him."

Turning to Goodman Lankton, Pynchon questioned, "Has Hugh Parsons seen you since about this errand?"

"Nay, sir, I have never seen him since."

"Excuse me, sir." Simon Beamon spoke up, as he waved his hand. Pynchon instructed him to rise and come forward if he had testimony to add. Henry Burt swore him in, and he testified he had seen George Lankton and Hugh speaking, but they did not talk about hay. Reice Bedortha, having also been present, swore that Hugh was with Thomas Sewell in the street but he did not speak to George about hay.

"Goodman Lankton, is it your contention that Hugh Parsons has never spoken to you about buying hay?"

"Aye, sir."

"Goodman Parsons, how do you explain?"

Hugh shook his head. What difference did any of this make, he wondered. He stared hard at Mr. Pynchon and answered. "I did not ask him because John Lumbard told me Goodman Lankton had sold more hay to Goodman Herman than he could spare."

"The court calls John Lumbard to testify."

John Lumbard was sworn in, and William Pynchon asked him about his conversation with Hugh. He testified that on the Wednesday before Hugh went to the Lankton's house, he and Hugh were working together. Hugh had mentioned he wanted to buy some hay from Goodman Lankton, who had just walked past where they were working. John said, he told Hugh then that Goodman Lankton had sold so much of his hay to Goodman Herman that he might not have enough left for his own cattle.

"Do you have anything further to add?" Pynchon asked John.

"Only that the Friday after, when the said pudding was so strangely cut, I told Hugh Parsons that Lankton had no hay to sell, 'tis all I know." John returned to his seat on the bench, he would not look at Hugh.

Pynchon seemed to mull over the testimony for some time. "It is evident that Hugh Parsons, coming to the door of Goodman Lankton presently after the burning of the pudding, which was the next day after John Lumbard had told him he had no hay to spare, that his errand to get hay was no true cause of his coming thither, but rather that the spirit that bewitched the pudding brought him thither."

Pynchon waited while Henry Burt worked to write all that had transpired. Hugh stood, fuming inside. John Lumbard would have lost his house and land if not for the work I gave him, and this, he thought, was how I am to be repaid for my generosity. I will never help that man again!

Finally, Henry put his quill down. He shuffled through some papers. "The court calls the wife of Reice Bedortha."

Blanche made her way to the front. What could she say against him, Hugh wondered? Henry stood to read her testimony back to the court:

*The testimony of Goody Bedortha taken on 27 February:*

*About two year ago since, Hugh Parsons being at our house, we had some speeches about a bargain with my husband about some bricks. Blanche Bedortha saith that she spoke something about the said bricks that did much displease Hugh Parsons: thereupon he said unto me, Gammer you need not have said anything, I spoke not to you, but I shall remember you when you little think on it.*

Henry Burt lowered the paper. Pynchon asked Blanche if her husband had been present during this conversation. She answered yes, as was Samuel Marshfield. Reice testified that he was much displeased with Hugh and said it was no good speech. Samuel corroborated their testimony, saying he had heard Hugh make such threatening speeches to Blanche. Pynchon asked if there was anything else to add to their testimony, all three shook their heads. He then instructed Burt to read the rest of Blanche's testimony:

*Soon after his threatening speeches she was going to bed, and put off her waistcoat made of red shag cotton, and as she was going to hang it up on a pin, she held it up between her hands, and then she saw a light as it had been the light of a candle, crossing the back of her waistcoat, on the inside, three times, one after another, at which she was amazed; and therefore she saith, that after she had laid it down, she took it up again to try if ye firelight might not be the cause of it, but she saith that the firelight being all one as it was before, she could not perceive any such light by it, and besides she saith it could not be the firelight, because there was a double Indian mat betwixt her and the fire; and she saith moreover that because the light was so strange to her, she took her waistcoat several other nights to try if the firelight would not give such a light as she saw at first, and held it up the same way that she did at first but she saith she could not perceive any such light afterward.*

*About a month after this, she saith that when she was in child-bed; and as well as most women used to be, and better than she used to be; yet at the week's end being desirous to sleep, she lay still, that she might sleep, and she did sleep; and yet about an hour or more after, she awaked, and felt a soreness about her heart, and this soreness increased more and more in three places, namely under her left breast and on her left shoulder, and in her neck; and in these three places, the pain was so tedious, that it was like the pricking of knives, so that I durst not lie down, but was faint to be shored up with a bag of cotton wool, and with other things; and this extremity continued from Friday in the forenoon till Monday about noon, and then the extremity of the pain began a little to abate, and by Tuesday it was pretty well gone; and suddenly after, my thoughts were, that this Evil might come upon me from the said threatening speech of Hugh Parsons.*

*I do not apprehend that I was sick in any other part of my body, but in the three said places only, and by the extremity of these prickings only.*

Henry Burt turned to the magistrate in anticipation of questions. Pynchon sat in thought, then inquired if there were any who could testify about her pain. Blanche replied that the Widow Marshfield had nursed her through her sickness. Pynchon looked about the courtroom, asking if she was present. Samuel Marshfield spoke up saying his mother had felt poorly that morning or she would have been there. Pynchon instructed Henry to write her a summons to court for a future date. Then he asked if Blanche had any other testimony she would like to add. She did.

"Your Honor, my child be about two years old, and a month or so gone, he stood near to his father, and he hastily run to him and strived to get up upon his knees. He was crying and saith he was afraid, 'I am afraid of the dog.' Yet there was no dog. His father asked him where the dog was, and he saith it was gone under the bed."

Henry waved his quill at her, and she paused in her speech, waiting for him to catch up. After a few moments, he motioned for her to continue.

"His father asked him, whose dog it was, and he said, it was Lumbard's dog. His father said, Lumbard has no dog. Then, my son said, it was Parsons' dog. But I know that the child meant to say Parsons' dog from the first. When Hugh Parsons did come to our house, the boy would call him Lumbard." She paused to take a breath. "Ever and anon he is afraid of this dog and yet Parsons hath no dog, neither was there any dog in the house. But the earnestness of the child doth make me conceive it might be some evil thing from Hugh Parsons."

The magistrate looked from Blanche to Hugh. "Goodman Parsons, have you aught to say?" Hugh felt numb. He had no answer for him.

Reice took the stand next, and he too said the child was frightened of a dog, saying it was under the stool or under the cradle or other places. My God though Hugh, bad puddings and the imaginary pet of a two-year-old child, what next? Startled, he jumped when Pynchon banged his gavel, calling for a dinner break.

# Deposition

1 March 1651 Day 1
Afternoon

The members of the court, witnesses and spectators dispersed to eat their dinner. Hugh was brought a plate of beans and cornbread. Thomas Merrick's wife was an excellent cook, so he could not complain of the food. He was only given a single mug of beer, and of this, he did complain. By 2 o'clock, Henry Burt banged a drum to reconvene the court. Hugh was once again placed in the front of the courtroom, next to Mr. Pynchon. When all was ready, Pynchon rapped his gavel and brought his courtroom to order. Henry Burt quickly tidied his papers. He glanced down as he scanned the page, then called Anthony Dorchester to the stand. His testimony was read aloud.

*Testimony of Anthony Dorchester taken 25 February 1651:*
*About September, that was twelve months ago, four men had equal shares in a cow, each had a quarter and the offal was to be divided as well. Hugh Parsons desired the root of the tongue, but he had it not, it fell to my share. And a certain time, after I salted it, I took the said root and another piece of meat and I put it into the kettle as it was boiling over the fire at Hugh Parsons' house where I was living at that present. There was nobody there but he and his wife and I and my wife who was ill with the consumption sitting on her bed who was not able to get off without help. Neither were any children able to get such a thing out of a boiling kettle, this being a sabbath day, Hugh Parsons and his wife went to church before me, and then I made myself ready and went presently after them and came home before them.*

*I took up my meat before they came home, but the root of the tongue which Hugh Parsons desired was gone.*

*His wife came home presently after me, but he was not with her. Then I told her and she wondered how it could be gone, and she went to the tub where it was salted to see if it might not be forgotten and it was not there. Then I said to her I am sure that I put it into the boiling kettle and she confessed that she saw me pick it up and wash it and being present did much wonder at the strange going of it away and said she feared her husband might convey it away. She told me that her husband went along with her till we came near Goodman Merricks. Hugh was very pleasing to her; more than usually he had been in a great while before. But, there he laid the child down and went no further. She saw him no more until the meeting was almost done. Presently after this he came home, and I spoke of it to him and all that he said was that he thought I did not put it in. But I told him I was sure that I put it in the boiling kettle. And I have ever since believed that no hand of man did take it away but that it was taken away by witchcraft.*

Mr. Pynchon listened intently to Anthony's testimony. When finished, he turned to Hugh and asked what he knew of the missing piece of meat.

"I confess that I desired the root of the tongue." Hugh admitted. "But I am ignorant as the child unborn, which way it went."

A murmuring went up in the crowd and several men said that it might have been taken away by his wife as well as by him. Mr. Pynchon thought on this before saying, "That is not so likely because Hugh Parsons went not with her to the meeting, but laid down her child and went from her, and she saw him no more till the meeting was almost done."

Hugh spoke then saying, "I do not remember that I went any whither, unless I might go into Goodman Merrick's house to take a pipe of tobacco, and though my wife saw me no more till the meeting was almost done, yet I might be standing without the door, though she saw me not."

Abigail Munn, sitting in the front of the women's section rose. Pynchon asked what she knew, and she said, "I knew by the talk of the strange goings away of this root of the tongue, what Sabbath was meant, and that I saw Hugh come that Sabbath to the meeting when the sermon was well onward."

Jonathan Taylor also rose and was deposed. He stated that he had heard Hugh say notwithstanding the root of the tongue was desired by Anthony Dorchester for his wife being sick, yet he said 'I will have it'.

Hugh remained stoic, not knowing how to defend himself against these baseless accusations made by people he considered his friends. He was aghast at how they had turned on him.

"The court calls Griffith Jones," boomed Henry Burt. Griffith, thought Hugh with disgust, a man who skips out on church more than anyone I know. He would cheat a church mouse if he thought there was profit in it. How can he come here to speak against me?

*The testimony of Griffin Jones taken 25 February 1651:*
*When I lived in my house near Hugh Parsons house about two year ago; on a Lord's day, I went home to dinner, but my wife stayed behind at a neighbor's house to dinner. I took up my dinner and laid it on a little table made on the cradle head. I sought for a knife, but I could not find any. I cleared the table where I dined to see if any were there and I searched everywhere about the house and I could find none. Yet, I knew I had more*

*than two, and when I could find none I went to an old basket where I had things to mend shoes with all, and there was a rusty knife, and with that I was fain to eat my dinner.*

*After I had dined, I took away my victuals that were left and laid it up; and then I laid the rusty knife on the corner of the table to cut a pipe of tobacco with all. But before I cut my tobacco, I first went out of door to serve a pig that was but a very little off the door and no man could come in but I must see them and as soon as I came in to cut my tobacco with the said rusty knife there lay three knives together on the table which made me blush; wondering how they came there seeing nobody was in the house but myself; and as I was going to cut ye tobacco, Hugh Parsons came in, and said, where is the man. Are you ready to go to ye meeting; I said by and by; as soon as I have taken a pipe of tobacco. So he stayed and took some with me.*

Again, Pynchon looked at Hugh for a response.

"I am ignorant of any such thing and in the sight of God can clear my conscience."

"Such a strange thing falling out, just at your coming in, does suggest an occasion of witchcraft." Pynchon mused aloud.

Hugh, all but defeated replied, "One witness is not sufficient to charge me with witchcraft."

The courtroom hummed with hushed talk as the magistrate conferred with his clerk. Hugh, as did everyone else, understood that his freedom depended on the outcome. He could be left at liberty or he could be locked up. What would become of his animals and his crops, he thought, fighting back a sense of despair. He silently berated himself for not speaking out in reply to these outrageous accusations. Griffith Jones was nearsighted, everyone knew. He was always losing his knife, pipe, his tools. Add a few cups of cider or beer, and he himself got lost.

Finally, Pynchon resumed court with his gavel. Looking serious and every bit the part of judge, he began to speak to the courtroom. "Whereas by these most serious testimonies, I find there is compelling evidence to remand you, Hugh Parsons, into the custody of the constable, Thomas Merrick."

The courtroom buzzed like a hive of angry bees. Hugh stood, shocked. All he had worked for was crumbling before his eyes. Thomas Merrick came forward and stood next to him as William Pynchon rose and walked out of the building, followed by Henry Burt. The spectators, as if now afraid of Hugh, rose and fled the building, no doubt headed to Francis Pepper's place to dream up more ridiculous charges.

Thomas and Hugh walked past Pepper's and headed for Merrick's house. Thomas informed Hugh that he would be chained and must remain on his property. At night his chain would be locked to a bolt secured to the wall. Not that there was anywhere he could run.

After a light supper with Thomas and his wife, Hugh asked how long Thomas thought the deposition might last. Thomas screwed up his face as he thought of an answer. "Well, let see there must be ten or so folks let to give testimony."

"What," said Hugh shocked. "'Tis well on half the town bent on making me into a witch."

Thomas nodded, then gave Hugh a grim look. "Then there is the testimony of your wife, Mary, yet to come."

# Deposition
3 March 1650/1 Day 2 of Testimony
Morning

Although the Merricks gave Hugh a comfortable bed near the fire, he barely slept. His mind was a whirl of emotions, doubts, anxiety and anger. Yes, he was angry. Mary had brought his whole world crashing down on him. Sometime after midnight, he drifted into a restless sleep. He woke at dawn with a sharp pain in his belly.

"What ails you Hugh?" Merrick must have heard him moaning, thought Hugh.

"My belly is in torment."

"I can take the chains off you if you need to ease your bowels." Thomas offered.

"Nay, 'tis just a pain. I have no need to relieve myself." Hugh muttered between clenched teeth. "Can Goody Merrick make me something to ease the pain? Mary would make me a brew to relieve the cramps."

Thomas went to find his wife to see what she could do to help Hugh. Sarah made him a cup of hot water with ginger and honey, which he sipped slowly. The pain gradually subsided.

By 9 o'clock the next morning, Hugh was back in court, his pain tolerable. Again, the room was packed. Looking around, he could see Mary cowering in the back, huddled next to Blanche. Mr. Pynchon entered and called the court to order. John Matthews was called to testify. His deposition was read to the court.

*Deposition of John Matthews taken 27 February 1651*

*A little before the trial with the Widow Marshfield, which was about May 1649, being in talk with Mary Parsons about witches, she said to me that her husband was a witch. I asked her how she knew it. She said the Devil came to him in the night, at the bed and fucked him and made him cry out one time. She could not tell what it should be else but the Devil. She said also that her husband was often tormented in his bowels, and cried out as though he were pricked with pins and daggers, and I know not what else it should be, unless it were the Devil that should torment him so.*

Hugh looked at Thomas Merrick, who looked back at him with astonishment. Hugh was dismayed, he could tell what Thomas was thinking. The very thing had happened but a day ago and in his house. Thomas quickly asked to testify and was sworn in. Pynchon indicated for him to proceed.

"This last night, towards morning, Hugh Parsons was lying by the fire and said to me several times, 'Goodman come and lance my belly, for I am in lamentable pain or torment'. I said to him, if you will go forth to ease yourself, I'll take off your chains and let you go. He said, 'No, I have no need that way'."

Sarah Merrick was also sworn in and testified to the truth of her husband's statement. Pynchon finally asked Hugh to explain what had happened.

"Your honor, I had but a pain in my belly. I never asked for it to be lanced. Who here has not had such a pain, I ask you?" Hugh said, with exasperation. Pynchon glared at him and reminding him to just answer the question.

"Now then," said Pynchon, looking at Hugh, "your wife saith that she suspects you may be the cause of all the evil that has befallen Mr. Moxon's children. She saith she hath spoken to you about the bargain of bricks that you undertook to make for Mr. Moxon's chimneys, and that she thought Mr. Moxon would expect the performance of the said bargain; there upon you said, 'if Mr. Moxon do force me to make bricks according to bargain I will be even with him or he shall get nothing by it'. She saith that these two speeches are very usual with you when you are displeased with anybody. What have you to say about that, Hugh Parsons?"

Hugh shook his head. "I said not that I would be even with him, but this I said, if he would hold me to my bargain, I would puzzle him in the bargain. That is all."

John Matthews indicated that he had something to share with the court and was sworn in. He told the magistrate that he had gone to Hugh, to pick up some bricks, and said to him, 'do you not make more bricks for Mr. Moxon's chimneys. He will stay with us now, and then I believe he will have up his chimneys.' John explained that he told Hugh, Mr. Moxon would hold him to his bargain, and Hugh had replied, he would be even with him if he tried. He then said, "When Hugh Parsons made me my chimney, he did often use the same speech and when he is displeased with anybody, it is his usual speech."

Mr. Moxon, who happened to be present, rose to have his say. "The same week I spoke to Hugh Parsons about the bricks, my daughter Martha was taken ill with her fits. I confess also, when I spoke to him of the said bargain, Hugh said, I could not in strictness hold him to the bargain."

Moxon made his way back to his front row seat. Pynchon directed a question at Hugh. "Hugh Parsons, do you think there is some witchcraft in the distemper of Mr. Moxon's children?"

Hugh was beginning to wonder if he were to be blamed for everything that befell his neighbors. "I question not that there is witchcraft in it, but I wish that the saddle may be set on the right horse!"

Pynchon demanded, "And who is the right horse, do you know of any other witches?"

"Nay, I am clear for myself, and neither do I suspect any other."

"What of your wife, do you suspect her?"

"No, I do not know that ever I had any such thought of her."

"Humph, have you naught else to say?"

"Nay, sir, I know naught of witches or witchcraft." Mary might throw accusations at him, but he could not in good conscious return the favor. If he was to get out of this alive, he needed to deny everything to do with witches, he thought.

"Are you ready for the next witness, Goodman Burt?" Pynchon looked over at Henry who was gently massaging his writing hand; he nodded in agreement. "Then I call Mary Parsons to the stand. The courtroom began to thrum, there was a palpable tension in the air, like being too close to a lightning strike. Hugh felt his skin tingle as his wife made her way forward.

Mary appeared haggard and worn, her hair and clothing unkempt. Gone was the pretty woman he married five years ago. Was it only five, thought Hugh, it seems like he had been putting up with her for an eternity. She would not look at him as he tried to catch her eye. She could put an end to this if she wanted to, they could patch up their miserable marriage and go on. But Hugh judged by the sullen look on her face that she had no thought to back down from her claims against him.

"Goodman Burt, please read the deposition of Mary Parsons."

*Deposition of Mary Parsons 24 February 1651*

*Mary Parsons saith why she doth suspect you to be a witch is because you cannot abide that anything should be spoken against witches. She saith that you told her that you were at a neighbor's house a little before lecture, when they were speaking of Carrington and his wife, that were now apprehended for witches, she saith that when you came home and spoke these speeches to her, she said to you, I hope that God will find out all such wicked persons and purge New England of all witches ere it be long; to this she saith you gave her a naughty look, but never a word; but presently after, on a late occasion you took up a block and made as if you would throw it at her head, but yet in the end you did not, but threw it down on ye hearth of the chimney. This expression of anger was because she wished the ruin of all witches.*

Mary Ashley was summoned as a witness as she was present that night. She testified that all Mary said was true. Hugh remembered the night as well. He and Robert Ashley were drinking late, and the women kept on and on about the Carringtons, until he had had enough. He told Mary to shut up about the witches and pretended to throw a loose brick at her.

"Hugh Parsons, what say you to this?"

"I deny it. I do not recall the occasion." Better to deny all, Hugh thought.

Pynchon questioned him further though. "Are you sure you cannot recall the night? 'Tis not often a man threatens his wife with a brick."

"I remember the occasion, yes, the talk of the Carringtons, but I do not recollect that I picked up a brick to throw at my wife."

"It might be well on that occasion," said Pynchon, "for not long since she saith that you said to her 'if ever any trouble do come unto me, it will be by your means and that you would be the means to hang me.' Did you not say such to her?"

Hugh sought for a reply, finally saying, "I might have said so. In my anger I am impatient and doth speak what I should not. Mary is the worst enemy I have considering the relation that is between us. If anybody bespeak evil of me, she will speak as ill and as much as anybody else."

"Goody Parsons, you may continue your testimony," directed the magistrate.

Mary faced Pynchon and cleared her throat. She did not look nervous as she spoke. "I have often entreated Hugh to confess whether he was a witch or not, I told him that if he would acknowledge it, I would beg the prayers of God's people on my knees for him and that we are not our own, we are bought with a price and that God would redeem from the power of Satan."

Hugh sputtered aloud, my God, she believes what she says. She hath never spoke such words to me in her life.

"Hugh Parsons, has yer wife spoken such words to you and asked you to confess?"

"Nay sir, not anything to me about witchcraft, that I remember."

Pynchon looked over at Mary as husband and wife faced off against each other. The courtroom was silent as everyone waited for Mary to speak.

"Husband, did I not speak of it to you upon the death of my child. Did I not tell you then that I had ideas that you had bewitched your own child to death!"

Hugh, shocked, stood still, aghast that she could say such a thing against him.

Pynchon, banged his gavel and called for a thirty-minute recess.

# Deposition

Hugh felt beleaguered. His wife was a mad woman. He did not know how to defend himself against her. Court had resumed, and Pynchon was taking his seat. Mary stood, once again, across from him. When Henry Burt was ready, she turned to Anthony Dorchester. Speaking to him, she said, "Anthony Dorchester, can you not remember how I charged my husband with the bewitching of his own child?"

Anthony squirmed in his seat. He looked straight at Pynchon when he answered, avoiding both Hugh's and Mary's eyes. He said, "I do not remember her speaking such words directly to Hugh, but I do recall her telling me she thought Hugh had bewitched his child to death."

Impassioned, Mary said, "When my last child lay ill, I told Hugh I suspected he had bewitched it as he had done his other child. I have spoken of it, to him and to other folks, at least forty times."

Pynchon looked from her to Hugh and then down at his stack of depositions. He read for a moment before addressing Hugh. "It is alleged that you might well be suspected to have bewitched your former child to death because you expressed no kind of sorrow at the death of it. What say you to that?"

"I was loath to express my sorrow before my wife, because of her weak condition. I did not want to add to her burden."

Mr. Moxon stood and desired to ask Hugh a question. "I spoke with Mary Parsons about your sick child and about her grief for it. Why should you forebear to express any sorrow before her? How would this grieve her?"

Hugh looked at Moxon, fixing him with a hard stare. "My wife might wonder at it, but that was the true reason of it."

Pynchon again referred to his papers. "Why did you not show more respect to your wife and child as it lay dying? You went into the Long Meadow and lay there all night when your child lay at the point of death, and when you heard of the death of it the next morning, you never showed any sorrow for it."

Before Hugh could reply, George Coulton stood and asked to testify. Duly sworn in, he said, "I went to Parsons' house and found his wife sitting by the fire with the child in her lap. She showed me the strange condition of the child and I was amazed at it. The child's secret parts did rot or were consumed and she said, though my child be so ill and I have much to do with it, yet my husband keeps ado at me to help him about his corn."

George took a breath and continued. "I said to her, your husband has more need to get you some help than to keep ado at you to help him." George nodded at the murmuring of women in the courtroom. "Then she spoke very harsh things against him before his face. If he had been innocent, he would have blamed her for her speeches, for she spoke such things against him as are not ordinary for persons to speak to one another and yet he being present, said nothing."

Pynchon fixed Hugh with an accusing look. "If you had been innocent about the death of your child, you would have reproved her speeches."

"Sir, I have such speeches from her daily. I made the best of it. And I set her not about business. I required none at her hands, except it were to throw in some Indian corn from the door. I have often blamed her for doing work and bid her do less."

Mary laughed mirthlessly at his reply. Anthony Dorchester leapt to his feet, coming to Mary's defense. "I have never known Hugh to blame her for doing too much work, except that she helped my wife at any time and that angered him as it did not bring in any profit to him. And, I say this, he need not say that he forebear grief for his sick child before his wife for fear it should trouble her in her weak condition, for he never feared either to grieve or displease Mary at any time." Anthony then turned to Hugh and asked, "Did you ever do anything to comfort your wife in her sorrow for the death of her child?"

Hugh ignored him.

Mary began to speak, again. "No, I will answer. No, he did nothing to comfort me but still when he came home, he kept ado at me to throw in the corn from the door and when I saw my husband in this frame it added more grief to my sorrow."

"'Tis clear, from the testimony of George Coulton, you showed no natural sorrow for the death of the child when you first heard of it in the Long Meadow." Pynchon stated. "Does anyone else have aught to say about this?"

Jonathan Burt stood. "At the time of the morning when I brought word to Hugh Parsons of the death of his child, which I think was about 8 or 9 o'clock in the morning, and the place where I told him was at a great oak and 16 or 20 poles from George Coulton's house."

George stood, and said, in agreement with Burt, "Hugh came into the Long Meadow when his child lay at the point of death. When Jonathan Burt told him of the child's death, he was not affected with it, but came after a light manner, rushing into my house and said, 'I hear my child is dead, but I will cut a pipe of tobacco first before I go home'. After he was gone, my wife and I did much wonder at the lightness of his carriage, because he showed no affection of sorrow for the death of his child."

Hugh shook his head at this testimony. With pursed lips he said, "I was very full of sorrow for the death of it in private, though not in public. I was much troubled for the death of my child when I first heard, before I came into Goodman Coulton's house."

George stood again and denied what Hugh had said. "He had just heard of the death not moments before he came into my house. When Jonathan Burt told him of it, they were just 12 to 20 poles from my house, and he came presently thither. Therefore, if he had had any sorrow for the death of his child, he could not but have showed some sign of it when he came to my house. But both me and my wife discerned no sign of sorrow."

Hugh looked around the room for someone to help him. He all but shouted at Benjamin Cooley. "Goodman Cooley, was I not affected with the death of my child when I came to speak to you to go about the burial. I could not speak for weeping!"

Benjamin stood, and took the oath before saying, "I cannot remember any sorrow you showed. You came to me with a pipe of tobacco."

Anthony too, testified that Hugh showed no sorrow as did Blanche, who agreed with the rest, that when Hugh came home for the Long Meadow, he did not appear to be affected by the death of his child.

But Hugh fought back, saying with passion, "When my child was sick and like to die, I ran barefoot and barelegged, with tears, to desire Goody Cooley to come to my wife, because my child was so ill!"

Mary burst out without waiting for permission to speak. "'Twas only a sudden fear at the first time the child was taken ill. For it was sudden and strangely taken with a trembling, that began in his toes and coming upward, and it stopped the child's breath."

Goody Cooley was asked to weigh in. "There were some speeches used that the child might be bewitched, for those that are now bewitched have often times something rise up into their throats that doth stop their breath. It does seem that the child was strangely taken, as George Coulton said."

When Pynchon looked around the room, asking for any other testimony, Mary Ashley and Sarah Leonard leapt to their feet. They had both been at the Parsons' house the night Samuel died. Both agreed with George Coulton, the child's secret parts were consumed or wasted away.

Pynchon banged his gavel and announced a dinner break. They would reconvene when he had eaten. Hugh was glad for the break. To stand and listen to his neighbors, and the men who he had thought of as friends, was difficult. To hear them claim he did not grieve for his son was painful. Hugh picked at his food; his appetite gone. He sat and wondered what was to come. He was soon to find out.

Mary was called back to the stand. She glanced briefly at Hugh. She looks at me as if a stranger, Hugh thought. And I do not know her either.

"We have heard of Hugh Parsons lack of sorrow. Mary Parsons, can you tell us what other reason you have to suspect your husband for a witch?"

"Well." she started. "When I say anything to anybody, never so secretly to such friends as I am sure would not speak of it, yet he would come to know it. By what means, I cannot tell. I have spoken some things to Mrs. Smith that goes little abroad, and I am sure would not speak of it, yet Hugh hath known it and would speak of it to me as soon as I came home." She paused and thought a bit. "Because he useth to be out at night till midnight (till of late) and about half an hour before he comes home, I shall hear some noise or other about the door or about the house." Mary was building up steam now. "Because he useth to come home in a distempered frame so that I could not tell how to please him, sometimes he hath pulled off the bed clothes and left me naked a bed and hath quenched the fire, sometimes he hath thrown peas about the house and made me pick them up."

Hugh stared at a spider spinning in the rafters. I am like the fly caught in its trap, he thought, as Mary went on spinning her tale. "Often times he makes a garbling noise but I cannot understand one word he says. When I did ask what it was that he talked in his sleep, he would say that the Devil and he were fighting, and that the Devil had almost overcome him but at the last he got the master of the Devil."

Hugh closed his eyes as he heard the collective gasp of the courtroom. She digs my grave with my own words, treacherous woman.

Pynchon stopped her asking, "Goody Parsons have you ever known your husband to do anything beyond the power of nature?"

Mary nodded vigorously. "Aye, sir, there was the time when my husband sent me to Jonathan Taylor to get him to work on the morrow."

Hugh stared at her puzzled as to what she was speaking of. She continued. "As I returned home in the twilight, I saw a thing like a great, nasty dog by the path side. I suspected it was done by witchcraft from my husband. He sent me on an errand but usually he doth such things."

The noise of the courtroom rose as the spectators exchanged stories of seeing the same dog on the river path. Hugh closed his eyes. He was tired, and he felt a pall of darkness covering him. He was beginning to fear for his life.

# Murder

4 March 1651

From her seat near the front, Mary looked around the courtroom. She felt vindicated. Everyone could see what she had known for some time; she had married the Devil, or at least his spawn. She was frightened at first, scared to come forward. Mr. Pynchon surprised her with his gentleness as he led her through her deposition. He never once laughed or gave her any sign he did not believe a single word she spoke. The man who had once scoffed at her and called her a papist, now looked on her as an example of an upstanding, puritan womanhood. Or at least, she assumed he must.

Hugh would get his due. She had him squirming like a toad in the stand. He would pay for the hell he had put her through, for all the years of their marriage. She smiled to herself as she watched her neighbors testify against him. After the second day of depositions ended, Mary walked home with Blanche. She returned to her own house, now that Hugh was in custody at the Merrick's.

They had not gone far when Blanche grabbed her arm and hissed, "Don't look back, the Devil is on our heels."

Mary could not help herself, she turned her head and looked back over her shoulder. Hugh was right behind them with Thomas Merrick at his side. Hugh caught and held her eye; she could not tear her gaze away. Blanche seeing what was happening, yanked her arm and hurried her down the road.

"Mary." Hugh shouted at her. "Mary, take care of my son, take care of Joshua."

How typical of him, she thought, he cares only for 'his son'. He cares not for me or his daughter. He did not give a whit about his first son. Mary stopped in at the Bedortha's, picking up her children. John Lumbard's wife had been watching the children while she and Blanche had been in court. Hannah ran to her and gave her mother a hug. Joshua, surprised his mother, wailed the moment he saw her. Joan Lumbard gave Mary a mystified look. "Poor wee mite, he was happy as can be all day."

Mary carried the squalling child home. The house, cold and dark, had a foreboding look. She had trouble starting the fire. It took several tries to get it blazing. Despite her exhaustion from her day in court, she looked around her neglected house and realized there was still much work to do. The animals needed to be feed, she sent Hannah to throw corn to the chickens, who pecked angrily around the yard. Joshua refused to settle, and Mary had no choice but to bring him to the barn with her. She laid him down on a pile of straw, then got oats for the horse and gave the cow a forkful of hay. Neither looked too happy with her or the noisy child; the horse neighing loudly when it saw her and pawed at the ground with its hoof. The pigs, followed her back to the house, squealing and rooting around her legs, nearly tripping her. They too, were hungry.

Mary had not cooked in days. Nothing prepared for her own dinner, never mind the pigs. She had to remind herself that Hugh was not there to get her water. She grabbed the bucket and headed down to the well to fetch clean water. She trudged back to the house trying to balance Joshua on one hip and the water on the other. She spilt about half a bucket of the water down her dress and into one boot. It was all but dark when she reached the door, cold, wet and tired. She put Joshua in his cot and carried the bucket into the lean-to. She groaned aloud when she found Hannah covered in cornmeal.

"Heaven help me, what are you doing child?" Mary asked, angrily.

"I'm hungry mother," she said pitifully. "I thought to make some cornbread."

"We are all hungry, and now I have another mess to clean." Mary brushed as much meal from Hannah's clothes as she could. "Go and see if ye can make your brother stop his crying." Mary directed her back into the hall. She got a pot and filled it with the water, added some beans and salt beef. Later, she would add some cabbage, onions and carrots to the pot. They would be having a very late supper. Hugh will be angry she thought, he does not like to eat so late. She smiled grimly when she remembered where he was, and then thought grumpily, he will be having a nice supper.

She set the kettle over the fire to boil and checked on her firewood and saw she would need more. She called to Hugh to fetch wood from the pile outside the door. Hannah looked at her with a pitiful face. "Father is not here, when is he coming home?"

Never, Mary thought as she collapsed onto a stool, he is never coming home.

"I am thirsty mother; may I have something to drink?"

Mary sighed and got to her feet. She sniffed the contents of her ale jug, she had not done any brewing for more than a week. She poured some into a cup and sniffed it again. It had gone off. Taking the crock outside, she poured it into the pig trough. Cider, she thought, we shall have cider. She poured a little into a cup for Hannah and added water before giving it to her.

"Brother is still crying."

"I know pet, I know. Go and sing for him and mayhap he will stop."

Mary poured herself some cider and took a sip. Ah, it tasted good. She longed to sit and enjoy it, but if they were to eat, she had work to do. Back in the lean-to, she got together the ingredients for bread. Eggs, damn she needed eggs. Again, she bit her tongue as she was about to call for Hugh to fetch eggs from the coop. Grabbing her cloak, she went back out into the cold and stumbled across the yard to the hen house. Fumbling about in the dark, she snagged a few eggs and put them into her apron pocket and hurried back into the house. Her batter ready, she poured it into a frying pan, and went to check her fire. She was dismayed to see it was dying. Agh, she wanted to cry, she could not make it even one evening without Hugh.

After several hours, Mary's stew was ready to eat. She put the cornbread over the coals to bake. They would have it for their breakfast, with milk and honey, if she had time to milk the cow.

Joshua continued to cry and whimper. Mary rocked him and rubbed his tummy, but he refused to settle. She tried nursing him, but he refused. If Hugh were here, she could heat some water and give the baby a warm bath to sooth him. She sipped more cider to calm her frayed nerves. Hannah had fallen asleep at the table, her face all but falling into her trencher. Her spoon clattered to the floor. Mary picked up the girl and laid her on Mary's bed.

Back in the hall, Joshua worked himself into a full wail. Mary picked him up and walked him around the room. She sang, she bounced, she patted his back and rubbed his tummy. Nothing eased him. Mayhap some rum would quiet him. She poured a cupful and wet a linen with the golden liquid. She squeezed some into his mouth, his face wrinkled up with the taste of the harsh liquid and squalled all the harder.

"Do you not like it then, you little demon. Your father certainly does." She paused. He was like a small demon. She had not been serious when the words had slipped through her mind, but now that she had said it, she wondered. Taking up the cup of rum, she tossed it back, felt the burn as it hit the back of her throat and roared down to her belly. She poured another cup. 'Tis why he looks so much like his father. He is a witch's whelp, the devil's spawn. She alternated between anger and fear. The child would grow up just like his father. Look at him she thought. Black hair, black eyes. He had Hugh's nose and chin. No one who looked on the babe could fail but comment on how like his father was his countenance.

She sipped her rum in silence and studied the child. He was too like his father. She thought herself brave to have stepped up and called Hugh out for what he was. He was a witch and he would hang for it. Justice would be served; he would be punished for his sins. Here, in front of her was another witch, albeit a very small noisy witch. She took another sip of rum. She needed to protect herself and Hannah from this imp. Nodding to herself, yes, she thought, 'tis my duty. I am being tested. Am I God's anointed? I am, I am. This is my destiny!

She poured another cup of rum. Joshua had quieted. He knows I am on to him, Mary thought. She circled his cot, looking down on him. He studied her in return, staring at her with those dark eyes. Hugh's eyes, those are Hugh's eyes. He is spying on me through this child. She jumped when a blast of wind whooshed down the chimney causing the fire the flare up. A sign, Mary mused, 'tis a sign.

Mary took up a linen cloth. She folded it into a small square while she recited a prayer. Slowly she lowered the cloth over the child's head. It's an imp, it's an imp, she muttered, not my child, not my child. She closed her eyes tight and pressed harder and harder, feeling the little limbs flail against her hand. A tear slid down her cheek. In no time at all, the child's movements ceased. She pressed a bit longer. At last she raised her hand. Opening her eyes, she saw that the child was still, his little chest would rise no more. Dropping the cloth, Mary collapsed onto the floor.

She woke with a raging thirst and a pounding headache. It was freezing and dark, the fire had gone out. She felt bile rise in her throat. Unable to make it to a bucket, she vomited onto her floor. The room spun above her head; any movement made it worse. Rising, she stumbled into the parlor and fell onto her bed. A small warm body lay across the coverlet. Hannah, she thought, what is she doing here? Mary pulled back the coverlet and crawl beneath it.

A little persistent voice, like a woodpecker, peck, peck, pecked its way into her head. God help me she thought, my head is about to explode. "Mother, wake up." She cracked open one eye; her daughter sitting on the bed next to her. She groaned and rubbed a hand over her face. She moved and felt the world tilt. Slowly she shifted onto her back and slid her way to the edge of the bed.

Holding onto the walls, she made her way into the hall. The room was frigid and dark. The fire must have burned out while she slept. She put her foot in something wet on the floor. She glanced down and saw she was standing in vomit. Scanning the room, she could make out a pan of blackened bread that sat on a trivet over cold gray ashes. What has happened here? The last thing she remembered was coming home and Joshua crying. Joshua. Where.... She looked wildly around in the dim light.

There he was, in his cradle. God, he must be cold. She crossed the room and bent to pick him up. Cold, why was he so cold? She jostled him. Nothing. She ran to door, throwing it open and stepped out into the cold dawn light. Looking down at her son, she felt a scream well up in her chest. She sank to her knees, cradling the body of her boy. Dead, dead, dead, my son is dead.

# Deposition

18 March 1651
Morning

Hugh lay on his back, hands behind his head. It was Saturday. He should be tending to his cows and working on his latest brick order. Instead, he lay here waiting for Thomas Merrick to take him back to court for another day of deposition. A pounding on the door distracted him from his thoughts. From his position on the floor by the fire, he saw Merrick's boots stomp by as he made for the door. He heard the murmuring of male voices as cold air curled around him. He shivered and pulled his thin coverlet up around his chin. The door slammed shut and Thomas stomped back towards Hugh and the fire. Hugh looked over at two booted feet near his head.

"Get up, Hugh."

"As you wish." Hugh threw back the cover and sat up. He rose to his feet and faced Thomas. Thomas could not seem to meet Hugh's eye. What is this, thought Hugh? "What is it, Thomas, is something amiss?"

Thomas, lifted his head and met Hugh's eye. His lips drawn into a thin line, a grim expression on his face. He shook his head.

"What?" said Hugh, concerned by Thomas' mien. "What is wrong?" he pleaded.

Goody Merrick bustled into the hall, still tying on her kerchief. Concern written on her face. "What has happened Thomas? Welcome news is not delivered in the dark. What did Reverend Moxon want?"

Thomas looked at his wife and patted her arm before he turned to Hugh. He took a deep breath, letting it out in a prolonged exhale. He reached out and placed a hand on

Hugh's shoulder. "Hugh, I am sorry to tell you-," he paused.

Hugh tried to swallow the lump in his throat. "I am sorry to tell you, your son, Joshua, is dead this day and his mother, your wife, has confessed. She hath been arrested for his murder."

Hugh heard Merrick's wife gasp as a shudder of pain ripped through his body. He closed his eyes tight, the sting of tears pricked as they formed behind his lids. Don't be true, please God, don't let this be true. He was numbly aware the sympathetic embrace of Goody Merrick. She made comforting noises which competed with the buzz in his head.

"Sit, Hugh. Sit you down. Let me get you something to drink." Thomas poured Hugh a tot of rum, setting it down in front of him before pouring a second cup for himself. "I'm off to see Mr. Pynchon. I will let you know what is about, when I return." Thomas tossed back the rum before he grabbed his cloak and threw it over his shoulder. "Hugh." Hugh raised his head and met Thomas' eye. "I am sorry." Thomas whirled and left the room.

Hugh felt his heart had been replaced by a stone; heavy, cold and without life. He sat with eyes closed, hands over his face. Silent tears slid down his cheeks. He could not remember the last time he cried, probably as a lad, he guessed. If ever man had reason to cry; this was it. His world, built with his blood and sweat, crumbled around him. His future dissolved, wiped away by the hand of his wife. He felt muted and alone. He still has his funny little daughter, but she was better off without him. Blanche would keep her. No daughter of her own, she would want her.

The next day, they laid Joshua to rest, buried next to Samuel. Thomas unchained Hugh so he could attend the funeral with some sense of dignity. He stood silent and unmoving as he watched his son's casket lowered into the earth. Mary was not there and Hugh had requested that Blanche keep Hannah away. In fact, he spoke to Blanche and asked her to keep her. Blanche agreed.

There was no food or drink following the funeral. The attendees came in hopes of excitement and diversion of standing in the presence of a witch, not to remember the dead. Many seemed disappointed not to see Mary. After the burial, they drifted away, back home or to Francis Pepper's, thought Hugh, to gossip about his family.

Later that day, Thomas Merrick informed Hugh that Mary was under arrest and detained at the Cooley's house, under constant watch. Mr. Pynchon would take her deposition over the next few days and decide her fate. Hugh's deposition was on hold until further notice. He whiled away the time until his hearing resumed. It felt strange not to be working. It was the first time since his childhood he was not engaged in some form of manual labor every minute of the day. He hated it. Endless stretches of boredom, interspersed with meals and naught to do but reflect on his life.

On the 18th of March, his deposition resumed. Thomas warned him that Mary would be present, her testimony needed. "You best keep me in chains then, err I tear her limb from limb."

Thomas led him to the meetinghouse, a crowd gathered outside. Henry Burt met them at the door. "Mr. Pynchon would like a private word with Hugh."

Thomas nodded and Hugh entered alone. Pynchon, already seated, did not stand as Hugh approached. "I supposed you might have questions about your wife and what has occurred over the last fortnight."

"Questions, yes. But I am not sure I wish to hear the answers."

"Best to be blunt about it then. Your wife, Mary Parsons, has confessed to the murder of her child, your child, Joshua. We have found evidence she tells the truth, and I have charged her with murder." He paused. "She has also confessed that she too, is a witch. She hath made a statement." Pynchon picked up a piece of paper and read:

*I lost a child and was exceedingly discontented at it and longed; Oh, that I might see my child again! And at last the Devil in the likeness of my child came to my bedside and talked with me and asked to come into my bed with me and I received it into my bed that night and several nights after, and so entered into covenant with Satan and became a witch.*

Hugh grimaced, and rocked back on his feet, no longer shocked by anything she said or did. "She is mad, mad with grief. She does not mean it. 'Tis the ravings of a mad woman." Why am I defending her, he wondered?

Pynchon studied him with a quizzical look. "I am amazed that you come to her defense. She killed your son, after all."

"I do not seek to excuse her, only to explain her," Hugh said, without emotion.

"Humph." Pynchon nodded. "She will testify today. Early next week, Henry Smith will transport her overland to Boston to stand trial before the Court of the Assistants. If, found guilty, which I'm sure she will, she will hang."

Hugh flinched. His fear was not for her, but for his own fate. He may soon face the same punishment.

"Goodman Burt, let the public in, we have much ground to cover today." The doors swung open, and the town poured in, humming with excitement as they jostled for seats.

Pynchon banged his gavel with force, and as the room quieted, he nodded at his clerk. "Goodman Burt, if you please."

Henry rose and summoned Samuel Marshfield to the stand.

Samuel was visibly nervous; his right leg shook. His voice quavered as he spoke. "Ah, when, he ah, when Hugh, um...." He looked at the magistrate, embarrassed.

"'Tis all right, son, just tell the truth of the matter and we shall discern your meaning."

Samuel nodded and began again, his confidence boosted. "When Hugh Parsons came to my mother's house to deliver the corn, the ah, 24 bushels of Indian corn that he, um, owed her, he desired my mother abate the fine by twenty shillings." Samuel took a breath and looked over at his mother, who gave him a smile of encouragement. "Mother told him she would give no abatement. She said 'I hear ye have said that the witnesses gave false testimony'. So, he, so Hugh saith, 'if you had not, it been as good you had. Then he threatened her by saying the corn would be, 'like wildfire in your house, like a moth in your clothes.' He made vile speeches, saying the corn would be but a loan and it will do you no good. And such like things."

"Anything else, you can tell us?" Pynchon questioned gently.

"Ah, yes. The next spring, my sister, Sarah my sister, was taken with strange fits." He glanced over at Mr. Moxon and said, "but never as bad as Mr. Moxon's children."

"Thank you, Samuel. You may step down. Mr. Burt, I believe we will hear from Widow Marshfield."

The widow stood ramrod straight before the court. The steely look in her eye revealed a glimpse of her inner strength. Unlike her son, she spoke with authority, clear and to the point. "Hugh Parsons came to my house to tender what he owed me from the slander case against his wife. He said, 'I hear you will abate twenty shillings.' I said I would not. I said I hear your wife hath said the witnesses gave false testimony. He got angry and threatened me."

"What threats did he use?" asked Pynchon.

"As my boy said, Hugh Parsons told me the corn would be as if lent, it would do me no good. It would be like wildfire in my house and moths in my clothes. The next May, my daughter suffered with her fits." She paused and then, said louder, "fits of witchcraft!"

The hum of the crowd became louder when the widow uttered the word witchcraft. Henry Burt asked for silence. The magistrate raked the room with his stern gaze.

"Hugh Parsons what say you to these accusations, did you threaten the Widow Marshfield?"

Hugh did not respond. He was not truly listening to the testimony.

"Goodman Parsons, we are waiting on you."

Hugh shook his head and asked when was he supposed to have given such speeches. Mr. Pynchon, frowned at him. "When you paid the corn to Widow Marshfield."

"I do not remember that I spoke such threatening words. In justice, the corn was due her. But we apprehended that my wife was falsely accused, that may well be the reason of my speeches."

"Anything further, Goody Burt?"

"Aye sir, we call Goodman Lumbard to the stand.

John Lumbard, my old friend, thought Hugh, with a slight shake of his head.

"I heard Hugh Parsons and his wife claim the corn, which they paid the Widow Marshfield for the slander, would do her no good and that it had been better if she had never taken it. I have heard both her and him say so several times, and I have often heard him say when he hath been displeased with anybody he would be even with them for it."

John stood still as Henry Burt wrote his testimony. He avoided Hugh's eye. When Henry set down his quill, he stepped over to have a quiet word with Pynchon. As he sat back down and took up his quill, Pynchon addressed John Lumbard.

"Goodman Lumbard, I understand you have your own incident about which ye would like to testify."

"Aye, sir."

"Well, go on." Pynchon encouraged.

"Well, sir, one-day last summer, I set a trowel and a stick, which I was using to hold my clay as I daubed on the ground, just without me door."

Hugh groaned aloud, which earned him a dark look from Pynchon. Hugh shook his head and stared with scornful eyes at his neighbor as he continued his tale.

"Like I said, I set down my trowel, and then two Indians came in and also presently went away again. I went out to look for my trowel and there was my said stick, but no trowel. My wife came out, and we looked very narrowly both in that place and also within the house and could not find it. Two days after," he pointed at Hugh as he spoke, "Hugh Parsons was at the door of my house, when I spied the same two Indians, and I called them to ask them for my trowel. Hugh asked me what do you want of the Indians and I said they have stolen my trowel. Then, said Hugh Parsons, look here it is and there it was in the very place where I laid it. I did not see him lay it there, but I do really think it came there by witchcraft."

"Parsons have you any reply?"

Hugh, angry that his friend had turned on him, shook his head as he spoke, "I do not remember putting a trowel down anywhere, he made no mention of it when I was there."

John Lumbard interjected. "He did not ask how it came to be there because I had been at Hugh Parsons but the day before to borrow his trowel, so I could make an end to my daubing. The trowel that was missing and reappeared was Goodman Lanktons."

# Deposition

18 March 1651
Afternoon

Pynchon banged his gavel loudly and nodded at Henry. "Goodman Burt, if you please."

The town clerk rose and called the first witness, Goodman Cooley, to the stand. He swore him in and then, in a loud voice, Burt read the deposition of Benjamin Cooley.

*Deposition of Benjamin Cooley, taken 27 February 1651.*

*Mary Parsons told me, about a year since, that she feared her husband was a witch, and that she so far suspected him that she hath searched him when he hath been asleep in bed. She could not find anything about him unless it be in his secret parts.*

Anthony Dorchester was recalled to the stand. His deposition was also read to the court.

*Deposition of Anthony Dorchester taken 27 February 1651*

*About a year since, I and mine, have lived for a time at Hugh Parsons house and that I have several times heard Mary Parsons say that she suspected and greatly suspected her husband to be a witch and that her husband once in 24 hours would be from home if not in the daytime then in the night time whatever weather it was; and that in his absence she hath heard a rumbling noise in the house, sometimes in one place and sometimes in another; and that she did much suspect him to be a witch because if she had any private talk with any he would come to know it by what means he could not tell being confident that those she revealed herself unto would never tell it.*

"Do either of you have anything else to add?" Questioned the magistrate.

"Aye, sir." said Cooley, who elbowed Dorchester as he stood there mutely. "Last night, Anthony and I, we were charged by the constable to watch over Mary Parsons." Anthony nodded in agreement. "She, Mary Parsons, that is, spoke of many things. She told us that if her husband had fallen out with anybody, he would say that he would be even with them." Benjamin stopped for a moment before adding, "He has said the very thing to me, in fact. Can I tell you about the time he threatened me?"

"Thank you, Goodman Cooley, we may save that for another day. But, for now, we are only interested in the testimony of Mary Parsons."

Benjamin looked sheepish as he continued. "Mary Parsons said also, that she found that her husband did bewitch his own child so she might be at liberty to help him in his Indian harvest. He expected help from her, and because, she said, her time was taken up caring for her child, and he being eager after the world, he seemed to be troubled at it. That is, he found fault with her spending so much time nursing the child. So much so, she suspected he wanted to make an end of his own child quick, so she might be at liberty to help him."

The spectators made much of this. A father, who would wish his own child ill, was a monster in their eyes.

Anthony spoke up. "Another thing she said made her suspect her husband to be a witch was, because most things he sold to others did not prosper. Ah, and another ground of suspicious was, because he was so backward to go to the ordinances, either to the lecture of to any other meeting. She saith she hath been faint to threaten him that she would complain to the magistrate. If not for her threats she thought he would not let her go once in the year."

Anthony paused before continuing. "One other thing she saith made her suspect him to be a witch. It was because of the great noise she should hear in the house when he was abroad. She heard a noise in the house as if 40 horses had been there. And oft times, after he was come to bed, he kept a noise and a galling in his sleep, but she could not understand one word. And so, he hath done many times formerly, when she asked him what ailed him, he would say he had strange dreams. She saith one-time, he said that the devil and he were fighting, and once he had almost overcome him but at last, he overcome the devil."

Henry Burt scribbled furiously to get down all the testimony, finally raising his head when he was done. He flexed his stiff fingers and then called Francis Peppers to the stand.

Pynchon waited for him to be sworn in. "Goodman Peppers, what can ye tell the court?"

Francis looked uncomfortable, but said, in a loud voice, "When I came to see Mary Parsons last Sabbath, that she kept at Robert Ashley's house, as soon as she saw me, she said unto me, 'ye heifer was bewitched.' I asked her how she could tell. She said, her husband had bewitched it, and now he had bewitched me, and he knows now that I say, and he now terrifies me in this place." He paused a moment looking around the room, "and then she began striking her hand upon her thigh as if against her will."

That got the crowd buzzing. Hugh remained stoic. Nothing they could say would hurt him anymore than he was already. He watched as the magistrate conferred with Goodman Burt. They rifled through some papers, and

Pynchon pointed to a particular page. Henry held it up and called Goody Ashley to the stand. She stood, looking smugly self-righteous, as she listened to her testimony being read.

*Mary Ashley deposition 27 February 1651*

*Mary Parsons was at her house last lecture day was sen-night before meeting and among other speeches she said 'as for the death of Mr. Smith's children, it lay very sad upon her, very,' she said. Why I asked, and she said, 'because my husband would have me nursed his children.' But, said she, 'doth anyone think me a fit nurse for them.' I asked her why he would have her to nurse them and she said for the luker and gain. And then she said, 'one may well know his reason. After this she fetched a great sigh and said, 'little doth anyone think how the death of those children lies upon me.' Finally, Mary Parson said, 'it would be better for others to bring Hugh out then for me, but I can speak a great deal of him if others bring him out'.*

Pynchon studied Mary Ashley and asked her sternly if she knew of anything else. He, Pynchon, would be most interested in this testimony, as Mr. Henry Smith was his son-in-law, and the children in question were his grandchildren.

Not waiting for Henry Burt, Pynchon called Mary Parsons to the stand. Mary had been made to wait just outside the door, guarded by the constable, Thomas Merrick. As she entered, the room hummed with whispered excitement. She shuffled up the aisle, hampered by her jangling chains. Her head hung low, she muttered to herself as she went.

The magistrate questioned her, asking on what grounds she thought her husband had bewitched Mr. Smith's children.

Mary lifted her head and spoke softly. The room quickly fell silent, and Henry Burt, who was a little deaf, strained to hear her. She looked only at Mr. Pynchon. "Because my husband would often say that he would be even with Mr. Smith if he denied to let him have any peas or to plow his ground or to do any other thing for him that he desire; he would often say I would be even with him."

"Humph," grunted Pynchon, disappointed. "Is that all?"

"Aye, sir."

"Well then, what about this matter of Thomas Miller." Pynchon pointed to the man himself, who sat in the front row, his leg propped up on a stool. "What do you know about that, Goody Parsons?"

Again, Mary spoke softly. "I suspect my husband to be a witch because all he sells to anybody doth not prosper. I am sorry for that poor man, Thomas Miller, for not two days after my husband and he bargained for a piece of ground, Thomas Miller had that mischance of that cut on his leg."

Thomas Miller was called to testify. He was helped to his feet and limped his way to the front. Hugh rolled his eyes, that man was all but healed the last time Hugh saw him walking in the street. After swearing in, Thomas looked to Mr. Pynchon for guidance. Pynchon nodded at him to begin.

"Well, sir, I was in company with several other workmen, we were about the timber trees and it was dinner time and we were merry together. Hugh Parsons sat on a bow, somewhat higher than the rest. Then one of the company started this question: I wonder why he sits there? So, I says, to see what we have. And then I began to speak about the cutting of the puddings in town. About half a quarter of an hour later, as I set to work, I cut my leg." Thomas stopped and looked around for confirmation from some of the men in court who were with him in the woods. Several men nodded in agreement.

Thomas Cooper was called up and sworn in. Pynchon asked him to tell what he knew of Thomas Miller's accident. He looked nervous but said in a croaking voice, "I was much troubled in my mind, because Thomas Miller spoke so plainly to Hugh Parsons. I feared some ill event should follow." He cleared his throat, and spoke again in a clearer voice. "Hugh Parsons was as merry and pleasant before this speech about the pudding as any in the company, but after this he was wholly silent and spoke not a word in reply about the pudding. He just sat there silent."

Cooper helped Thomas Miller back to his chair, while Henry Burt called the next witness, Thomas Burnham.

Thomas Burnham came forward. He seemed eager to talk. Mr. Pynchon had to silence him as he had yet to be sworn in. After that formality he began to tell his story. "I was in Goodman Pepper's establishment having a mug of beer when Hugh Parsons come in and sat down near to me. This being a little before his apprehension. Now I said, to him, 'here is strange doings in town about cutting of puddings, and whetting of saws in the night time.' Hugh Parsons heard these things, but he remained silent for a while. Then he said, he had never heard of these things before tonight. So, I said to him, this is strange that you should not hear of these things and I being but a stranger in town, do hear of it in all places wherever I go."

He stopped a moment to look around, before continuing. "Hugh would not speak of the puddings, but he did speak of other things, planting fields and corn crops and such. He was as pleasant as any can be and would answer any question, lest it be about the puddings. I spoke of the pudding and the saw several times on purpose to see what Hugh Parsons would say to it, but still he continues silent and would not speak anything about these things. Then Goodman Munn being present said, 'I would that those that whet saws in the nighttime and on the Lord's day were found out.' Then I said, 'you sawyers you had need to look to it'. Hugh Parsons being also a sawyer, never returned an answer, but still continued silent. This matter about the pudding and whetting of saw was often tossed up and down between several persons and many said they never heard the like. Hugh Parsons was often spoken to, in particular, and asked if he ever heard the like, but still he continues wholly silent."

The magistrate thanked Thomas Burnham for coming forward, he being but a stranger in town. He then asked if anyone else was present at Francis Pepper's that night. Joan Warrener and Abigail Munn both raised their hands and admitted they were there. The pair acknowledged that they remembered all things that had been related by Thomas Burnham, and that Hugh Parsons was wholly silent.

As Henry Burt finished transcribing the women's testimony, William Pynchon asked aloud who had heard the whetting of saws at night. The room was filled with murmured conversation as the towns people consulted each other on who had told who about hearing saws in the night. There was much shrugging of shoulders and finger pointing.

The magistrate asked Burnham who had first told him about the whetting of saws, or if he had heard them himself. He declared he could not recall who had told him, and confessed he had not heard them himself. The noise in the room grew louder as the folks started shouting across the room at each other. Losing patience, Pynchon brought the court to order with a resounding bang of his gavel.

"Am I to believe, not one person in this room can recall hearing the whetting of saws on any night?"

The room remained silent. Pynchon gave them a moment to jog their memories. No one admitted to hearing the saw. "Mr. Burt, please make a note that no one present can recall the origin of the complaint of saws being sharpened in the night."

"Constable Merrick, escort Goody Parsons back outside, or rather take her to my office. 'Tis cold and she does not look well."

Mary shuffled back, not looking at her husband. Little did Hugh know; it was the last time he would ever see his wife. As she left the room, Henry Burt called Thomas Cooper to give his testimony. "I was appointed to watch Mary Parsons last week, among other thing she told me that she was now hampered for her relating so much as she had done against her husband at Mr. Pynchon's. But, said she, 'if that dumb dog could but have spoken, it would have been better with me than it is'. But, said she, 'I would make that dumb dog to speak.' I said to her why do you speak so of your husband, me thinks, if he were a witch there would be some apparent sign or mark of it appear upon his body, for they say witches have teats upon some part or other of their body, but as far as I here there is not any such apparent thing upon his body. She answered, 'it is not always so; but, said why do I say so, I have no skill in witchery.'"

Cooper looked around the room as if he were enjoying himself. He took a deep breath, and in a storyteller's voice, he began to tell more of Mary's story. "It were right queer." His eyes shone with excitement as he spoke. "She said to me, 'that night that I was at Goodman Ashley's-, the Devil told me that night, that he may come into my body, only like a wind, and so go forth again. I think I should have been a witch afore now but that I was afraid to see the devil, lest he should fright me. But the devil told me that I should not fear, that I will not come in any apparition, but only come into thy body like a wind, and trouble thee a little while, and presently go forth again'." Cooper pause again, "and so I consented."

The low murmur of the room rose to a loud gaggle of voices as neighbors leaned over each other to exchange reactions. Thomas Cooper waved his arms, and Pynchon pounded on the table, shouting for quiet.

When the room fell silent, Thomas continued. "Mary Parsons saith to me, 'that night I was with my husband and Goodwife Merrick and Bess Sewell....'." He was interrupted by a loud gasp. " We were in Goodman Stebbing's lot. We were sometimes like cats and sometimes in our own shape, and we were plodding for some good cheer. They made me go barefoot and make the fires because I had declared so much at Mr. Pynchons'."

Hugh looked around as the room went wild. Bess Sewell fainted dead away.

# Deposition

18 March 1651
Afternoon

The Magistrate pounded his gavel on the table, trying to regain control of the room. "Everyone out. Every out of the meetinghouse." He shouted, to raise his voice over the gabble of the crowd.

Goody Sewell, limp and weeping, was carried out and taken to Francis Pepper's for a stiff libation to calm her hysteria. The constable tried to console his wife, Goody Merrick, who cried uncontrollably in the corner, saying over and over, through her tears, "I am no witch, I am no witch."

Hugh, for the first time in weeks, found himself ignored. He sat on the floor of the meetinghouse, hands over his face. He listened to Goody Merrick's weeping and tried to conjure sympathy for the woman, but there was nothing but a hollow feeling inside. He should be angry at Mary for her betrayal of her friends, innocent women, but his anger had gone, bled out over the course of his confinement.

When the room emptied, Henry Burt led Hugh to the Pynchon's barn and chained his manacles to a post. A servant brought out a trencher of food and ale. After an hour or so, the servant unshackled him and escorted him to the outhouse to relieve his bladder and then returned him to the meetinghouse.

The atmosphere in the packed room fairly crackled with tension. Neither Goody Merrick nor Goody Sewell were present. As Hugh glanced around at his former friends and neighbors, none would meet his eye. God, please let this end soon, he prayed, before more innocent lives were shattered. He flinched as Pynchon pounded his gavel and called the room to order. "Mr. Burt, will you please read to us the testimony of Goody Edwards, the wife of Alexander Edwards."

*Deposition of Sarah Edwards taken 27 February 1651*

*About two years since, Hugh Parsons being then at the Long Meadow, came to my house to buy some milk. I said to him, I will give you a half penny worth but I cannot let you have any more at this time. This was at that time when my cow gave three quarts at a meal. But the next meal after she gave not above a quart, and it was as yellow as saffron. I could not discern that the cow was ill. The next meal the milk altered to another strange odd color and so it did every meal for a week together it still altered to some odd color or other and also it grew less and less. All the while the cow was as well as at any time before, so far as I could discern. About a week after she began to mend her milk again without any means used. Upon this I had thoughts that Hugh Parsons might be the cause of it.*

Goody Edwards' deposition did not warrant much of a response. The expectations of the crowd disappointed, colorful milk did not compare to the naming of witches. Alexander Edwards and George Coulton confirmed Sarah's testimony but neither elicited more than a mild murmur.

"Hugh Parsons can you explain this bewitching of the cow?"

Hugh sighed, everyone in town must be concocting some mystical story involving him. "I swear," he said wearily, "I did not lie one night at the Long Meadow that summer. I did lie there in the spring of the year, either in

March or in the beginning of April, when I was setting up fencing there and I never had any milk of her but that one time and at that time of the year." He added, "I do not think her cow could give three quarts at one meal."

The magistrate listened intently to Hugh's testimony. He then read through some papers on his table and consulted with Henry Burt. Finally, he cleared his throat, looking at Hugh, he said, "Parsons, Alexander Edwards has sworn that you did lie in the Long Meadow that summer."

Hugh stood a moment, racking his brain, before saying, "I may have spent the night at Long Meadow at planting time, mayhap about the end of May, I sometimes do."

Pynchon recalled George Coulton and questioned him further. He scratched his head and thought for a moment before stating, "I remember Alexander Edwards come to me to tell me of this accident and he said that he was persuaded that Hugh Parsons had bewitched his cow. But I did not believe him at that time. I rather conceived that the cow was falling into some dangerous sickness; for such a sudden abatement I told him was a sign of some dangerous sickness at hand." He scratched his head again before adding, "but seeing no sickness followed, I am now persuaded such a sudden change could not come from a natural cause."

"And what do you suppose the cause may be?" Questioned Pynchon.

"Witchcraft, sir."

Henry Burt looked around the courtroom for his next witness. "Is Simon Beamon here?"

"Here he is," someone shouted, "he be sleeping in the corner." Another said, "Wake up man, 'tis your turn to testify."

The crowd snickered as Simon made his way forward, a sullen look on his face.

*The deposition of Simon Beamon*

*About February last, Hugh Parsons came to me at my Master's, Mr. Pynchon that is, for a piece of whitleather, to make a cap for his flail. I had my horses already hitched to my cart and was going out with them into the woods. I told Parsons that I could not stay but would give it to him another time.*

*Now the same day after, I was loaded with a piece of timber under the cart and coming home the horses set a running suddenly as if they were scared. But I saw nothing that would scare them. As I held down the thill-horse to stay them, I was beaten down with the cart. As I fell, I kicked out with my foot and hit the horse which stopped. If not for that the cart would have run over me. The cart wheel went over part of me jacket and was so close to me body. As I lay there, I saw the wheels run over a great stub of a pine, 'twas two-and-a-half foot high, it were, yet the cart did not overturn.*

*I thought there was some mischief in it from Hugh Parsons for my horses had often gone that road and never did the like before, nor ever since.*

*This deponent also sayth upon oath:*

*About the end of the last summer, I being at the mill to fetch home meal, Hugh Parsons being there, desired me to carry home a bag of meal for him. When I refused, Hugh Parsons was offended. Now, I got my meal and when I had gone about six rods from the mill my horse, being a gently quiet horse, I fell down from the horse and the meal upon me. I laid the meal on the horse again and got up and was well settled and being gone about two or three rods further, I fell down again and the meal upon me. The horse never started. I laid the sack again and the third time I got up and when I was well settled and gone a rod or*

310

*two further, I fell yet again, with the sack upon me. The horse did not move, just stood quietly in his place. Finally, the fourth time, I was able to get home.*

The courtroom burst into laughter. Simon stood red faced, twisting his cap in his hands. Hugh, who would have joined in the laughter under different circumstances, had nothing to say about either story.

A bang of the gavel brought the room to order and William Branch called to testify. He came forward and began to speak in a low, dramatic voice. "Well now, let's see, about a year ago, no make it two years ago, when I lived in town, I went to bed within about two hours of night. Before I was asleep, there was a light all over the chamber, like fire."

His face grew animated and his hands waved about in the air as he spun his tale. The crowd sat silent with anticipation. "There came a thing upon me like a little boy with a face as red as fire and put his hand under my chin, as I apprehended. And I felt something like scalding water on my back and then I heard a voice saying it it done, it is done...."

A female cry reverberated around the room as Goody Axtell, a look of wide-eyed terror on her face, leapt to her feet and dashed from the building, hands covering her ears.

Goodman Branch continued his story. "Then, I waked my wife and told her of it, and I have been ill ever since. I have thought Hugh Parsons to be naught and have been troubled that he hast made so many errands to my house for several things, and yet, I could not tell how to deny him what he desired. About summer, twelve months ago, I went to the Long Meadow, and as I was going before Hugh Parsons door, I was taken with a strange stiffness in my two thighs as if two stakes had been bound to my two thighs, so that I was faint to thrust myself forward with great difficulty. This stiffness continues all that day, and after this, I fell into such a distemper as burning heat in the bottoms of my feet that I never had the like before, and this heat in the bottoms of my feet continued near twelve months err, I was well. I thought then, it was some work of witchcraft from Hugh Parsons, and so I think to this day."

"Do you have anything to add, Goodman Branch?"

"Only this, I hath often heard Hugh Parsons say, when he is displeased with anybody, 'I do not question but I shall be even with him at one time or other.' I remember he said so to Goodman Bridgman, upon the difference that was between them about a tree, and I heard him say, he would fit John Matthews, speaking about a bargain of bricks. 'Tis all I know."

"Thank you, Goodman Branch."

Henry Burt wrote furiously. The murmuring in the courtroom drowned out the scratch of his quill. When finished, he called Thomas Miller to the stand.

"Please tell us your testimony."

"My wife, being in one of her fits said…" Thomas was interrupted by Burt, who wanted to know the date of her fit.

Miller began again. "My wife, Sarah, had a fit on 17 March 1651, and she said thus, 'get thee gone, Hugh Parsons, get thee gone, if thou wilt not go, I will go to Mr. Pynchon, and he shall have thee away'."

Mr. Pynchon looked at Hugh and frowned. "Are there other witnesses to these fits?" Miles Morgan, Prudence, his wife, and Griffith testified upon oath and confirmed the fits.

Francis Pepper testified that it is a usual thing with Goody Miller, in her fits, to use the word 'Sirra' and 'thou witch'.

John Stebbings said, "My wife too, has had fits. When she was entering into one, she looked up the chimney. I asked what she looked at, and observing her, I fixed on something, asked her again for she did not answer at first what she looked on, and she said, with a gesture of strange wonderment, 'O dear! There hangs Hugh Parsons upon a pole', for there stood a small pole upright in the chimney. And then, she gave a start backward and said 'Oh! He will fall upon me'; and at that instant, she fell down into her fit."

Rowland Stebbings being present doth also testify the same upon oath.

William Brooks testified that, the same day that Hugh Parsons was apprehended and about the same time of the day, the constable brought him along by the door of Goody Stebbings, she was first taken with her fits and cried 'Ah! Witch! Ah! Witch!' Just as he was passing by the gate.

The witnesses took their seats as Pynchon called for any other witness to these events. There was a collective shaking of heads in the room.

"The court will recess for an hour and then reconvene for our final testimony." Pynchon banged his gavel.

# Deposition

When the court reconvened, a line formed for admission into the meetinghouse that any minister would envy. Hugh was led in and stood before them. Pynchon called the room to order, and Henry Burt asked Jonathan Taylor to come forward to have his deposition read before the court.

*Testimony of Jonathan Taylor:*

*Sometime this winter on a night, a pair of good Mr. Matthew's pails fell down with a noise, and going out presently to see the occasion there of, could not perceive anything; but going into his house again it being very dark. Hugh Parsons was at his back, his hand on his door as soon as he was of the bidding him sit down which he did. Parsons saying Goodman Colly's boy nothing but beat my calf. His master will take no order of him, but I will. Anon after Goody Colley came and inquired after her boy, whether this deponent had seen him, he telling her no, she replied, I sent him to Goodman Matthew a good while since and I cannot tell what has become of him and desired him, this deponent to help her look for him which he did in all the hay mowes and houses with  hooping and hallouing for him but could not find him nor hear of him; at last they gave over looking him and ye deponent inquired of ye said Goody Cooley whether Hugh Parsons had not met him and took order with him as he threatened him for beating his calf; and after they were parted a while the boy came home, and his dame asking him where he had been, he said, in a great cellar and he was carried headlong into it, Hugh Parsons going before him and fell down with me there and he afterward willed into it.*

*One night I was at the Merrick's and when I was ready to go home I asked Goody Merrick for some beer; she said go down into the cellar and draw it, so I did, but could not wring out the tap with all the strength I had; then I took a piece of Inch board and knocked the tap on each side to loosen it, and then I tried to wring it out again with my hand till the blood started in my hand with wringing at it and ye I could not get it out. I came up and told Goody Merrick and she laughed at me and said I am persuaded I will fetch it out with my little finger; I told her it was impossible, then she said light a candle and go see; so I lighted a candle and she and Hugh Parsons went with me, and as soon as ever she touched it, the tap came out. I said to her what, are you a witch (though I did not think so) but I do verily believe it could not have been so except it were bewitched.*

*After I came home and when I was abed there was a light in the room as if it had been daylight I was amazed to see such a light; I thought it could not be day; I sat up in the bed to see if it were day or no; and as I looked over the bed I saw three snakes on the floor and I was in a maze to see them; I stranged that snakes should be abroad at this time of year; two of them were great ones, and the other was a little one with blackish and yellow streaks; and the little one came to the bed side and got up upon the bed with that I struck it down with my hand ; it came up again, and I struck it down again; then I began to fear that if my wife should see them being then very near her time, it would half undo her with fear; therefore I did not wake her, but lay down again; and then I thought thus; let God do what he will; and as soon as I was laid down ye snake ran up a third time and hit me on the forehead which pricked like a needle; then I heard a voice that said; Death, and that voice was like Hugh Parsons voice to my best apprehension; and now I was a little revived in spirit,*

316

*and I said Death; that is a lie, it was never known that such a snake killed a man; then it was dark again; and I was taken with such strange shaking as if every limb had bin pulled in pieces; then my wife awakened , and she said husband what ails you that you shake so, are, are you cold; no said  I am hot enough, but I am very ill, she said shall I rise and warm you some clothes; I said no; but this extremity continued all night as if one limb had been rent from another, and in the morning she arose and called in some neighbors; this was on Friday night, and I was held so til Tuesday morning, as if I had been rent into pieces; one fit began at my forehead, where the snake bit me, and ended at my knees, and then the next time it began at my knees and ended at my forehead, and in this order it continued all ye fore said time.*

*Tuesday was a day of humiliation, I said to my wife, though I be ill, yet I will go thither; I am persuaded I shall be better, and so I was; but yet I have been troubled with gripping pains ever since, and am not after my former usual manner.*

*Two nights ago Mary Parsons, I watched her; she said, I have two things to say to you; one is that I forgive you the wrong you have done me; the other is about the three snakes that you saw; they were three witches, said she; I asked who they were; she said one was my husband. I asked her who were the others, she said, I have pointed at them already.*

*But you will not believe me; I am counted but as a dreamer; but when this dreamer is hanged, then remember what I said to you; ye town will not be clear yet; then said she if you had believed ye voice that spoke to you you had died; but seeing you spoke to it and resisted it, it had not power to kill you; for you do not know how my husband hath threatened you.*

Hugh stood, eyes closed, shaking his head slowly back and forth. His shoulders slumped; his body weary. He had lost weight, his clothes hung limp from his large frame. I cannot believe it's come to this. Snakes, witches and beer taps. 'Tis madness for sure, but not of my making. He opened his eyes and glanced around the darkening courtroom. The spectators, for that is what they were, spectators, hung on every word of the testimony as it was read. Henry Burt sat after reading the last deposition. Pynchon leaned over and they had a quiet conversation for some minutes. Hugh watches as his fate was decided.

William Pynchon rose from his seat, his face grim. "We have come to end of the testimony against the prisoner, Hugh Parsons. We have listened to grave accusations by the people of Springfield, in this most serious of matters. After careful consideration of this evidence, we hereby declare that Hugh Parsons is to be remanded into the custody of the Massachusetts Bay Colony for trial in Boston, on the charge of witchcraft."

# Release

May 1652
Boston

Hugh blinked and covered his eyes. The bright sun blinded him. He looked down at his feet, unshackled; they felt weightless. His arms rose, feather like, without the resistance of his chains. He stepped outside the prison walls for the first time in a year. I am a free man, he thought. I am free.

Hugh stepped away from the doorway. He took a deep breath to clear the dank air from his lungs. He looked left and right. The citizens of Boston streamed by in both directions, oblivious to the newly released prisoner, fresh from his cell.

Hugh was still in shock. The Court of Assistants had declared him guilty of witchcraft. He believed he would die at the end of a rope. After a year in a Boston prison, it sounded like relief. He welcomed death and its release from his current hell. But the court had reversed its decision, and here he was, a free man.

The court had given him a bill of credit, pending the sale of his house and goods in Springfield. Henry Smith agreed to forward the funds to Boston. Hugh walked, welcoming the stiffness of his legs, as he moved about the town. He looked around in amazement, the place had changed from a shantytown with mud streets to a proper town.

A sign, waving in the slight breeze, stopped Hugh in his tracks. He stood in front of the Blue Anchor Inn. Tears burned behind his eyelids, and he had to steady himself against the sturdy walls of the building. He could almost smell beef stew, his first meal in Boston all those years ago.

He pushed inside and found a seat in a corner, ordering a mug of ale.

Hugh sat at an empty table, crowded with memories. His scowling face discouraged any would be companions. But Hugh was not alone, here was Goodman Brown, there Samuel Chapin and Captain Holloway. He recalled his first days in New England, his life stretched before him filled with uncharted potential.

Now, here he was a broken man. His wife dead, his sons dead, his daughter lost to him. Hugh had another ale before he requested a room. A serving girl led him upstairs to an empty chamber. Hugh stretched out on a bed; it was only just past the noon hour but he felt bone tired. He slept, unmoving, for close to 24 hours, waking near dawn of the next day.

The next morning, Hugh walked the length and breadth of Boston, scouting out brick buildings under construction. At every building site, he asked the name of the brickmaker. The following day, he called at the office of each business inquiring about employment. On his third stop, he was able to speak with the brick master, Goodman Wilson. Wilson quizzed him on the brick making process, and happy with Hugh's answers hired him on the spot.

Hugh spent a few weeks at the Blue Anchor before securing a small house on a narrow side street near his work. He kept to himself, worked hard but spoke little. He returned each night to his simple home. He paid a neighbor to keep house, cook his meals and ensure that he had a steady supply of ale. He worked six days a week. On the Sabbath, he avoided the meetinghouse, defying the local authority. Instead, he walked along the Boston shore or trudged up the hills, gazing out at the deep blue ocean.

A few years after his release, his housekeeper was widowed. Without relatives or children, she was alone in the world. Some months after her husband's death, she and Hugh found themselves together, two lonely people. They married, Hugh moving into her more commodious home. His wife was at the later end of her childbearing years and was surprised when she bore not one, but two children, both girls, Ruth and Anne.

The years rolled past. He grew old, his girls grew up and married. His wife died. When he could no longer work, his son-in-law, Ruth's husband, took him in. He spent his days dozing by the fire, dreaming of a farm in Lincolnshire, surrounded by watery fens. He never talked about his life. If asked, he dodged and evaded, happy to forget his years in Springfield. Only on his worst nights was he haunted by dreams of witchcraft.

# Boston

Testimony against Hugh Parsons began on 27 February of 1651 and lasted until 7 April. Mary was sent to Boston ahead of him, accused of witchcraft and the murder of her son Joshua. She was tried for witchcraft in Boston before the General Court on 13 May 1651, for which she was acquitted. Mary then plead guilty to the charge of murder and was sentenced to death. She was not hung immediately but was given a reprieve until May 29th for reasons unknown. There is no record of her execution and the consensus is that she was gravely ill at her trial and died in prison before her punishment could be carried out. It is possible that she was so ill that the court was certain she would die naturally in a matter of days or weeks.

There is not much to be found in the records of the General Court concerning the case against Mary, but it does contain the following excerpts, which I leave in their own original spelling:

*The Court understanding that Mary Parsons now in prison, accused for a witch, is likely through weakness to dye before trial if it be deferred, doe order, that on the morrow, by eight of the clock in the morning, she be brought before and tried by, the Generall Court, the rather that Mr. Pynchon may be present to give his testimony in the case.*

*May 13th, 1651:*
*Mary Parsons, wife of Hugh Parsons, of Springfield, being committed to the prison for suspicion of witchcraft, as also for murdering her oune child, was this day called forth and indicted for witchcraft; by the name of Mary Parsons you are heer before the Generall Court chardged in the name of this comon-weath,*

*that not having the fear of God before you eyes nor in your hart, being seduced by the divill, and yielding to his malitious motion, about the end of February last, at Springfield, to have familiarity, or consulted with a familiar spirit making a covenant with him, and have used diverse divillish practises by witchcraft, to hurt the persons of Martha and Rebeckah Moxon, against the word of God, and the laws of this jurisdiction, long since made and published. To which indictment she pleaded not guilty; all evidences brought in against her being heard and examined, the court found the evidences were not sufficient to prove hir a witch, and therefore she was cleared in that respect.*

*At the same time she was indicted for murdering her child, by the name of Mary Parsons: You are here before the Generall Court, chardged in the name of this comon-wealth, that not having the feare of God before your eyes nor in your harte, being seduced by the divill, and yielding to his instigations and the wickedness of your owne harte about the beginning of March last, in Springfield, in or neere your owne howse; did willfully and most wickedly murder your owne child, against the word of God, and the lawes of this jurisdiction long since made and published. To which she acknowledged herself guilty.*

*The Court finding hir guilty of murder by her own confession, proceeded to judgement: You shall be carried from this place to the place from whence you came, and from thence to the place of execution, and there hang till you be dead.*

Whether Mary Parsons really killed her son is unknown. The residents of Springfield believed she did. His death was recorded in the town records by Henry Burt who wrote:

*Josua Parsons, the sonn of Hugh Parsons, was kild by Mary Parsons his wife, the 4 day of ye 4 mon. 1651.*

The testimony heard against Hugh Parsons began on 27 February 1651 and last until mid-April of that year. Thirty-five of his neighbors testified against him. Because he was accused of a capital crime, with the potential punishment of death, he was sent to Boston for trial. Pynchon did not have the legal authority to try such cases. Hugh's trial however did not occur until the following year in May of 1652.

In the meantime, William Pynchon found himself in hot water with the General Court. He had written a book; a theological treatise, called *The Meritorious Price*. Printed in London, it arrived in Boston on 15 October 1650 and was immediately banned and burned. Pynchon left Massachusetts in 1652, the same year as Hugh's trial. He returned to England, where he lived for the remainder of his life.

After a year in prison, Hugh was finally brought before the Court of Assistants. The court records tell us:

*October 24, 1651: It is ordered, that on the second Tuesday in the 3d month next, there shall be a Court of Assistants held at Boston, for the trial of those in prison accused of witchcraft, and that the most material witnesses at Springfield be summoned to the Court of Assistants, to give in their evidence against them accordingly.*

*May 31, 1652: Whereas Hugh Parsons of Springfield, was arraigned and tried at a Court of Assistants, held in Boston, 12 of May 1652, for not having the feare of God before his eyes, but being seduced by the instigation of the divill, in March, 1651, and divers times before and since, at Springfield, as was conceived, had familiar and wicked converse with the divill, and hath used diverse divillish practices, or witchcraft, to the hurt of diverse persons, as by several witnesses and circumstances appeared and was left by the grand jury for further triall for his life.*

It would seem from the use of the words "those in prison" and "evidence against them" that Hugh was not the only person on trial. Were Goody Sewell and Goody Merrick also on trial? Was Mary's naming them as witches enough to have them arrested? The records do not give us any hint of their fate.

Hugh was found guilty of witchcraft:

*The Jury of life and death finds against Hugh Parsons, by ye testimony of such as apeard in corte soe much as gives them grounde not to cleare him, but considered with ye testimonies, by divers that are at Springfield, whose testimonys were onely sent in writeinge as also ye confession of Mary Parsons, and ye impeacment of some of ye bewitched persons of ye said Hew Parsons, which if ye General Corte make ye confession of Mary Parsons and ye impeachment of ye bewitched persons or other of them, and ye testimonies that are in writeinge but appeared not in person authentik testimonies according to law, then ye jurie finds ye saide Hugh Parsons giltie of ye sin of witchcrafte.*

From this, it's clear that only a few of the thirty-five accusers made it to Boston for the trial. The verdict must have made some of the Assistants uncomfortable as they sent it to the General Court for further review. The records say:

*The jury of trials found him guilty. The Magistrates not consenting to the verdict of the jury, the cawes came legally to the Generall Court. The Generall Court, after the prisoner was called to the barr for traill of his life, perusing and considering the evidences brought in against the said Hugh Parsons, accused*

326

*for witchcraft, they judged he was not legally guilty of witchcraft, and so not to dye by law.*

*31 May 1652: The jury of trialls found him guilty. The Magistrates not consenting to the verdict of the jury, the cawes came legally to the General Court. The General Court, after the prisoner was called to the barr for triall of his life, perusing and considering the evidences brought in against the said Hugh Parsons, accused for witchcraft, they judged he was not legally guilty of witchcraft, and so not to dye by law.*

On 1 June 1652, his life in ruins, Hugh Parsons was a free man. He never returned to Springfield. John Pynchon, William's son, sold Hugh's property and effects and sent the proceeds to Boston. In contemporary accounts of the trial it was believed that Hugh left Boston for Narragansett and then Long Island. In Bond's History of Watertown, it is said that he was the Hugh Parson of that place.

## Author's Notes

I fell in love with genealogy about ten years ago. I have loved history since I was a teenager. Writing this book was my way of combining both loves. I first encountered Hugh Parsons while doing genealogy research on my family. Writing is a new love. Several years ago, I started writing a blog about my genealogy research. I currently write two, one on my family genealogy which includes many Puritan immigrants to New England, like Hugh and Mary and a second blog on mythical Native American ancestors. If you are interested the web address for these blogs are:

The Family Connection: www.jeaniesgenealogy.com

Indian Reservations: www.indianreservations.net

I am currently working on my second novel, *Blood in the Valley.* It is set in the Mohawk Valley in New York during the American Revolution. Like *Weave a Web of Witchcraft*, it is about real people, many my ancestors, and their struggle to survive in desperate times. I will be posting on my blog, The Family Connection, as the novel progresses.

Made in the USA
Coppell, TX
19 December 2020

45993193R00194